WHEN IT'S
NO LONGER NIGHT

Among These Bones — Book 2

AMANDA LUZZADER

KNOWLEDGE FOREST
PRESS

Published by Knowledge Forest Press
P.O. Box 6331
Logan, UT 84341

ISBN-13: 978-1-949078-04-6

Cover design by Damonza.com.

For my husband Chadd

*Let's experience life's adventures
while holding hands.*

I'll love you always!

CHAPTER 1

Sorrow is watching a person suffer; misery is knowing you've caused their suffering.

I couldn't sleep. Again.

Moonlight poured past the bars on my bedroom window and through spaces between the bedroom curtains, illuminating the white-painted cinder blocks and lending the room an iridescent shimmer.

Out in the front room, my husband lay on the couch, his back turned to me, as always. I had a narrow view of him through the bedroom door and the hallway beyond. I could just make out the rise and fall of his breathing, and I knew he was sleeping.

After my reawakening and the few days it took for me to fully recover, it was his idea for us to sleep in separate rooms, his idea for him to sleep on the couch and me in the bedroom.

"I should take the couch," I had said. "Really. I'm the newcomer. I can't take your bed."

"No," he said, as though there were never any debate to be settled. "I insist."

That was over a year ago.

At the time, I was grateful, because he really did feel like a stranger to me, and I knew I couldn't lie in bed with him in the dark, let alone be a wife to him. I thought sleeping apart would only be temporary though. Even though it had been explained to me that I would never—could never—really remember him, I guess I thought that we would get to know each other as wife and husband again eventually, and perhaps even fall into the patterns and ways we'd shared before.

But there he was, over a year later, his back to me, down the hall and on the couch.

And here I was, pulling the blanket up to my chin, then my nose. The room wasn't cold. It wasn't freezing. The heater sighed on and then hushed, and the entire apartment maintained a constant, comfortable temperature, but I felt cold anyway. The man on the couch remained a stranger of sorts, but I wanted him to cuddle into me, or at least to add his body heat to mine beneath the blankets. I wanted someone who would share his warmth.

More than anything, I wanted someone to touch me. I wanted to be touched, even if it was only a hand on my back, or the touching of feet down at the end of the bed.

Maybe then I'd sleep.

I often laid awake at night, thinking there was something I needed to see to, something urgent that needed doing. Something I needed to fix.

But what? And where?

Was it the knowledge that I needed to make things better for that poor guy out there lying on the couch? Maybe. Was it to atone for what I'd done? Maybe.

What had I done?

He was there at my reawakening, and probably when I was put to sleep, as well. He'd brought flowers—daisies—to greet me when I woke up.

Disorienting is not the word for it. Confusing is not the word for it. To slowly awake, like a child, and then to open your eyes, remembering nothing about yourself—but to see a man smiling down at you. You don't know who he is, but from the way he smiles at you, you know he knows you. Like when you bump into someone on the sidewalk and they know your name but you don't know theirs—that's the kind of awkwardness I'm talking about, but you don't know who you are, either, and so it hardly matters whether you know the other person or not.

"Hey, sweetheart," he'd said. "Hey, Alison." He was nodding. His hand lay on my shoulder.

I blinked a few times and lay there propped on an elbow in the bed in the unknown room. I frowned up at him. My pulse and breathing quickened.

"Try to just focus on breathing," he'd said hastily. "You're safe. There's no need to be afraid or panic. Don't try to figure it out. Not yet. Just breathe in and out."

My crazed gaze roamed around the room. It was mostly bare but for the few medical items you'd find in a hospital room. A blood-pressure cuff, a latex glove dispenser. Cinder block walls.

The man, the stranger, spoke to me in a voice meant to be soothing.

He was saying something about going home and getting things back to the way they were supposed to be, the way they'd been before. He said something about an Agency, about a project. I tried to listen and to process, but it was like drinking from a five-gallon bucket tipped up to my mouth. I only understood every few words.

Why don't you start with where I am, I thought. Why don't you tell me who you are, I thought. How about who am I? Start with that.

I went back-and-forth thinking this was a dream and knowing that it wasn't. I couldn't rest my glance on anything for more than an instant. My perception faded in and out of focus.

Then he kissed me on the top of my head before I had a chance to flinch away. I would definitely have pulled away if I hadn't been so befuddled. And it wasn't his disfigured face that I'd have pulled away from, though that had something to do with it. It was more because I was lost, floating. I knew I was in a "bed." I knew this must be some kind of "hospital." I knew that if someone would just hand me a hair-tie, I'd pull my brown hair back into a ponytail to get it out of my face and that would help me calm down a bit and sort this out. Because I knew that I knew things. I could think and speak and put words to objects.

But I didn't know this man. And I didn't find his tone comforting. Not at all. If anything, his purring and cooing did more to worry me than waking up in a strange room without any immediate recollection of how I'd gotten there.

So, he kissed my head before I could react and then he left the room at a purposeful, though limping, half-jog.

"I'll go down and get a wheelchair," he said. "Won't be a minute."

That's when I realized there was another person in the room. A nurse. She was tall and broad-shouldered. I got the impression she might have been selected to assist the man in case I needed to be restrained.

"Where am I?" I asked. "Why can't I remember anything?"

She gave me an understanding but unfriendly nod and from the look on her face I knew she'd been asked this before. "You'll be briefed," she said impassively. "Really, you should just try to focus on breathing and not going into panic mode."

Interestingly, her unconcerned tone was more comforting than the man's urgent attempts to keep me calm. She was icy, but she was in control, and that was maybe what I wanted to know—that someone was in charge. I took a breath.

"What happened to him?" I asked the nurse, with a gesture to my face to indicate the scars and droopiness of his.

She turned away from me to make notes on a sheaf of papers. Without facing me again, she shook her head. "Be still," she said in a firm tone. "You'll be told everything."

I exhaled again, loudly this time. "What is this?" I demanded. "Am I being detained? You can't detain me. Why won't you tell me anything?

The nurse turned and took a step or two toward the bed until she loomed over me. Then she shot a glance at the door as if judging when the man might return.

I thought she was going to hit me. I drew back.

"You really want to know what happened to him?" she said, her voice acid.

There were so many other things I really needed to know more, but I looked out the opened door too. And then I nodded.

"You did," she hissed. Her fists were balled up. "You did that to him. You betrayed him, betrayed us all. And he paid for it. And here he is anyway. To take care of you." All at once she frowned and glanced at the door and then turned away from me again.

I lay down on the bed and drew up my knees. What was this place, I thought. What was happening?

"Who is he?" I asked in a quiet voice.

She sighed wearily. She turned her head and over her shoulder she said, "His name is Gary. Gary Gosford. You're his wife."

CHAPTER 2

In the days that followed, I was told everything that had happened. Officers from the Agency came to brief me. They told me about the worldwide viral plague that almost wiped out all of us. They told me about how, in the rebuilding of society, memories were now almost a kind of privilege, and how some people who struggled to contribute to society were kept in a perpetual state of forgetting until they could improve. It was for their own good. The Starting Zones they called them, mere camps really—depopulated residential neighborhoods that had been walled off. These neighborhoods were where the Genpop, the general population, were kept. The Agency officers explained how those in the Zones were watched and screened and tested for moral rectitude and ethics and even physical stamina and strength.

"Whenever there is a crisis, there is also an opportunity," Gary told me. "If we have to rise from the ashes of a catastrophe, we may as well make a good start of it, don't you think? In fact, not doing so would only lead to a future downfall."

Then Gary told me of how terrorists and assassins had infiltrated the Zones and even the Agency, and a small group of them had managed to make contact with me and had somehow corrupted me or turned me to do their will. I'd somehow been forced into betraying the Agency. There was a battle, and I had detonated a bomb that had killed dozens of men. The blast had nearly killed Gary.

"It was a tremendous setback," said Gary. "I don't mean because I was hurt, and I'm not even necessarily talking about the people we lost. We lost good people, and I was hurt, but the worst part was that it stopped our momentum. I can't tell you how infuriating it is. We're trying to make things better for everyone, and certain people just want to stop it, to ruin it. There've been other security problems, other insurgents. So now half our time and effort are wasted on investigations and security and rooting them out."

He stopped and looked at me. His eyes were narrowed and his jaw was clenched. He held the look for a few moments, and then his expression softened.

"We'll be back on track, eventually. We're playing the long game here. We'll get back on track."

Gary told me that he wasn't supposed to tell me any of this, that those who had their memories confiscated were supposed to wake up and start fresh, but the nurse knew who I was, who I had been, and she let her loyalty and commitment to the Agency get the better of her.

"Susan's good at her job," said Gary. "I shouldn't have left you two alone. She was reprimanded—quite severely if what I heard is accurate," Gary said. "The point is, she contaminated your new start. I feel like you have to know the whole story now. Just don't let anyone know we had this talk. I could get into even more trouble."

"More trouble?" I asked. "What do you mean 'more' trouble?"

8

"Some of my superiors didn't understand my"—he paused for a second and pressed his lips into a tight line—"my approach. I was accused of putting people in danger. Long-story-short, I was transferred. Lost my job as Zone supervisor."

"Because of me. Because of what I did."

Gary shrugged faintly. Then he shook his head.

"I don't know. It was them. It was me. I should have dealt with them differently from the start."

"If I was one of them," I said, "then why didn't they throw me in prison? Or worse? Is there a worse?"

"You weren't one of them. You were never one of them. I convinced them to allow you to stay if—well, everything's arranged now."

"If what?"

"Doesn't matter. It's all arranged now. You're here and we're still together and—"

"If you stepped down."

Gary didn't say more, but I knew that was it. He'd given up the position he cherished to make sure I wasn't kicked out into the Zones or put in prison.

I think it was Gary's disfigurement and scars that made him sleep always facing away from me. He often spoke to me and others with his face turned away. He didn't want to be seen, by me least of all. He didn't want anyone to see the parts of him that were damaged—the parts that I had damaged. But that of course wasn't everything. Even so, it was nearly impossible to know to what degree he held me responsible. He theorized at times that the terrorists had threatened me or blackmailed me into playing my treacherous role. With my memories of the whole affair now gone forever, it was difficult to say if I were really to blame or not. I thought about it for weeks without

9

ever arriving at any conclusion except that Gary's injuries weighed him down so deeply that I wondered if he'd ever be well.

"You know, it doesn't bother me—the scars, the injuries." That is what I wanted to say to him. That his disfigurements, the way he looked, did not matter to me. In addition to Gary's face, the right side of which was pitted with the shiny wrinkles of burn scar tissue, his right arm was shriveled and useless, and he shuffled when he walked, favoring his right leg. He'd evidently angled his right side in the direction of the explosion, as though his own uprightness would be enough to stop it.

I'm sure the same could be said of the other survivors of Gary's team, the men who'd survived my treachery. They saw past the scars, too. Some of them had lost hands and arms. One of them was blind. They visited Gary sometimes and you could tell they still looked up to him, despite his dismissal and demotion.

But that didn't matter to Gary. His injuries seemed to run deeper than his pink puckered skin and ruined limbs. He'd been kind to me when he first brought me to our apartment, and for a week or two he'd been consumed with the nervous energy of new beginnings. He talked of things we might do, like picnics or hikes, and earning a house. Soon after, however, Gary turned quiet, sullen, and even resentful. He'd lie on the couch for hours, or he would sit on the steps outside watching the crows in the courtyard.

Gary provided for me. He took care of my needs. Aside from his breezy, downcast neglect, he never mistreated me. But we barely spoke, and when I spoke to him, he was nearly always turned away.

And underneath it all was the nagging and ever-present certainty that all of this was my fault. No matter that I couldn't remember even the faintest impression of what had happened. No matter that I had to take Gary's word on all of it. It was my fault, and the fact that I couldn't remember it made it impossible to ever resolve the situation.

"Oh my god. I am so sorry," I'd said to Gary when he told me the stories.

"You weren't then," he said without the slightest hint of irony.

"I can't imagine ever wanting to hurt you," I said, "or anyone else."

He nodded, but in his face was disappointment. Gary was the husband I didn't know, couldn't remember. He was the husband I had ruined, the one I betrayed. I should have loved him, but I didn't. I knew Gary didn't love me either, or I thought I knew. I often wondered what had really happened. Because every story is colored by its teller, and certainly someone as wrecked as Gary would have certain biases. Moreover, did he love me before I betrayed him? Did I love him? Could he forgive me?

At night, our Agency dormitory was noisy with the sounds of the other tenants, water pipes, squeaky floors. I tried so many things to sleep—herbal teas, soothing sleep tapes, exercise, reading. But night after night, sleep didn't just evade me, it mocked me.

If I rose from my bed and opened the curtains, I could stare at the moon. But bars crossed the windows—for our protection, Gary said, to keep out those living down in the Starting Zones that sprawled in the shadow of the immense Agency housing blocks like a garbage dump inhabited by phantoms. The bars protected us from those phantoms who occasionally rose up in their muddled rage to hurt us.

Most maddening of all, I knew what I needed to sleep. I knew what would bring me peace and sleep, and it wasn't tea or recorded sounds or an unobstructed view of the sky.

I needed to talk.

As strange as it sounds, the thing I knew would put me straight to sleep was companionship. Human voices, human laughter. I needed to speak with people and be spoken to.

And touch, human touch. When my body was utterly overcome with fatigue accumulated after a week or so of no sleep, I would sleep, and in that sleep, I'd dream of someone holding me.

I hadn't had any meaningful companionship since I'd been awakened that day with Gary and the big nurse in the recovery room. Gary had touched me that day, and I'd wanted to cringe away. Now I'd pay a ransom for a side hug or a pat on the upper arm. When I handed him a glass, I'd try to arrange my grasp so that we'd touch fingers for a split second.

I couldn't go out much—there was nowhere to go, or at least nowhere I could go. There was unrest outside, trouble in the Zones. I couldn't remember the last time I had a conversation, or was embraced, and that made it feel like it had been forever.

I stood at the bedroom window as Gary slept on the couch. The bars cast a crisscrossing of shadows across my nightgown and the floor behind me. I don't know how long I stood there, but after a while I went back to bed and lay there awake, wanting and needing to do something, my mind screaming at me to do something but knowing nothing, remembering nothing, and having no idea where to start.

***

In the morning, Gary arose from the couch in the front room, folded the bedding, and set it on the floor to one side of the couch. He made almost no sound. I sat on the bed watching him. I could see only a narrow slice of the front room. I watched him cross the room and go into the kitchen, but I didn't need to see him to know why he'd gone into the kitchen. Every day was the same. I could close my eyes and picture every move he made and every move he was going to make.

Because every day was exactly the same.

That's not true—every day was *almost* exactly the same. There were small differences, variations. For one thing, we spoke a little less each day. We interacted less often with each passing week. But aside from such subtleties, the days were all alike.

Except today.

Today would be different.

Today would be different because I would make it different.

From my place on the bed, Gary was out of my view for the moment, but I knew he was filling a filter with coffee grounds and then he would turn on the coffee machine. I could count it down. Three, two, one—and the coffee machine hissed to life.

Next he'll come into the hallway, I thought, and a few seconds later there he was in the hallway. If I hadn't watched this routine a few hundred times before, I might have said that he was limping down the hallway to the open bedroom door and straight to me. Like maybe he was coming to the bed to give my foot a friendly squeeze and to say good morning.

But he wasn't.

13

I thought, will he look up this morning? Some mornings he looked up and sometimes not. It was one of the variations. At this step of his routine Gary sometimes looked up and made eye contact with me. Spotting and noting even small things like this had become part of my day.

He didn't look up. Ninth day in a row.

Next he made a sharp left off the hallway and disappeared into the bathroom. He still made very nearly no sound. I sat on the bed, on the right side, because when I'd first come home to the apartment, Gary's things were on the nightstand on the left. After a year I was still sleeping on one side of the bed.

The toilet seat clunked open. The toilet seat clunked shut. The toilet flushed. Shower water running. Shower curtain rattling open. Shower off. Shower curtain shut. Like clockwork. Sink faucet on. Sink off.

Only after he was showered and shaved did he come into the bedroom. He wore a bathrobe, and he shuffled into the room. At this point Gary finally established eye contact and gave me a head nod. It was the dying remnant of the more lengthy greetings he'd once given me each morning. At first he would tell me good morning and we'd exchange a few words, but that had devolved into a muttered "morning," which had devolved over weeks to a mere "mm." A few more months later it was just the eye contact and a nod, and I knew that sooner or later it would all vanish until there was no acknowledgment at all. What would that be like? To live with someone and simply never have any contact?

But that day wasn't today. Today would at least be much different from the last couple hundred. And maybe they'd be different from now on.

From the closet Gary removed a pair of slacks and a shirt and his underwear. I could describe how he rotated through his pants and shirts so that he dressed alike each day but not exactly the same, and I even knew how he selected his underwear—it had taken me a while to piece that together, but even I had grown bored with tracking it.

He returned to the bathroom to dress.

Only a few more steps remained in the morning routine. I had made attempts to break him out of this strict regimen. I made him breakfast a few times, and he politely ate, but eventually he said, "You needn't bother with all of this. I'm not a big breakfast eater. I have coffee and toast. That's it."

Now I lay in bed as he moved through the same ten or twelve almost-silent steps with their four or five variations.

I heard the toast pop up, and then the faint scratching of the butter knife against the bread, and I knew there was less than five minutes until he was gone. I looked at the clock. Four minutes and ten seconds later, Gary crossed the front room again, this time on his way to the front door.

Before what Gary referred to as "the incident" (by which he meant the explosion that maimed him), he'd worked as a supervisor out in the Zones.

"It was rough work," he'd told me, "but I was making a difference. I really was. It was a job that mattered." Then he had let his gaze fall, and I knew he was thinking of what he'd lost, what had been taken from him.

He worked at a desk now, doing some kind of data entry and record keeping of people who lived in the

Zones. I'd asked him about it several times but he seldom wanted to talk about it.

"It's busy-work," he'd told me testily one day. "Okay? They've parked me at a desk, and they give me tasks that a monkey could handle."

I'd never been to his office, but I had a mental picture of it. The ubiquitous cinder block walls painted white, frosted plastic panels over fluorescent light tubes. Beige computer and keyboard. He sat there typing, pecking and poking at the keys because his injuries left him unable to properly home-row.

I didn't have a job.

"There's no need," Gary said. "In fact, it'd be a bad idea. You'd have to travel to the Depot every day and there's just so much trouble out there right now. It's a weird time."

Terrorists had somehow made contact with me, which had led to the trouble he referred to. He never said it explicitly, but I knew he worried about it happening again. When I did occasionally leave our housing unit to pick up provisions or visit the doctor, Gary would question me.

"Did you come straight home?" he'd say.

"Yeah, of course," I'd answer. "Where else would I go?"

"I don't know. Just expected you sooner."

"I went slow. The sidewalks are all covered in snow."

"Talk to anyone?"

"Yes."

"Who?"

"The dentist."

"He say anything?

"That my gums look good."

"Maybe in a few months we can look for something you can do," he'd said. "Maybe we can find something you can do here in the housing blocks."

"I'll do anything," I said. "Clean, wash windows. I'll clean the toilets."

"My rank and position are more than sufficient for now."

He was right, but of course this had little to do with clothing or getting enough to eat. It would be nice to have a little income to put away in my account for extras like chocolate and mango-scented body wash, but what I really craved was some kind of break from the endless, quiet, eventless days. And contact with other people—if I'm being honest, that's what I wanted most of all.

There were people in the housing block to speak to, but most of them certainly must have known what had happened with Gary and me, and almost none of them would say more than a few words to me. I'd become acquainted with Mrs. Carlyle, a resident in our housing block, but she wasn't a friend—she'd posted a note by the entrance of the commissary saying she was interested in someone to wash her linens for a pitiful weekly sum, and I'd responded immediately—mostly because it meant someone to speak to, but aside from a few brief conversations to set things up, she now communicated strictly through the written notes she'd pin to the laundry bags she left outside her door each Sunday morning.

These days if I got a curt nod in the courtyard from one of the guards, I counted that a good morning. If one of them said, "Hey, Mrs. Gosford," it made my day.

Members of Gary's old team would sometimes visit him, but I never spoke to any of them—barely even saw them.

A few weeks after I'd first come home to the apartment, Gary sat me down and said, "Okay, a few of my old team are going to stop by later tonight."

"Oh, really?" I said. "I'll make something for dinner. Beef stew, maybe. Or lasagna. We can go to the commissary and get ice cream—"

"No, no. That's not actually what I was getting at. They're gonna stop by, and I'll be leaving with them. We'll be gone until late."

"Oh, I see. Of course. A night out with the boys, huh? That'll be good for you. Sure."

"Right," he continued, "but what I'm trying to tell you is that it might be best if you were in the bedroom when they get here. Or maybe at the commissary. We'll only be a minute, and then we'll be gone. My concern is that I don't want you to feel awkward. So."

"I understand. I'll be in the bedroom. It's no problem."

"Good."

At first, the team came to get Gary a couple times a month, but soon it was pretty much every Friday, then Fridays and Saturdays. As his morning greetings became more curt, his nights out with his team became more frequent. After a few months he was gone more nights than he was home, and his absence became the new routine in these days that all looked alike.

Today would be different.

I heard the deadbolt unlatch, and the front door open. The final step of the morning checklist.

"Have a good day, Gary!" I yelled.

18

This was a variation of my own—provoking him into interacting with me. Sometimes he'd answer, "Yeah, you too," and other times it was, "Okay, thanks."

I listened. I knew he'd heard me because there was no sound. I closed my eyes and I could picture him with one hand on the door knob and the door open, maybe halfway out the door already and looking over his shoulder, deciding how he'd reply.

This time there was nothing. After a few more seconds, I heard the door close. No reply at all. That was new.

"Doesn't matter," I said under my breath. "Today's gonna be full of surprises."

I got out of bed.

CHAPTER 3

My only real responsibilities in Gary's apartment were cleaning the house and preparing dinner. This meant that my only responsibilities in the entire world were cleaning and dinner. I suppose some people would think that wasn't a bad deal. I heard of people who worked jobs that were much more difficult and distasteful than mine—backbreaking jobs, or jobs that simply never ended. I heard about Agency security personnel who spent three days marching on border patrol and then just two off before starting again. I heard about Agency drivers who were on call twenty-four hours a day and sometimes worked that long at a single stretch. There were those who worked in production facilities for twelve hours a day and more if told to. People in the Zones were given manual labor such as farming, construction, and road maintenance—without the benefit of machines and electrical power.

And so I cooked little dinners for Gary and kept the already-tidy apartment tidy. I made casseroles and pot roasts and lasagna. It turned out I wasn't much of a cook, but Gary was easy to please, despite his almost never paying me a compliment. With no kids or pets—which in a funny way made my simple chores even more challenging—there wasn't enough to keep my mind occupied.

When I complained of boredom and tedium, Gary replied, "Find meaning in the things you do each day. You can't just sleepwalk through your tasks. We all have a part to play in this project, and even if those tasks seem inconsequential, we have to believe in them."

This was much easier to say than to do, of course.

Without true human companionship, it all seemed pointless. The rooms were clean but not comfortable, the food adequate but not a source of any kind of satisfaction. It was what I imagined a prison hospital would be like—not a dismal place, not a desolate place, but hospitable only in the barest sense of the word.

I tried to find a purpose in my existence, but what I arrived at more easily were small moments of distraction. In the courtyard I sometimes fed food scraps to the ravens and magpies that lived around the apartment block. If I put my ear to the heater vents I could sometimes hear my neighbors bickering about petty things. He accused her of being too critical. She told him he was lazy. He said she was rude. She said he didn't spend enough time with her kids. They never shouted at one another, but they were sharp and they hurled the most shocking insults. I listened to them, not caring who was right but wishing to be with someone who cared enough to raise an objection or to argue and shout.

And then there was the bathroom window.

The bathroom had only one window—in the wall where the shower was, and it was made of frosted glass—you couldn't see out of it unless it was open. But scaly deposits of hard water residue built up on the inside every week, and the outside would become grimy with tiny spider webs and windblown dust. So I removed the window every so often to clean it.

The window looked out on an alley between two apartment buildings—the view was just another wall of windows. But one day I removed the window panes and heard voices and shouted commands down below. I put my head out the window and at the open end of the canyon between the two adjacent buildings, there was a crowd of people.

It turned out to be a queuing station where some of the people from the nearby Zone came to collect their weekly rations and supplies. I couldn't see the entire line, but if I looked out at just the right angle, I could see the front of the line and the Agency people who dispensed food and other needs.

Even from that distance I could see that they were shabby and tired-looking. Men, women, young people, old people. They came with their frowzy sacks and busted baskets to collect whatever was on offer. Sometimes it was packets of food or coarse bundles of vegetables, sometimes bundles of clothing, sometimes cans of fuel.

When I figured out this was a weekly event, I set my bathroom window cleaning schedule to match it, and I would watch them for an hour or more at a time, thinking of who they might be and how they got along. Sometimes the schedule changed, and on days when there was no queue, I wondered how they could get by without a weekly re-supply.

One night, in an attempt to make conversation, I asked Gary about it.

"You watch them from the bathroom window?" he asked, eyebrows raised.

"Yeah. Well, I saw them by accident, but now I watch them sometimes after I take the windows out."

"Don't do that anymore," he said. "If the security personnel see you, they might think you're up to something. They'll come and question you."

"I'm just looking out my own window."

"Don't do it anymore."

"They seem so sad. So broken. Those people down there."

"Most of them are lazy," said Gary. "Or they have no useful skills. They're weak, unproductive. Freeloaders."

I deduced that I used to be one of them. Gary didn't say so, and I couldn't remember, but I'd been told that we all began in the Starting Zones. And when Gary had first brought me home to the apartment, I'd shown obvious signs of malnutrition. I was underweight and my heart palpated at times. My gums were shrunken, like they were drying out. My hands were hard, cracked, and calloused. My fingernails were grimy and worn down to mere patches of rough keratin. I used to be one of them, out there beneath my bathroom window. I was watching myself down there.

When the people reached the front of the line, they'd bow their heads. I couldn't make out what this meant at first, but then I figured out that the guards were passing a wand over the backs of their necks to read an implant of some kind that held their identity. Only after being identified could they have their rations.

These tiny distractions and the slight variations in the routine of Gary's comings and goings didn't seem to hold any real significance, but they were in fact the only things keeping me from losing the will to even get out of bed.

But that was about to end. That is what I'd told myself. Today was the day I would change things between Gary and me. And I was partially right—things were about to change, but not in the way I thought.

As soon as Gary was out of the apartment, I was up. I had coffee with toast and eggs and I even allowed myself a few curls of bacon. The apartment was already fairly tidy, but I cleaned it from top to bottom anyway. Then I showered, set my hair in curlers, and retrieved the cardboard box I'd hidden under my side of the bed. Inside the box were a few items I'd bought from the commissary with the money I'd earned by doing my neighbor's laundry every Sunday.

First out of the box was a pair of simple, open-toed shoes. I had only two other pairs of shoes—a pair of gray sneaker-type sensible shoes like the ones nurses wear, and a pair of brown work boots that I wore when it was cold out. My new shoes were made of navy-blue canvas with white piping and a cork wedge sole. I thought they would be good for the summer, for a walk on a beach. They were shopworn, or more probably they were previously owned, but I liked the way they looked on my feet.

Next was a simple dress with cap sleeves and a pattern of white and blue flowers. It didn't exactly match the shoes, but I thought it was reasonably flattering.

The pièce de résistance was a small tube of red lipstick. Ordinary lip balm was scarce enough; actual red lipstick was a real luxury. I almost never saw anyone wearing lipstick, and this tube had cost me more than the dress.

There were a few other articles in the box—a blue hair band, some trial-size make-up samples, and a little tube of scented hand lotion that might function as a substitute for perfume.

These were the tools I'd assembled to make Gary accept me—or at least notice me.

My plan was not to seduce him. I was pretty sure Gary found me attractive, and I longed for human touch and companionship, but this wasn't so much about getting turned on as it was about prying him out of his routines—and my routines, for that matter. I thought that if I could make something different happen, if I could just change a few of the mundane variables in our day, it might lead to one real conversation. After that maybe we could sit on the couch now and then and open up to one another. And after that—anything might be possible. Gary and I had been living this way for almost a year, and even though I had no memories of my previous life, I knew it was insane to go on. I knew Gary wouldn't sweep me up into his arms at the sight of me in my mismatched finery, but I was hoping he'd smile and be just a little delighted at my efforts.

I did wonder what it would be like to kiss. I knew the mechanics of kissing, knew I wanted to kiss someone, but I, of course, had no memory of ever doing it. The thrill of it, the tingle of it, was like something I'd read about but had never felt for myself.

As I looked at my paltry collection of almost-contraband supplies lying there on the bed, I felt a sudden pang of despair and doubt. Gary was obviously resentful of me, or ashamed, or dissatisfied. Probably, it was all of these. Probably, it was more than these. How could lipstick or open-toed shoes change that?

I took a deep breath. It didn't matter. I had no way of knowing what would happen, but I had to try. I had to make a change happen.

I didn't want to put on the dress or make-up until just before Gary got home, so I left my bathrobe on while I made dinner. It was shepherd's pie, which Gary seemed to appreciate slightly more than most of the other dinners I made.

I started my plan first thing in the morning, but I ran short of time nevertheless, and I had only just enough time to put on the dress and lotion and make-up and shoes before Gary came through the door. The table was set and the food ready. We had no tapered candles, so I'd turned off most of the lights and lit one of the plain, squat utility candles we used during power outages.

Gary stood at the threshold for what seemed like a long time, looking at me, at the table. From the hallway fluorescent light poured into the candle-lit space.

I stood at the table. Gary kept staring.

After what felt like several minutes, I squeaked out a "hello."

Gary blinked a few times and shut the door. Then he turned to the coat rack and slowly removed his scarf, his coat. He hung them on the rack. He set down his shoulder bag and turned to face me again.

"Hello?" I repeated.

"What's this?" he said, waving his finger in the direction of me and the table and me again.

"What's what? It's dinner time. Shepherd's pie. How was your day?"

"Same as usual, I guess. Why do you want to know? Is that a new dress? And—lipstick?

"Yeah, do you like it?"

26

"Where'd you get it?" His expression hadn't changed. He was confused, suspicious.

"I've been saving. I've been doing laundry for a lady here in the building. That Carlyle woman. And I've been saving the money." I straightened the already-straight hairband and smoothed the already-smooth dress over my tummy and waist. "I really wish everything matched better, but it's all just from the commissary, and you know they don't have very many—"

"Alison," Gary said, "what is this all about?"

"I told you." I tried to stay in the moment, tried not to consider the possibility of failure. "It's dinner. Sit down. Tell me what's going on with you. You said something about quarterly filings. Are you finishing those up?"

He opened his mouth but frowned as if unsure whether he should reply at all.

"You know what?" I said. "I'm being dumb. You don't want to talk about work when you just got back from work. Sit, sit, sit. We don't have to talk right now. Sit down and let's eat before it's cold."

He blinked a few times more and then shook his head as if surrendering a little. We sat down and the little candle flame quivered with our movements. I served the shepherd's pie, and we ate awhile.

"I had a dream that I was flying last night," I said abruptly, with a nervous titter. "Do you ever have those? Flying dreams? I never know if I like them or hate them. It's so exhilarating, but then I'm always afraid I'll fall."

Gary shrugged and nodded his head a little—without looking up from the food.

"Everything taste okay?" I asked.

"Mm," he muttered with a slight nod, eyes still on his plate.

"A little less chili powder this time. It's not easy to get. I think it tastes better with less."

"Mm."

The candle flame was still now, hovering over the wick.

Gary pushed the last of his shepherd's pie into the center of his plate, scooped it up with his fork, and put it in his mouth. He set down the fork.

"Gary, there's more. Did you get enough?"

He looked across the table at me. In the candlelight he looked wary. A few seconds ticked by.

"Thank you," he said flatly. "I'll have a little more."

My god, it's working, I thought.

He passed me the plate, and I spooned up a second serving for him.

"I'm not sure it's a good idea for you to be taking odd jobs," said Gary. "It's—not encouraged."

"Oh, it's just a couple hours a week. I just do it while I do our laundry. I don't even speak to her most of the time—she sets it outside her door and I bring it back the same day."

"Still."

"So, tell me what's going on," I said. "Is it still really nasty out there? Shootings and attacks? Can you say anything?"

"Not really."

"You used to. At first, I mean. You told me how things had gotten out of control. And that they were going to change. You can't say anything now?"

Gary pushed his plate away and sat back in his chair. He dabbed his mouth as he looked at me again.

"What's wrong? Food's no good?"

"I told you it's fine," he said in a low voice. He placed his elbows on the table and knitted his fingers as though he might pray. "But you know what would go really good with it?"

"What?"

"A little peace and quiet to eat it."

I didn't know what to say.

"The dress, the lipstick, a candle," he said. "And all these questions? What's going on?"

"I just want to talk," I said. "I thought we could open up to each other a little and talk."

"I've told you what I do. I've told you who I work with. It's not work that's rewarding. It's not work that's exciting or worth talking about. It's the job they gave me after—after what happened to me—and I do it, and I try not to complain but when the day is over, I don't want to think about it, talk about it, explain it. I just need peace. Rest."

"But we never talk. We never do anything together."

"I'm not sure what you want from me, Alison." He ran a hand over his face. "Times are hard. What should we do? Play Backgammon? Go for a walk? Hmm? Arm in arm?" He held up his shriveled arm. "I can't work all day and provide for us and then come home and think up ways to keep you entertained, too." He stood up, but he bumped the table and everything clanked loudly. A glass of water splashed on the table.

I felt like crying.

There was a shelf on the wall by the table that held all the books I'd managed to collect. I'd read all of them. Many of them several times.

"What about your precious books? Here. Read. *The Old Man and the Sea. Gone With The Wind. Great Gatsby.*" He tossed them one by one onto the couch.

"Why did you bring me here if you don't want me here?" I blurted. "You go days without saying anything to me! You barely even look at me! I'm trying to be good to you!"

"If this is your idea of having a conversation, I think even being at the office would be better. Don't wait up." He went to the door and slipped his feet back into his shoes. With his good arm, he took his coat from the rack and struggled into the sleeves.

"Wait, Gary," I pleaded. "Don't go. I'm sorry. Please just don't go."

But he was already opening the door. The fluorescent light flooded in from the hall, and then the door closed.

Failure. The exact opposite of what I'd planned. I slumped onto the worn leather couch and watched the spilled water drain off one edge of the table and onto the floor. I sat in the candlelight and the quiet.

One of the books in the meager little housing block library was a college textbook on human development. It told of infants in orphanages in what were called "third world countries" back before. The orphan babies were furnished with food and formula and water and clean diapers and even toys, but they often became unresponsive or catatonic for no apparent reason, and many of them died. Later the book explained it was a kind of starvation they died from—not a starvation for food, but human contact. Odd to have found that book in my situation, I'd thought, but I understood the hypothesis perfectly. Understood what would have made those babies better, what would've kept them alive. How long before I became catatonic? How long before I died?

A tiny sound broke into my thoughts. A scratching or rattling. It was the doorknob. Someone was quietly turning it. I sat up and smiled and turned to look at the door. It turned gently. It was Gary, fumbling with his key, coming back in. Had he softened? Did he realize I was right or did he just not want to be in his office at this hour? I wasn't even sure how long he'd been gone, how long I'd sat there on the couch. But it didn't matter how long it'd been and it didn't matter why he was coming back. I took some deep breaths and thought hard for a few seconds.

I told myself: When he comes in, don't make demands. Let him talk—or let him not talk. Don't pester. Maybe the plan had been too much all at once. I'd shocked him out of our routine, all right—but maybe the timing was wrong. Start over, I told myself. Go slow. This can still work.

I stood up from the couch, straightened the dress again.

I unlocked the door and opened it.

It wasn't Gary.

CHAPTER 4

Electricity.

It was electricity I felt there on my arm where he touched me—it was his right hand, my left arm. Just above the elbow. There is no other way to describe it. It was a mild electrical shock that originated from that place where he grasped me, and it radiated all the way up into my shoulder and down into my chest, and down my forearm and into my wrist and hand, and it seemed to dissipate from the fingertips. But it lingered, too. My arm tingled that night until I fell asleep.

He'd put his hand on my arm and gripped it firmly enough that it felt as though I would not be able to easily pull away from him, and yet it did not feel forceful or in any way hostile.

"Al," he said, "I would never hurt you."

He was tall and what most people would describe as rugged. Even in the uncertain light I could see that his skin was dark from long days spent outdoors. But he was also more than a little disordered—several days of stubble on his face, hair wild and badly in need of trimming. His jacket and flannel shirt were battered and frowzy, and his trousers were spattered and streaked, as though he'd been crawling or hiding in the mud.

When I'd opened the door, he'd been crouched at the doorknob, working at the deadbolt with picks. He stood up quickly, as though embarrassed, mouth working without forming any words.

I'd let out a panicked yelp and shuffled clumsily backward through the front room and into the kitchen where I blundered into the table and set the dishes and knives clanking again.

The man must have known I was drawing a shuddering breath to raise hell, because in an instant he'd stepped inside and closed the door silently behind him, holding out his palm to me and with his other hand shushing me with a forefinger at his lips.

"No no no no no no no!" he said in a furious whisper, finger still crossing his lips. "Don't do it, Alison. I will not hurt you. Shh. Shh."

I was breathing hard already. He knew my name. I did not know him. Tucked into the waistband of his pants I saw the handle of a pistol. I fought to keep my wits.

"I'm Chase," he explained in a rush. "You're Alison. You don't remember me, but we're friends. You just don't remember."

There was a panic button next to the thermostat on the wall. It was by the hallway, only ten or twelve feet away. I might not even have to press it. If I could just lean back on it, maybe I could activate it. I edged around the kitchen table, taking small, sideways steps, but I'd leapt out of one of my new shoes when I'd opened the door, so it must have looked like one of my legs was longer than the other, or that I was stepping into small holes with every other step.

"Your memory was wiped," said the intruder. His words were quick and urgent, yet measured. "You know that, right? 'Bout a year ago? Right? You don't remember anything before that, do you?"

I stopped for a moment.

"Yes. Good." He held his hands out, palms toward me. He spoke slower now. "That's where I'm from. From that time you don't remember."

"I don't know you."

"Well, now, that's a matter of interpretation. Semantics. I know you and technically you know me, but you don't remember me, so do we know each other? I don't even know. We could argue about it all night."

I edged a little farther.

He took a step in my direction. It wasn't quick or startling, but it was a long step, and smooth. He'd halved the distance between him and me. The panic button was still at least seven feet away, and it was dim in the room. I pictured myself scrambling toward the thermostat and tripping over something on the floor, or running smack into the wall.

"Don't come any closer," I muttered, my voice hitching in my throat. "I'll scream and scream. These walls are paper thin."

He stood still, hands still outstretched.

"What do you want?" I asked.

He smiled. "Well, it might sound funny, but I'm here to rescue you."

"Rescue me? From what? I don't need rescuing."

"Maybe rescue is the wrong word," he said, shoving a hand into his pocket. With the other hand he scratched his beard. He looked at the floor and sighed. "Again, it's semantics. We could argue about it forever, and we both know you would."

That sounded right.

"I'm here to remind you of who you are." Chase looked around the darkened room, eyeing the barred windows, the spartan furnishings, the weird candle-lit table-setting. "You don't belong here. Alison, I know you. Really well. And this? The Agency? If you could remember what they did to you, you'd know. This isn't for you. Come with me."

"The Agency has given me everything. They even gave me a second chance."

Chase laughed. "They wiped your memories, Al! How can you be okay with that?"

"They had their reasons."

"Sure. Of course. They told you—what?—that you're bad? That you're a criminal? Al, you're not. You're annoying as hell. And you're stubborn as a goddam donkey. But you're not bad. You're good."

How could this intruder, this unkempt stranger with a gun in his belt, confront me in this darkened room alone and in less than two minutes put me almost at ease? An odd sensation was rising from my gut. Some unreconciled blend of feelings like a sharp, spiky ball was coming up through my body. I glanced at the wall where the thermostat waited in the uncertain light.

"Let me ask you one thing," said the man. "Did they at least tell you about your son?"

Without meaning or wanting to, I took a step in his direction. "Son? What? My son? Gary and I have a son?" I almost laughed at the absurdity.

The man seemed to intuit my confusion. "No," he chuckled, "not with him." He pinched the bridge of his nose and then continued: "I don't have time to explain it all right now. We've got to move."

With this, he stepped to one side, bowed slightly, and made a gentlemanly gesture toward the front door.

"I'm not going anywhere with you."

With another long, smooth stride, he closed the distance between us and stood just a couple inches from me. His face was tilted down, mine upturned. With only the slightest movement, we could have kissed.

That's when he put his hand around my arm. His hand was hard and calloused, like mine had been. And yet his grasp was tender. It was so gentle—tears started in my eyes.

"Al, I would never hurt you."

I remained still, letting the voltage of that contact course up and down my arm, letting it nourish me. But then something in my mind turned or snapped and I was seized by a fit of panic and shame. It was my past, the past I didn't remember. There was betrayal and subterfuge there. Had this been how it had started before? With some stranger offering rescue? I'd done something, and the man I'd lit a candle for just hours earlier had been hideously maimed and broken because of it, so broken he couldn't even look at my face anymore.

And now I'd been so starved for attention that I would apparently take it in any form, even from this thug, this conman.

"Don't touch me," I screamed, and then I lunged across the room and palmed the panic button.

He came at me, arms spread as though he'd scoop me up in a bear hug, but some instinct or dormant training activated like an alarm in my brain. I dropped into a sly crouch and drove my shoulder into his solar-plexus. As his diaphragm seized, he gasped deeply with a croak and staggered lamely backward. I scrambled forward and took the gun in his waistband by the handle. As I shoved him to the ground, I pulled the gun free.

Now the intruder scrambled toward the door. I brought the gun up, my arm straight, and pointed it at the man as he clawed at the doorknob. I placed my thumb on the hard, knurled lobe of the hammer and drew it back.

When had I learned to use a gun? Who had taught me?

The intruder once again raised his palms toward me, but this time it was defensively, in a surrender.

"Put the gun down, Al," he said. A high-pitched keening sounded out in the hall, like a fire alarm. I knew security personnel were on their way.

"Shut up," I said. I kept the gun pointed at his breastbone, but my hands were shaking.

We stared at each other for a moment, neither one moving nor speaking. I could almost see him deliberating, plotting.

I opened my mouth to warn him not to try anything, but he was fast. In an eye-blink he feinted right. I tried to track him with the muzzle of the pistol but he sprang to the left and with a strong, swift motion he hurled the coat rack at me. As I dodged the heavy wooden rack and the coats fluttering in my direction, the man got the door open and he was gone.

But I wouldn't be blamed for this. I wouldn't have my memories wiped again. I could already hear Gary debriefing me, defaming me, demanding to know who'd been in the apartment, why I'd let him in, what I was planning.

As quickly as I could manage, I stepped into the hallway. The man was nearly at the stairwell. I raised the gun and fired. The man stiffened and spun around and crashed onto the floor. As he struggled to his feet, I took aim and fired again, and I kept firing until the bullets were gone.

CHAPTER 5

For all the days I had spent wishing to be around other people and to have conversations, now I just wanted to be alone. Within twenty minutes of my encounter with the man who called himself "Chase," five Agency officers were tromping through the apartment. One of them told me to sit on the couch and keep my hands in view. Two of them stood in the living room looming over me, watching. One of the others roamed through the rooms, searching the place, taking photos, and going in and out of the front door. The one who introduced himself as Jensen was apparently the officer in charge although he also seemed like he might be the youngest of them. He took notes, and examined things that were found, issued orders, and muttered into what was apparently a small recording device.

I sat on the couch as I was told.

After a while, a few of the officers left the apartment, and Jensen made a show of coming ominously into the living room. He brought a kitchen chair into the room and, without taking his eyes off me, he set it down opposite me, between the two officers who'd been standing over me. Then he spun it around and swung one leg over the seat back so that he sat backwards in the chair—his eye still locked on me. He draped his arms over the chair back. The two other officers stood motionless, watching. Jensen looked at me for another long while, making a point of saying nothing.

He wasn't very old. Not exactly a kid, but younger than me. Late twenties? Early thirties? He wore a stony expression, eyes narrowed, jaw firmly set, staring at me like I was someone he'd just caught slashing his car tires. But there was something uncertain in his face, too. I could see it. Something tentative, as though he were new to his job and wanted badly not to mess things up. I knew there'd been shake-ups in the security services—killings, defections, corruption, and officers who'd simply vanished.

Yes, I thought, Jensen is new.

He took the recording device from his jacket pocket and placed it on the small coffee table with a deliberate gesture, and then he finally broke eye contact with me.

"This will be recorded," he said, jabbing a finger at the device.

Was he trying too hard? Was that what I was detecting? Or was he just unsure about what was expected?

Still, although I didn't know the intruder who'd come to my apartment, didn't welcome his presence, and had even emptied his own gun at him as he fled down the hallway, Jensen had succeeded in making me feel like I had done something seriously wrong. And so I tried to play it safe—without telling any actual lies, I stayed as vague and imprecise as possible.

"How did he get in?" asked Jensen.

"It's—it's kind of complicated," I stammered.

"Complicated?"

"Well, I heard the doorknob turning, and I thought it was Gary—that's my husband—"

"We're acquainted with Officer Gosford. Continue."

"Well, so, he'd left the apartment and—"

"What time was that?"

"What time? I've no idea."

"Continue."

"So, after he left the apartment—"

"The intruder or your husband?"

"Husband. My husband. I'm trying to tell you how the intruder got in. He's not in the apartment yet. If you'd just let me finish my—"

"There's no need to get agitated. Just tell me what happened."

"I heard someone at the door."

"Could you speak up a little?" He inclined his head at the recording device.

"Someone was at the door," I said, raising my voice. "You know, turning the knob."

"The door was locked?"

"Yes. But I unlocked it. I thought it was my husband. And then I opened the door."

"That's when the intruder entered?"

"Yes," I said.

"In other words, you let him in."

Maybe he wasn't that new, I thought.

"No," I said. "I mean, I did, but not on purpose. I opened the door, and he just came in."

"He didn't force his way in?"

"Well, no."

"So, you allowed him to enter."

And it went on that way. It felt like the other two officers had closed in on me and now formed a wall.

41

The guy who'd been going in and out of the apartment was back again. He muttered something into Jensen's ear, and Jensen nodded his head curtly, but then the in-and-out guy didn't go back out. He stood there with the others and so now there were four of them staring at me, and my mind became increasingly disordered and flighty, like a bird trapped in a house, flying into the windows and not understanding how to get free.

"Describe the man."

"What did he say to you?"

"And what did you say to him?"

"Had you ever seen him before tonight?"

"Have you ever been contacted by anyone else like this?"

Jensen repeatedly asked me the same questions, phrased slightly differently each time, and my confused answers kept coming back on me to hold me liable. Remain vague, I told myself. But Jensen wanted me to recite the entire conversation word-for-word, and I couldn't even if I'd wanted to. Jensen's rapid-fire questions kept on coming. He interrupted, changed the subject, and twisted everything I said to make me seem suspicious.

He excused himself a few times to leave the apartment while his men stood silently over me. When he came back, he'd swing a leg over the backwards chair and then look at me for a few moments again before speaking.

"Do you always dress like this?" said Jensen.

"What do you mean?"

"The dress. The hair. Lipstick. Eye shadow."

"Is there a law against trying to look nice?"

"It's unusual. Like you were dressing for a special occasion."

"I made a special dinner for my husband." I pointed in the direction of the kitchen table. "He's been working really hard lately. I wanted it to be a nice night. But then he had to go to work."

"That's not what he says. He says you two had a fight. I have him outside. He says he has no idea why you're dressed up like this and you've never dressed this way before. No offense, but it sounds to me like maybe you were planning to meet someone else and your husband showed up instead. When your husband left, the so-called intruder showed up."

I opened my mouth, but didn't know how to answer. "No!" I managed to blurt after spluttering incoherently for several seconds. "I mean, yes, we did have a fight. But no, I wasn't expecting anyone besides him. No one ever comes here to see me."

"Hm."

Jensen continued, but he seemed to have gotten the information he wanted. He asked a few final questions of little consequence, and then at last he retrieved the recording device and slipped it back into his pocket.

"We're going," he said. "Don't leave the premises until cleared to do so. I mean do not leave this apartment. Someone will be in touch." He stood and all of them turned to leave.

"Can I ask a question?"

He didn't say yes or no. He just turned and looked at me again.

"Is he dead? The man."

He looked at me and blinked a few times. Then he said, "Yes."

Liar, I thought. You are a newbie. He's alive.

When Jensen and the others finally opened the door to go, Gary immediately rushed in.

"Alison, are you all right?" He crossed the room and sat on the couch with me.

"I don't know. I'm not hurt."

Gary put his good arm around me and hugged me to him. It was a strange sensation. Not unwelcome, but it did little to comfort me.

"I shouldn't've left," said Gary, more to the officers than to me.

"Officer Gosford," said Jensen. "I've instructed your wife to remain in the apartment until cleared to do otherwise. She's in your custody right now."

"Okay," said Gary. Then he turned back to me and with his face close to mine he said, "You sure you're all right, Alison? I'm so sorry I wasn't here."

"I'm fine I think," I said, but now I wasn't sure who was on the couch next to me.

"You shouldn't go out either, Officer Gosford. At least not tonight. We're still sweeping both of these buildings and patrolling the area. If she needs medical attention, we'll send somebody over," he added.

"Oh, thanks," said Gary.

"I'm fine."

"That's good. I'm glad," said Gary, hugging me close again. "I'm here, Alison," he added, but again it was my impression he was saying it for the benefit of the security personnel.

Jensen went out the door, and the others followed him.

They shut the door behind them, and I could hear their footsteps proceeding down the hallway to the stairwell. When all was quiet again, Gary stood.

"Who was he?" he demanded.

"Who was who? The guy who came here? I've no clue. He wanted me to go with him. He was going to take me by force. I shot him."

"You did what? How?"

I told him what I'd told Jensen—the barest version of what had actually happened. I didn't say that the man had told me that his name was Chase or that I knew he had told me the truth about my past. And I didn't say anything about what I felt when he touched my arm, but even as I avoided that part of the story, my hand went to that place, and the tingle started again.

When I finished, Gary was quiet for several minutes. He sat at the kitchen table where the dinner I'd made lay in ruins. His elbows were on the table, his mouth and chin buried in his heels of his hands.

"What is going on, Gary? Who was that guy? I feel like you know who he was."

"I've got to think."

"About what? What's going on?"

"Why don't you tell me," he shot back.

"Me? What did I do? Besides trying to get along with you?"

"You've got a history, Alison. You don't remember, but I know all about it. And they do, too." He pointed at the door in the direction the officers had gone.

"Yeah, but you know who doesn't know anything? Me! They took my memories! So how could I be responsible for any of this?"

"I'm just warning you, Alison," he said, voice raised, "if you know something you haven't said, you better spill it. You better not try to hide anything. This could be very, very bad for me."

"For you?" I yelled. "Is that all you care about? A guy broke in here and I chased him out with a gun, Gary," I shouted. "I didn't do anything wrong."

"No more talk tonight," said Gary. "Go to bed. Get some sleep. I'm almost sure they'll be back tomorrow."

"Fine," I said, and I got up to go into the bedroom.

"Alison."

"What?"

"Did you kill him?"

"No."

"Jensen told me he was dead when they got here."

"He lied."

"How do you know?"

"Because he asked me for the guy's description."

Gary thought about this and then gave a little shrug.

"Rookie move," said Gary. "He's only been on the job for a few weeks."

CHAPTER 6

Gary offered to stay home from work the next morning, but the offer felt half-hearted, a gesture he hoped I wouldn't accept.

"If you think you might not be okay alone," he said, "I could maybe stick around, go into work late, or maybe not go in at all. You had one hell of a night, I know. I mean you're okay, right? You said you were. But, you know, I'm sure I could probably arrange it if you maybe wanted me to be here for a while."

I figured he was still trying to cozy up to me for the sake of appearances, perhaps laying cover for himself if I were questioned more about our relationship. He'd put on such a show for Jensen and the other Agency cops—he'd almost fooled me, but now his heart obviously wasn't in it.

"No," I answered. I was in the front room with my back to the kitchen doorway, arranging my books on their shelves after Gary had tossed them around the room.

"You should go into work," I continued. "I'll manage. In fact, I wouldn't mind being alone. To decompress from it all."

"Okay, good," he replied.

I heard him pour his coffee and set the decanter down. The toast popped up.

"Yeah," he said from the kitchen. "You're right. It's better if I go in. Someone would notice if I wasn't there. Might lead to questions I'd rather not deal with right now."

I rolled my eyes. Not even twelve hours ago, a man had come into this apartment with a gun and he was considering the inconvenience of idle gossip in his office.

Gary came to the kitchen doorway. "Alison," he said.

"Yeah," I said without turning his way.

"Are you sure—" he stopped mid-sentence, chewed his lower lip. "Never mind. I'll get going."

"No, Gary. I had never seen him before. Hadn't talked to him. Don't know him. I did shoot him though. Those big splotches of blood by the stairs? I did that."

"Yeah," he said. "All right. I'll get going then."

I stood at the book case while Gary gulped down his coffee and then set the mug in the sink. He left the toast in the toaster. Then he went to the coat rack—the one that had been thrown at me last night—and shrugged into his coat.

"Call if there's a problem," he said in a quiet voice as he opened the front door. "Call me right away if they contact you again. And remember, you're not to leave the apartment."

I nodded. He went out.

I'm not really sure how I spent that day. It didn't seem to drag on, but it didn't pass quickly, either. It was just a day, one that could have been pieced together from parts of all the other eventless days I'd already

48

lived through. I sat in the apartment awhile. I must have cleaned up after the disastrous dinner. I stowed away the 30-hour survival candle—which I judged to have perhaps twenty-seven hours of life remaining. I made soup, I think. I laid my dress and make-up and shoes back in the box, slid it under the bed. I read some from one of the books on the shelf; not sure which one. I remember wondering if I might befriend one of the cats wandering around the courtyard—if I were ever cleared to leave the apartment again, that is.

And then the afternoon light came in through the bedroom window as the sun lowered in the sky.

I expected Gary within an hour after that, so I went to the kitchen and looked in the cupboard to see what I might make for dinner. Certainly nothing would top that candle-lit shepherd's pie, but maybe some rice and pinto beans would work.

As I filled a pan with water to boil, the front door swung open and banged against the stopper embedded in the baseboard. Gary limped inside without removing his coat or hat. He continued through the front room and burst into the kitchen without even closing the front door.

"There's a problem," he said. He was short of breath, and his eyes were wide. He paced the kitchen. "Big problem."

I set down the pan.

"Let's go over everything you told them. One more time." He shuffled back to the door, slammed it shut, locked the knob, and latched the deadbolt. I heard him try the knob to ensure it was secure. Then he was in the kitchen again.

"I told you everything I told them," I said. Technically true. I'd been purposely vague with Jensen, but I'd told Gary everything that I had said.

"Think, okay?" said Gary.

I studied his face. He was trying to keep his voice even, but it quavered, and the muscles in his neck were pulled tight.

"Think hard. Did you say anything—anything— that might be construed as anti-Agency? Anything, you know, subversive?"

I chuckled. "Me? Subversive?"

"You're being called in," he blurted. "A guy at the office tipped me off. I'm surprised I got here before they did."

"Called in to what? To where? Nobody called here."

Gary shook his head. "No, not a phone call. They're *taking* you in. It's serious. I think you're being rendered."

"My god. What's 'rendered' mean?"

"It's like—" he chewed his lip and ran his good hand over his damp, pallid face. "It's like being indicted, but there's no presumption of innocence. Kind of the opposite, actually."

"But I didn't do anything wrong. All I did—"

Gary waved his hand in front of my face to shush me.

"Focus," he said. "Were you cooperative? Fully? When Officer Jensen interviewed you—did you resist the questioning? Were you evasive?"

"No. I answered the questions."

"Yeah, but did you hold back at all? Or even act like you might be? Like were you reluctant? Or vague?"

My throat constricted at that word. Vague. I couldn't speak for a moment and stood there blinking and trying to swallow.

"Well?" demanded Gary. His voice was strained, cracking.

"I answered the questions, Gary! Isn't there anything you can do about this?"

"It depends," he said, raising his hand as if to slow me down. "Tell me. Did you say anything about me?"

"No, not really. I mean—no, I didn't." My heart thudded against my ribs like something wild that had been shut up in a cardboard box.

"Well, did you or didn't you?" he groaned.

"No! I didn't! He told me you were being held outside. He said you said you were suspicious about what I was wearing, how I was acting."

"Yes, I understand, but you spoke of me. Right? He said things; you said things. Right? What—things—were—said?" he implored.

I heard footsteps in the hall. Two sets. Or three. Gary heard them, too.

"Quickly. You have to tell me," said Gary. "I have to know in case they question me so that—"

There came a pounding at the door. Three fast thumps, and not polite raps with knuckles, but booming thumps from a balled fist. We turned in unison toward the door.

Then a muffled voice outside in the hallway: "Mrs. Gosford? Come to the door. It's Officer Jensen."

Gary faced me and put his hand on my shoulder. He lowered his voice. "I should tell you that you might not come back from this."

"Jesus, Gary! What are they gonna do to me?"

"I don't know," he hissed. "Nobody does."

51

Another trio of heavy thumps landed on the door. "Now, Mrs. Gosford. Right now."

CHAPTER 7

I didn't have a wristwatch, but it felt like we drove for more than an hour. It was the first time I'd been in a car since I had awoken. The sensations were familiar—the car smoothly banking into curves and surmounting hills, the sun flickering between the trees as we sped past them. But there was also a newness to it, and at times I forgot that I was probably being "rendered," the word that Gary had used so ominously before the officers came to the door, the word that could only mean disaster.

There comes a point in any crisis when the psyche simply tops out, when the anticipated hazards trip the breakers in one's mind. When that point is reached, desperation and panic retreat like dismissed defenders, replaced with a sense of acceptance or capitulation, and these can be mistaken for calm.

I sat in a large SUV behind a thick-necked driver, my head reclined on the seat. Jensen sat in the passenger seat. He spoke little. I asked him why I was being taken and where we were going, but he only shook his head. I wondered if the driver even knew I was in the vehicle.

But wrapped in the odd sense of calm I felt, I didn't press Jensen or ask him anything else. I could not remember being anywhere but the housing block campus, and my eyes were constantly drawn to the SUV's windows. Gary had driven me home from the Agency Depot when I'd first awoken, but I was groggy and confused and didn't remember much. I had seen glimpses of the Starting Zone nearest to our apartment—it looked like a fairly normal residential area, but with an abandoned, unkempt aspect, choked with dead weeds and derelict cars and little knots of dark, shabby people.

Now I saw open countryside and mountains and open sky. I saw a massive flock of starlings wafting and warping in their peculiar unison through the sparkling air. The flock veered, compressed, veered again.

On the utility poles there were red-tailed hawks watching the ground like sentinels. A small herd of deer made its way along a roadside barrow, nosing the grass and nibbling at the new spring growth. Everywhere I saw the signs of spring.

I slouched into the seat and watched all of this speed past my window view. I may have dozed for a few minutes.

Eventually we arrived at a tall, glass and steel building, tall and well-maintained. I'd never seen it before. The big driver of the SUV stepped out and opened my door, and I stepped out. The air was cool and fresh and alive. Was that fresh-cut grass I smelled?

Jensen and the driver walked on either side of me, but I wasn't handcuffed or handled roughly.

"This way," said Jensen. He pointed to a glass-enclosed entryway.

A few other people could be seen along the walkways around the building. They looked at me and the officers without concern.

We went in and came to a security checkpoint. There was a showing of badges and paperwork and there was a clipboard to be signed.

I kept remembering that I was in the complete control of a governing organization I knew nothing about. I knew nothing about it because they had made me forget everything. Anything I might have known or that might have helped me was removed from my mind—by them. And yet, if there were any panic or fear left in me, I wasn't feeling it.

Jensen still remained silent, steering me through the immaculate corridors by pressing on the small of my back with his hand.

"Will you ever tell me where you're taking me?" I said in a low voice.

No answer.

"Am I in trouble? Do I have any rights at all?"

We got into an elevator—an actual elevator, clean and functional. Again, the sensations were familiar, but it was in effect my first time.

As the doors slid open, there was a chime, which struck me as very out of place to hear just before being thrown into jail or meeting some even worse fate. We were on the third floor now and we walked down a long tile hallway.

At last Jensen led me to an office and told me to sit. Then he and the driver left without so much as a word or a nod. They did not even shut the door behind them.

The office had a big window and a magnificent mahogany desk with the surface so shiny I could see my face in it. The desk was bare but for a simple office telephone, writing blotter, and green-shaded reading lamp. A few files lay on the blotter. Behind the desk were neatly organized bookcases and a bank of wooden filing cabinets. On one wall there was a smartly framed map of some unknowable region, but there were no other wall hangings nor any framed pictures on the desk, and no mementos. There didn't seem to be anything of the room of a personal nature. Everything seemed to be job-related and purpose-oriented.

Time passed, and I noticed more. Certainly this office was better appointed and tidier than any place I'd ever been since waking. But there was more to it than that. I hadn't visited a great many other offices, but I'd seen a few, and in them there was always a sense that everyone was doing too much with too little. There was always a frantic aspect of impending trouble, of undeserved consequences. There was shouting, arguments, and a grim edge to every conversation.

This office was quiet. Very quiet. No, "quiet" wasn't even the right word for it. This office was peaceful. The door of the office where I waited stood ajar, and from out in the corridor I heard voices. Calm voices, conversations, even some laughter.

I'd immediately noticed the large window in the office and its view outside. I noticed right away that it did not overlook a bleak ruined neighborhood where disheveled survivors were penned inside. And it didn't overlook some wild and bushy unkempt abandoned place that nature had rudely taken back. The window instead looked out on a swath of green valley, and not just any valley but a checkerboard of agricultural fields that had been cultivated. Beneath the springtime sunshine, the shades of light green and fertile loamy brown shone brightly like promises of better days. Again, there was an impression of order, and I felt myself relax further into the chair.

By now the sun was just beginning to set, blushing the sky and reflecting off a series of ponds in the distance. I knew about sunsets, but to my remembrance, this was the first one I'd ever seen. The sight of it nearly brought tears to my eyes, and I considered how marvelous it was to see something as gorgeous as a sunset in adulthood, for what was for all intents, the first time. As a child I suppose I saw a few thousand sunsets but most likely failed to fully acknowledge how miraculous they could be. And so I thought suddenly that this was a gift. I might be arrested and in the deepest kind of trouble, but I certainly did not feel that way now.

Climate control. This office had climate control—outside it must be growing colder, early spring as it was—but it was perfect in here.

It was difficult for me to mark the time, and soon I tugged at the sleeves of my sweater, feeling as though surely I'd been forgotten or that the officers had placed me in the wrong office. It seemed ridiculous that they would bring me here to wait in silence for hours. I tried to estimate how long I'd been in the office, but the best I could do was somewhere between fifteen minutes and two hours.

I thought about Gary. What did he know? What didn't he know? Did he know the man who called himself Chase? Why had he been so worried when Jensen had come to the door?

As I thought about the sound of the security forces tromping into the corridor outside our apartment, I heard another sound, a rhythmic sound like those footsteps, but sharper.

It was the clicking of heels on tile. I heard the heels of a woman's shoes clicking smartly on the tile on the floor of the hallway outside. Click, click, click, click. Purposeful and powerful, but unhurried. Somehow, these footsteps were reassuring, and something told me that they were headed in my direction.

CHAPTER 8

She was poised, polished, perfect. The impression I got from the woman who at last entered the office where I waited was that she was in charge, that she was in control. She was tall and thin but not gaunt or lanky. Her hair was blond and tucked into a neat chignon, and in the coppery light from the window, it glistened warmly. The woman was my age, or maybe slightly older, but this was difficult to determine because she wore her years very lightly, as though she were simply too busy to show her age. She was dressed in a simple but well-tailored slate business suit with attractive, but not flamboyant, black heels.

There could be no mistaking this woman for an assistant sent to relay a message, or even an executive who played some secondary role. This person was second to no one.

When she came into the room, I leaned quickly forward in my chair and gripped the armrests to stand up. It was as though I'd been caught sleeping. It was the only action that seemed appropriate.

But she immediately said, "No, no. Don't get up. Relax."

She walked behind the desk, pulled out the big chair and sat down, and then placed her elbows on the desk with her fingers lightly tented. She smiled. Not a clinical smile or the smile of someone who is about to administer a punishment, but a smile of contentment. The sun was now shamelessly pouring in from the window behind her lighting her like some legend. I really expected her at any moment to float away on the sunbeams up into heaven.

I gawked at her elegance, in spite of myself.

"Alison," she said warmly, "thank you for agreeing to meet with me. I'm Rachel."

I nodded. I think. And I blinked. I can't be sure.

"So," said Rachel. "We will get to know each other very well in the next few days and weeks, you and I. We have a lot to talk about, but right now I want to get right to it: that was a very brave thing you did yesterday."

I blinked some more. "I was just trying to protect myself. You know. I did what anyone would."

Her smile broadened. "I'm not sure *I* would have the sense or skill or whatever it takes to grab an intruder's gun and then chase him out of the building with it," here she laughed, "but okay, Alison, I'll take your word for it."

This made me smile. She seemed to wait for me to say more, but I had no idea what to say next. Instead I looked around the office as if this were all some sort of cruel and elaborate pre-prison prank.

Rachel said, "You thought you were in some kind of trouble. Those security officers—so grim and tough with their uniforms and their guns. But we've had so many attacks, you know. There's security everywhere now. Unfortunate. But you thought you were in big trouble coming here, didn't you?"

"Yes!" I blurted before she had finished. "I'm not? I didn't do anything wrong?"

Rachel examined the surface of her desk and thought about this for a few seconds. Then she raised her eyes to mine again and said, "Alison, you certainly *were* in trouble."

My eyebrows went up. "I was?"

"Yes," she said. "The trouble was that you were a wasted asset out there in those Agency apartment blocks, making dinners and folding underwear. You are needed here. I want you here."

"Here?"

"I am director of Lotus," she announced.

I was unclear about the Agency's various levels and chains of commands. Gary told me very little aside from the crimes I'd visited upon him. But it didn't matter—what Rachel said came as no surprise. I knew almost before she had entered the office that she was director of something important.

Rachel opened one of the files lying on her desk and turned over the pages inside. "Alison, you are a perfect example of what the Lotus project was designed for. Do you know why your memories were erased?"

My heart sank a little. I'd only met Rachel moments earlier, but she was the last person I wanted to talk to about my former problems, my treason. She was at once so powerful and yet so accessible and sincere.

"I don't know everything," I said. I swallowed, and it made a clicking noise in my throat. I gazed at the floor. "I know I was a criminal. I made mistakes, I guess."

"What happened? You've been told, I assume."

I hesitated. I suddenly felt very small. I stared at the floor and chewed at the inside of my cheek. I could feel

Rachel's gaze on me as she sat at her desk, straight and seemingly flawless.

"Are you all right?" she asked.

"Yes," I said. "I'm okay."

"Go on, then. Tell me what happened."

"I'm responsible for what happened to Gary. And his other officers—their injuries. And Gary's removal from his job in the field. Other people died. Gary almost did. I was a traitor. He said I made bad choices. Terrible choices. I somehow got involved with the terrorists, criminals. I don't know everything." I shut my eyes to squeeze back tears. I felt like a child who'd been taken to the principal's office.

Rachel closed the file. "You weren't supposed to know any of that. You weren't supposed to be told. And do you know why?

I shook my head.

"Because you were not being punished for what you did. You were being given a new start. And what good is a new start if you're just burdened with guilt and shame? We choose every day what kind of people we will be."

I listened and said nothing.

"How do you feel right now, Alison?"

"Not very good."

"Guilty. Right? Ashamed?

I nodded.

"With the technology we have access to now, we have a unique opportunity as a society—as a species. We have the opportunity to be free of our past mistakes, to stop repeating them, and to be free of the shame that stops us from moving past them."

"I'm not sure I understand," I said. "You wipe people's memories every time they make a mistake? So they won't feel guilty?"

Rachel leaned back in her chair. "Let's back up." Her expression was of a parent explaining a dense topic to a young child. "You don't remember what it was like before the serum was first developed, but I do. There aren't very many of us left who do, but I remember. It was chaos. A complete collapse. Human society was balanced on the edge of a knife. The violence, the fear. The only thing I can say is that it was truly breathtaking. Some people gave up. A lot of people did. Most survived by simply growing more and more brutal, devolving into animals."

She spoke in low, even tones. She had broken her gaze with me and now stared into the middle distance.

"But as terrifying as that was, it was exhilarating, too. That sounds awful, doesn't it? But think for a second. When primitive humans a hundred thousand years ago came in from the savannas or down from their trees, who were they? Animals, right? Not people. They had no law, no bond, no order. They were murderous, savage. But that wasn't the ending of them, was it?"

I shook my head slowly, trying to understand. "No, it was the beginning."

"As we stared into that chaos," Rachel continued, "some of us saw something else. We saw a new beginning."

She looked at me, and I could tell that she knew I understood.

"Do you know anything about forest fires?" she said, as if this were the next logical topic we should cover.

"Forest fires? You mean like put out your campfires and be careful with matches?"

"Yes. Precisely. Forest fires are bad, right?

"Yeah, I guess they are."

"Forest fires are destructive," said Rachel. "They burn down our beautiful forests, they kill wildlife, they ruin rivers—and they're a threat to nearby houses and towns. So back before, they used to send airplanes and helicopters and firefighters to contain the fires and put them out."

"Sure," I said. "Right."

"But what people don't realize, is that forest fires are necessary for the survival of the forest. They're part of the growth cycle of forests and prairies and many ecosystems. Fires clear away undergrowth and deadfall and even pests like insects that infect tree bark. Fires thin out the trees so that new forest growth is always occurring. Some trees and wildlife are consumed, but healthy trees can survive small, periodic fires, and with forest growth pruned back, the entire forest gets healthier. But protect the forest entirely from fires, try to prevent all fires, and that is when fire becomes truly devastating. Because undergrowth and deadfall build up, creating massive fuel loads so that when fire finally does break out, it burns for longer and much more intensely, so that the forest isn't just cleared and thinned, but burned completely to ash. By trying to prevent all fires, forest managers make each fire worse."

I was still trying to understand.

"It's the same throughout the natural world. When populations become too large or weak, or when they lose their way, there is always a predator or disease or some other force that corrects them. The Black Plague of Europe was followed by several hundred years of

64

great prosperity and enlightenment. Yellowstone National Park actually benefited from the fires that nearly leveled it decades ago."

She got up from her desk and walked around to me. She leaned against the edge of the desk.

"Picture this," said Rachel, "a world where you didn't have to constantly worry about crime, rape, violence, theft. A world where people just live their lives in order and peace. We have a chance here to not only make this possible, but to do it compassionately, without prisons or death sentences, so that everyone has a chance to enjoy it."

"Mm," I said, "it all sounds very good. How do I fit into it, though?"

"You, Alison, and this incident you were involved with, are a great example of how the system we're creating can work. You made mistakes, you sided with the wrong people, and you caused a tremendous amount of trouble. And if you'd been allowed to keep your memories of that time and those choices, things might have gone differently, don't you agree?"

"I guess so."

"But you didn't side with them again. You didn't go down the wrong path. Not only were you brave, you stood up for what's right. I find this very encouraging. That's why you're here. I think you have the potential to be a great help to Lotus. Lotus is a new kind of place, away from the Starting Zones, where we've begun rebuilding society. I'd like you to move there and be a part of this project. What do you think of that?"

"It sounds exciting. More exciting than what I've been doing for the last year or so."

"Oh, it will be. I can assure you it will not be boring. It won't be easy, either. We face challenges on a virtually daily basis. But let's first get you moved in and settled and then we can talk about details."

She stood up straight and held out her hands. I put my hands out, and she took them and pulled me to my feet. Then she clasped my hands in a sort of double handshake.

"I know you will love Lotus," said Rachel, her teeth flashing white in a broad smile. "Do you have any questions? Is there anything I can clear up before we move you out of the Agency housing?"

There was a big question that had been pressing on my mind ever since Rachel had entered, ever since I realized that I wasn't being arrested or rendered or sent to prison. I didn't know if this was the right time to ask, though.

"No," I said. "I guess I don't have any questions right this second."

Rachel cocked her head to one side and showed a small, wry smile. "Really?" she said.

"Well," I said, "maybe. There was something that man—the intruder—said. He told me I had a son. Is that true?"

"Jensen told me. We checked into it," Rachel said, nodding. "And I have news."

She paused for a moment. It was probably a very brief moment, but in the time it took to pass I thought that my heart might explode. After what felt like a very long time, she continued.

"His name is Arie," she said, opening the other file that had been lying there on the desk. "He's almost eighteen, and like all those who have proved themselves worthy to advance from the Starting Zones, he is living in Lotus."

A sob escaped me. I hadn't known it was there. "I'm sorry; I don't know why I'm so emotional," I said. "I didn't even know until the other night. I don't know him."

Rachel placed her hand on my shoulder. "We're going to reunite you."

"Really?"

"Yes," she said. Then she raised a hand. "We will if that's what you'd like. Have you thought much about it?"

I had thought about it. Probably not enough to weigh all the implications—whenever I tried to look ahead and puzzle through what it might mean to have a son, my mind would simply stop and stick at the overwhelming impulse to see him, meet him. I couldn't seem to think about it in a way any deeper than that.

"The Agency in general and the administration of Lotus in particular all agree that families should be together if at all possible. We have found that related people really do restart better when they are not alone. So I'll go ahead and recommend that you and Gary join Lotus, and we'll transfer Arie to your household and family. We can move you there by the end of the week. Would you like that?"

"Does he know? Does he know about me? Does he remember me? When was the last time we were together? Oh my god. I have so many questions."

"That is understandable, Alison. Really, it is. Within Lotus, situations like this come up all the time. Don't be upset or disappointed, but I'm going to ask you to just hang on to those questions. You're going to be making some really big changes in the next few weeks, and it's important to take things step by step."

I bit my lower lip hard and nodded deliberately. "Okay," I said. I took a deep breath and breathed out through pursed lips. "Wow. Yes. It's probably better. One step at a time. Okay."

Rachel nodded, her brows knitted up to show how sorry she was to have to defer all my queries. "I can practically feel your excitement. That's just really encouraging to see. And it's infectious. I'm looking forward to seeing your contributions."

"It's like a dream come true," I said. "A dream I didn't even know I had."

The setting sun had almost disappeared, and its ruddy light made the room glow. Rachel laughed, and I laughed.

"Well," said Rachel. "Let's get you back on the road. There's lots to do."

"Okay," I said.

I waited for her to go on or lead me out, but instead an impish expression flashed in her eyes.

"I shouldn't do this, Alison." She stepped around the massive desk and looked down at the file folders. She picked up Arie's file and opened it again. "You know, as we rebuild and re-make everything, certain things we took for granted back before can sometimes be, you know, scarce and rare." She cradled the file for a moment and unfastened something from the rest of the papers. Then she passed it to me across the desk. "Take this."

A photo of Arie.

"Don't tell anyone I gave it to you," she said. "Paper and printing supplies aren't easy to come by these days. I could get in trouble."

She laughed, but I didn't pick up on the joke. I could only stare at the photograph.

It wasn't a portrait I'd frame and hang on the wall. It was just a small and simple snapshot for identification. But there he was, Arie. He stood straight facing the camera, his back to a plain white wall. It might have been a police booking photo, except that Arie wore the hint of a smile on his face. His bangs were long and hung down into his face, but his eyes were clear and bright, and in them I could plainly recognize the signs of wit and intelligence. And contentment, I thought. The young man was thin but handsome, and I could see my face in his.

I felt warm. A warm sensation was seeping into my core. Not necessarily the warmth from a hearth or a cup of tea. This was something deep, spiritual perhaps. A void inside me was filling, a longing was in the process of quenching. I had felt Arie's absence in my life but did not know—did not remember—why.

"All right?" said Rachel. I felt a touch on arm. "Alison?"

I blinked and looked up at her. "What did you say?" I asked, my face reddening. "I'm sorry. I guess I spaced out."

She chuckled. "It's okay. I get it. It's been a big day, and it just got even bigger."

I blinked some more and shut my eyes to squeeze away the tears that had started. "Gosh. I'm sorry."

"No, all I said is that we should go downstairs and find you a driver now, and make some other arrangements, if that's all right?"

For the first time I could remember, I felt happy.

The car Rachel assigned me sped through the last light of the evening and just when it was dark, the car reached the barred gate of the housing block. I saw the apartment towers and their dimly lit windows rising into the dark. The guard waved us through and in the electric lamp I saw his face—expressionless, without affect. I saw a few people moving along the sidewalks and corridors, and my nerves thrilled to know I would soon leave this place. I thought this is what it must feel like to win a lottery and move out of a slum. Having been in such a gloom for so long, I felt pangs of actual guilt at my fortune. In fact, I briefly felt as though I must have been selected in error, by some mistake, and I panicked that someone might find out and cancel the whole deal.

But then I slipped the little photo of Arie from my pocket and looked at it again, and even in the glaring, brutalist lighting of the housing block campus, the knowledge that I truly belonged to someone and that someone truly belonged to me erased those feelings of uneasiness or guilt or error.

I had a son. I would be with him now. Nothing could be more fair than that.

After taking the stairs two and three at a time, I came to the front door of the apartment, but I felt so different now, it was almost as if this were a different door, and I paused in front of it to mentally assure myself it was in fact the door to the apartment where I lived. Used to live. Past tense. Because it actually seemed different, looked different. Same shape, same color. Same apartment number and same nicked-up lock and knob. Same everything, but smaller, less significant, and with no meaning to me whatsoever. I put my key in the lock to open it, but it was unlocked.

Inside, Gary sat on the couch in the dark with a drink on his knee. In the darkness I made out a bottle on the low coffee table. Gary squinted a little at the light that came in from the corridor, but he did not turn his head to look at me.

"Gary," I said, trying to keep my voice even, "I have incredible news."

He sipped his drink. I fumbled around and turned on the lamp on the side table. He squinted more but ignored me still.

"Gary," I repeated.

He turned his head, regarded me coolly, blinked, and then looked away.

I sat down in the easy chair and waited. Gary only sipped his drink again. His eyes were glassy and his cheeks were flushed. I'd never known him to drink anything but a little dinner wine produced by the Agency, and in fact did not know there was anything else available to drink at all. How much had he had to drink? The bottle on the table was almost empty. Where had he gotten it?

"Gary?" I said after what felt like a full minute, but was probably only a few seconds. "What's the matter?"

"They already told me," he said, without turning to me. "Your news. Your 'incredible news'."

"You mean *our* news. About Lotus. And our son. Gary, what is the matter with you? Are you drunk?"

"He isn't my son," Gary said. There was a slur in his diction. He gulped the rest of the drink and rested the glass on his knee.

"But—"

"He's not my son, Alison. He's not."

Rachel hadn't told me, and I couldn't begin to guess why not. I still had so many questions, but all at once I knew Gary wouldn't answer them even if he knew. And I knew that he'd run the entire plan aground. Why did he hate me?

"Well, it doesn't matter," I said, trying to salvage the plan, trying to press through Gary's dark and silent objections, or maybe to go around them. "I just spent the afternoon with the director of Lotus. The director. She says we're going. You. Me. Our son—my son— Arie. We can leave this awful place and start new lives."

"This awful place, huh?"

"You know what I mean," I said. "It's dreary here. The guards, the rules. Your job—you hate it there. I think we'll be safer, too. A man came in here with a gun, for god's sake."

"Yeah, the people who live here aren't any good, either, I guess."

Gary had rarely, if ever, been particularly kind to me, but suddenly I felt sorry for him in spite of all of it, and sorry for insulting him, although I hadn't meant to.

"Wait a second," I said, "Isn't this what you've been working toward? An assignment in Lotus? This is the next step. We're going. Who knows? Maybe it will change things between us. I have this really great feeling about it all. I met the director. She's amazing. She's the first person I've met here who seems to know what she's doing."

"Is that so."

I dropped my face into my hands. "Gary, stop. You know what I mean. I just think it will be good for us. I can tell things will be different there."

When I looked at him, he was watching me sideways with his eyes without turning his head.

"I'm not going," he said. "I don't belong there. Look at me. Do I look like I belong there?"

"I don't think Lotus has anything to do with the way people look."

Gary scoffed. "Ah. So I really don't look like I belong there."

"That's not what I meant, Gary. I mean there's nothing wrong with the way you look and it's irrelevant anyway. We're going to Lotus. I'm very unclear about everything and my head is just spinning a million miles an hour over this, but if I understand everything correctly, this is it—Lotus is the goal of all this. Lotus is how we rebuild after all the terrible shit that's happened in the world."

Gary held his glass over his mouth and shook the last drop from it. Then he emptied the bottle into the glass and took another drink.

"Gary, please don't ruin this. They said Arie will be with us. My son. I have a son. Are you saying we can't go?"

"I have no say in the matter. I was informed about it just as you were, except I was told over the phone. Go on. Go to Lotus. I can't stop you. I can't do anything."

CHAPTER 9

Rachel had given me a whole week to pack, but when it came down to it, I found I needed almost nothing from the apartment, and the few things I decided to take with me fit into one backpack and one small cardboard box. Although my time with Gary had not been overly happy, I packed a few keepsakes—a favorite teacup, a wool throw blanket that I'd snuggled in on cold mornings. I took some of my books, although I had a feeling that books would be easier to come by in Lotus.

I didn't see much of Gary during those few days, though in spite of myself I hoped we would meet at some point. I wanted to repair things with him, to make sure we didn't hate each other when we parted ways. But he simply quit showing up at the apartment.

When the day came for me to leave, I was up early—I hadn't slept much anyway. After a cup of coffee, I made the bed and straightened the place up. I cleaned the few dishes I'd used and toweled down the shower. It was like I was trying to sanitize the place to make it so Gary might forget I'd ever been there if that's what he wanted. That's what I would have liked if he were leaving me. Or I may have been stalling, lingering to see if he might show after all. I knew I wouldn't miss Gary, but I guess I also wanted to know if he thought enough of me to meet with me for a last time, or to say goodbye. So I worked slowly and sat around for an hour or so before calling the number Rachel had given me. And I finally did call, but the lady who took my call said I should wait two hours before going to an appointed meeting place to be picked up. So I waited some more, and I thought with the extra time he'd be sure to come to the apartment, if only because he'd figure I would be gone by then.

But he didn't.

To hell with him, I thought. I left my keys on the kitchen counter and walked out. I walked out of the housing block campus, past the guards and barricades, past the barren concrete quads, and as I went my way, I made a point of not looking back.

I'd been told to wait at the outdoor rest area adjacent to the housing campus. It was a sad little place, shaded all winter by the apartment buildings and still choked with little banks of dirty snow. There were benches and a few big concrete landscaping beds, but nothing grew there but weeds and wild grass, which hadn't greened up yet. Some urban eddy of wind apparently deposited piles of litter and leafy debris. Security guards came there to take their breaks and smoke cigarettes. And even though it was late morning, it was still cold there and it would be all day.

I waited there for an additional hour, and to my surprise, Rachel picked me up herself in one of Lotus' large SUVs. Her clothing was a bit more practical this time, but she again looked sharp and purposeful—cotton pants and walking boots instead of slacks and heels, and she'd traded the blouse for a work shirt and a functional, close-fitting jacket. A ball cap and aviator shades finished the outfit. To me she looked like a very beautiful but formidable military officer.

"Such service," I said, placing my backpack and other things into the vehicle. "I feel like a celebrity."

Rachel smiled her winning smile and looked at me over the aviators from her place behind the wheel. "You know what, Alison? You are. You really are. I actually don't do a lot of driving like this, but I wanted to show you how glad I am that you're joining us. And I thought the trip might give us a chance to talk some more."

I got into the passenger seat and buckled my seatbelt.

"Ready to go?" she asked.

"All set," I said.

And we drove away.

"Well?" she said, after she swung the SUV onto the highway. "How are you feeling?"

"Honestly? I'm a bit overwhelmed," I confessed. "In a good way, I mean, but still overwhelmed. Maybe it just hasn't sunk in?"

"Yeah, could be," she said, nodding.

After a few moments, I said, "I noticed that you didn't ask about Gary. I guess you already know he refused to come."

"Yes. Unfortunate. Really it is. I'm disappointed but not surprised. But this is no tragedy, Alison, and it has nothing to do with you. I don't want you to worry too much about it, either, because I've got too much for you to do to have you distracted."

I nodded. I didn't want to be distracted, either. But I certainly was at the moment. I remembered that it took around an hour to get to the big Lotus campus I'd visited a week before to meet Rachel, but I could only guess how much longer it might be before I met Arie. I couldn't ask Rachel without feeling presumptuous, so instead I tried to appear calm as we drove along the same road Jensen and his driver had taken a week before.

It was another beautiful spring day, and that was a big help. A little rain had fallen that morning, and it had left everything newly green and freshly rinsed. It was exhilarating to be on what I guess others would call a "road trip," especially with someone like Rachel, this strong and forceful person who had taken such an interest in me. We drove along without speaking much for a while, and I really did begin to feel calm and content. Rachel broke the silence.

"I have a question for you, if you don't mind," she said.

"Sure," I replied.

"Have you been looking forward to this move? To Lotus, I mean."

"Well, yeah, of course," I said. "I thought the wait was gonna kill me."

"Good," she said. "Why?"

"Why what?"

"Why were you looking forward to joining Lotus? I mean I know you're going out of your mind waiting to meet Arie, and to start over with him, and I know things with Gary weren't great, but what is it about Lotus specifically that you've been looking forward to?"

"Gosh," I said, "I dunno where to start. I've just heard so many fantastic things. Better housing, better food. I've heard it's safer and I've even heard it's prettier, cleaner." I looked at Rachel to see if she thought I was babbling, but she looked back and nodded in a way that told me to continue.

"Let's see—I've heard the houses have flower gardens? And they say the electricity stays on all the time. And hot water. I'm sorry, I don't know why. Just everything. What's not to look forward to?" I laughed.

"Well," she replied with a laugh of her own, "I will tell you that everything you've heard is basically right. Better homes, better food, better everything. Flower gardens? Yep. The rumors are true, I'm happy to say. But—and you might not understand this right away—but unfortunately all of that is kind of a P.R. failure on my part."

"No, I don't understand. Why's it a failure?"

She thought for a moment before answering. "Is there anything else you're looking forward to?" Rachel had a way of doing this—answering questions with questions.

"Well," I said, "this might sound dumb, but I'm really wanting to meet new people, you know, like friends. And I really want to have an actual job and meet people there."

Without taking her eyes from the road she nodded long and slowly. "Not dumb at all. I'm glad to hear you say that. I think you're really going to like Lotus, because the living conditions really are better—but it's actually more about people."

She looked over at me to gage my reaction. I nodded a little.

"That's the real advantage we have," she continued. "In Lotus we're really trying to eliminate this notion that we're all survivors. Back in the Agency, everyone's a survivor. We're all just trying to survive, you know, to hang on until some new calamity arrives."

"Yes," I said, loudly, and almost in spite of myself. I'd often felt that the Agency was simply an extension of our collective but feeble will to scrape by.

"And we did survive, yes," added Rachel, turning to me and gesturing emphatically. "But let's live now. Let's live and advance."

I was nodding and nodding.

"And you know what you need to live and advance and prosper?" she asked, more rhetorically I think than to get an answer from me.

"People?" I said.

"Yes. People. Not just survivors. Not just ghosts from the back before, but people. Family. Connections. Community." With her finger she drew invisible lines between her and I and everyone else.

The building where I'd first met Rachel came into view ahead.

"We're not stopping here," said Rachel, breaking off her monolog. "You need anything? Need to stop? Bathroom break?"

"No," I said hastily. Don't stop, I thought. Keep going.

"Good," she said. "Where was I? Oh. See, Alison, we gotta be looking ahead to what our society is going to be like after we're gone. You know, in fifty years and a hundred years after that. And so on. What are we doing here? What are we building? What will we leave behind? Ever think about that?"

I was tempted to say I had, not only to ingratiate myself with Rachel but because I felt guilty for not having thought about these things. But I thought she'd probably see through that, so I said, "No, I guess not."

"Right, see, that's what Lotus is for," with each mile she spoke more rapidly, but she was also utterly clear.

"Under some of the harsher circumstances of society as it stands right now—you know, scarcity of basic needs, memory loss, living in fear—it's easy to totally lose sight of our responsibility to future generations. Hierarchy of needs, you know, basic needs before higher ones. Right? Well, Lotus is where we meet those needs. Food, water, shelter, clothing, security—you got it. We give you fruit. We send you electricity and hot water. Why? Well, fruit is delicious and hot baths are awesome, but it's not a reward for behaving, or being a robot. We give you those things so that you can spend your time focusing on important matters, like working and thinking and dreaming."

"Wow," I said. It was all I could say. She was a powerful speaker, and she seemed wiser than her years allowed. We drove on for a while, and Rachel expounded on her philosophy and her grand ideas about laying the foundation of not just new towns filled with happy, productive people, but an entirely new world, one with new rules and ways fashioned by her, and me, and everyone else in Lotus. And I can honestly say it was the most hopeful thing I'd ever remembered hearing, but I also had difficulty deciding how much of it would ever be realized and how much was the grandiose imaginings of an obviously ingenious and ambitious survivor of the back before.

We drove on for several hours through increasingly open country. I saw farmhouses and barns along the highway and in the distance, but they were vacant, with yards overgrown and windows gone. Telephone poles stood in their never-ending single-file along the road, but their drooping wires showed that they, too, were disused. We even drove through a few blink-and-you'll-miss-it towns, all abandoned and crumbling, of no use, mere relics of the past civilization.

At last we arrived, or at least I thought we were getting close, although close to where or what I couldn't say. The only indication that we had gotten anywhere was that Rachel braked, and we slowed down as we approached the highway's intersection with a smaller road. At the crossing stood a guard shack and a gate that barred passage to the side road. The shack was small but tidy looking—one could almost call it "cute." I judged it to be newly built.

"Almost there now," said Rachel as she turned the wheel. We eased around the corner, off the highway, and pulled up to the shack. "Sorry for the long drive."

"No problem," I replied. "It's actually been really relaxing."

The SUV rolled to a stop and Rachel pressed the button to lower her window. A guard stepped out of the shack.

"Afternoon, Rachel," he said, with a casual salute.

"Hey there, Hassan."

"How was the drive? Any problems?"

"Very nice drive. No problems."

"Good to hear. My day's been quiet, too." He smiled, gesturing vaguely at the wide-open space around us.

Rachel smiled and then said, "Hassan, this is Alison, the resident I was telling you about. She's moving in. Alison, Hassan."

I waved and said hello.

"Hi, Alison. Welcome to the neighborhood, as they say."

Now that I could see the gate up close, I knew it would never keep out an intruding vehicle. Even a small car could knock the little gate aside or drive around it. A larger vehicle could probably plow through the guard shack itself. The gate was apparently a formality meant perhaps as a friendly reminder to stop in and say hello to the lonesome guard. But all at once I was struck by the contrast between this little barricade and the heavy, military-grade fortifications erected on all sides of every Agency building I'd ever been to. I thought briefly about if I should feel safer here or less so.

Hassan released a counterbalance, and the gate swung upward in an almost cheerful manner.

"Drive safe," said the guard. He seemed mildly disappointed our visit was so short, but he made his friendly salute again.

"Thanks, Hassan. See you around," said Rachel, and we drove on.

Rachel was speaking to me about Lotus and other things, but now I was beyond distracted. Arie was waiting out here, wherever here was. I would meet him. At last. I gave curt, half-aware answers to Rachel's side of the conversation as my mind buzzed with questions—trivial questions, but they preoccupied me nevertheless. What would Arie think of me? What should I say? Was a hug in order? What would he call me?

Rachel must have sensed what was going on, because after a while she looked over at me and laughed and shook her head.

"What?" I said, but I knew.

"You can hardly stand it, can you?"

I covered my face and managed a choked and nervous laugh. "I've never been so nervous. I'm sorry."

"No, no." She said. "It's good to see you like this."

The weather of the prior few weeks had been cold and gray, and as I left the Agency campus that morning, I'd stepped through patches of dirty, slushy snow, the last ragged fragments of winter. And I knew we'd only driven three or four hours to the east, but there was no sign of winter here. As we drove farther down the Lotus road, I saw trees showing buds and even a few with blooms. Spring had arrived at Lotus and it seemed it had arrived for me, and I doubted that I'd ever forget the way the warmth and brightness mingled in me just before I met Arie.

"Have you met him?" I asked.

"Arie? I meant to, but no, I haven't had the pleasure. I may not be as excited as you are, but it'll be exciting for me, too. I've heard he's super smart, well liked, a hard worker."

"It's just so crazy," I groaned. "What if he doesn't like me?"

"Oh, don't say that," Rachel said, giving me a playful backhand on the arm. "You're his mother. You know, so many families have been separated and moved and a lot of them will never see each other again. I mean, it is what it is. It's too bad. It's terrible. But you'll be with your son. You've got DNA results—this was meant to be."

I nodded. That's how I felt, too—that this was meant to be. I wished that I could remember Arie as a baby, as a boy, but this was the hand we were dealt, and I had already accepted it, and I wouldn't trade the chance to know him now for anything.

"You know, Rachel," I said in a low tone. "I don't really have any way to thank you for all this."

"Sure you do. You can do your best. Be yourself. That's how it works here. And besides, you should thank yourself. You belong in Lotus."

"I'm really happy to be here," I said.

She grinned and then reached over to give my wrist a squeeze.

We drove down into a shallow valley where we crossed over a small creek flanked by cottonwoods and sycamore trees. The sunshine winked between the new leaves. Then we crested the rise on the far side.

Off in the distance, about a mile further on, I saw houses and buildings. Even from that distance, I could see that these were also newly built, tidy, and yes, cute. As we came closer, Rachel slowed the vehicle. The homes had a quaintness, painted and trimmed in cheerful colors, a rainbow of cottages. The small lawns were richly green and lined with little fences or neatly groomed hedges.

I felt instantly at home.

Rachel turned to me and said, "Welcome to Lotus."

CHAPTER 10

There was a second, more formidable checkpoint, one that appeared to have heavy concrete reinforcement and steel gates that could be shut against vehicle passage, but it was tastefully landscaped and it was unobstructed when we arrived and so Rachel whipped through with a carefree wave of her hand and without slowing.

We drew closer and passed by smaller residential streets. The homes were arranged in loose, roomy groupings, with lots of open space between them, along with trees and greenery. The streets were flanked by wide walkways with street lamps and benches. Everywhere I looked there were people walking and riding bikes. I didn't see any other cars aside from Rachel's, and I thought she might stop and tell us that we would go on foot.

The place was like the set of a movie, or a better yet, a musical. The overall effect struck me as orderly but not regimented, uniform but not anonymous, although perhaps slightly sterile. It looked as if the team who'd designed the place was thoughtful and smart but perhaps just a bit fussy.

"It's incredible. Better than I imagined."

Rachel only nodded.

Between the groupings of homes, there stood windbreaks of trees and shrubs, open pitches grown with deeply green grass, and parks with gentle hills and ponds and pathways of wood bark. And, just as Rachel had told me, there were beds of flowers everywhere. Some had been recently filled with dark-brown soil and little green starts, but others were blooming like crazy already.

A couple on bikes passed slowly by and waved at us.

"Lots of bikes," I said, waving back.

"That's how we get around, mostly," she said. I could tell she was very proud of the place. "Most areas are designed around pedestrian and bike traffic."

"Oh, I'd love to have a nice little bike," I said.

"We have one waiting at your house."

"Oh, thanks."

"I think it's red," she said with a laugh.

"What do people do if they can't ride a bike?"

"Hm. Hasn't been an issue to this point."

A flock of children on bikes rolled past. They waved, and through the SUV's windows I heard them shouting and giggling.

Despite my nervousness, I realized all at once that the homes had no garages or driveways, and this was something that gave the whole place a certain quietude and quaintness. The homes were cottages in the truest sense—small, simple, but well kept and handsome. Functional but friendly.

One of these is mine? I thought. Just for Arie and me?

"Ascension Avenue," said Rachel cheerily, nodding at the street ahead. "This is where you live now."

We turned the corner to find all the trees along the avenue had large and bright yellow ribbons tied in bows around their trunks.

"They wanted to make you feel welcome," Rachel said.

A very nice gesture, I thought, but my heart was tripping along now as though it might break free from my chest and continue on down the road. My hands were trembling.

Rachel gave the horn a couple quick honks, and a few people on the sidewalks and yards waved at us as we went by.

We stopped at a blue house with white shutters and flower boxes that had been planted with pansies. Over the door was a paper banner painted with the words, *WELCOME HOME MOM*.

That got me. I'd been on the verge of tears since we'd passed by the second security gate, but now they spilled down my cheeks and I heard tiny *tap-tap*s as they landed on my coat.

"We're here," said Rachel. She raised her eyebrows and grinned broadly as she switched off the SUV.

I stepped out of the passenger side to find that my legs were slightly shaky, too, and I suddenly felt a bit light-headed, enough that I steadied myself momentarily by leaning against the SUV's fender.

The front door of the little blue and white cottage swung open. A young man stepped out. He didn't burst out as if meeting some grand and long-awaited reunion. He stepped onto the stoop and paused there to smile at us. Then he swept the bangs from his face with his hand, waved diffidently, and hopped onto the walkway. His face split into a wide grin as he came closer.

Arie.

I recognized him at once, of course. I had the photo, but more than that I again saw his face in mine. I'd imagined myself running to him with my arms flung out, but instead I stood there at the SUV for what I thought must have been several minutes, just watching him. Even the way he stood and smiled and walked was familiar to me, I suppose because there were echoes of myself in them, but I also fancied that I could maybe remember. Maybe unconsciously? It didn't matter. The nervousness was gone now, and I felt strongly that we hadn't been separated for very long at all. On the other hand, I could have imagined all that, so anxiously had I been looking forward to meeting with him this way.

Rachel said nothing as Arie approached the SUV. She only maintained her grin and made a sweeping gesture in my direction, like a showman presenting an assistant.

But Arie appeared to need no help in identifying me. He crossed the grass, walking easily and with a confidence that I knew or imagined I knew—whichever; it didn't matter. And when at last he stood before me, he held out his arms and we hugged. My tears were just gushing now, and I felt pangs of embarrassment, but I let them flow. Arie held me and I held him.

"Wow," Rachel said, dabbing her eyes.

Arie broke the embrace but held onto my arms and stood looking at me with a big smile on his face.

"I really thought I'd be able to control myself better." I laughed but sniffed and wiped my face.

Arie laughed.

"I told myself I wasn't going to cry," I added. "I mean I knew I would, but I thought telling myself I wouldn't would maybe make me cry less."

"I think the opposite happened," Arie said with a snicker.

"Gosh, I'm a mess."

"It's okay," Arie said.

I reached for his hand and squeezed it. "I can't believe you're really real."

"I feel that way sometimes, too," he said, patting himself all over. "But I am."

So, he's funny. Of course he is.

Rachel joined us and said. "Arie, I'm Rachel."

"Yeah, of course," said Arie.

He wasn't quailed by her, but there'd been an immediate change in his voice—a deference or respect. So, he's mannerly, too.

"I'm Arie," he said. The two shook hands. "You're our director," Arie continued. "I've seen your photo. And I know you're very busy, or at least I assume you are, so I'm honored and very grateful. Thank you for delivering my mother safely." He bowed his head to her.

"Oh, no," she said, "this has made my day, my week."

"Shall we go inside?"

The home was clean and warm. The furnishings were simple but to me they seemed as smartly arranged as a kid of seventeen could manage—simple but welcoming.

So, he's not a slob, I thought.

And in the air was the smell of food. Chicken, I thought, and something spicy. Chili peppers.

So, he cooks, I thought. This must be some kind of dream. Was I allowed to be proud of him? Was this my doing, or was he just that kind of kid? I decided that he was probably just that kind of kid, but I could be proud anyway.

"Um, Rachel," said Arie, "wait—do I call you 'Rachel'? Or—"

"No, no—don't you dare call me ma'am or madam or something. Everyone calls me Rachel."

"Okay, gotcha," said Arie. He clasped his hands politely and went on with a kind of nervous courtesy. "Well, Rachel, so, could I ask—I mean would it be, ya know, like presumptuous, if I asked you to stay for dinner? I have been trying to sort of build up my cooking repertoire, and I'm not like a chef or anything, but I have a chicken enchilada recipe and I think it's pretty good. There's enough for everyone. Enough for the whole block, probably. So, *te quedarás a comer?*"

I turned to Rachel and said, "Oh, please say yes."

It was plain to see Rachel had not anticipated this invitation and was likely due back soon for some meeting or engagement, even though evening was coming on and she had what I knew to be a long drive ahead of her. She blinked a few times at us and opened her mouth without saying anything while we stood waiting.

After a moment she said, "You know what? Sure. I was planning to have an apple and some trail mix in the car on the way back but, no. I want enchiladas now and I especially want to hang out with you two. Yes. I'll stay. Thanks, you guys."

Arie ushered us into a dining room where there was a small round table. He had set out beautiful little place-settings complete with cloth napkins and properly arranged silverware—the knives even had their edges turned in. The arrangement of tableware was another one of those things that in without remembering how I knew it or where I'd learned it, and I wondered if I'd taught it to Arie sometime in the back before when I was his mom and he was my little boy.

"Oh, my," said Rachel. "Look at all this. I think I may need to drop by unannounced more often."

"Smells delicious," I said.

"Thank you, kind ladies," he said with light-hearted cordiality. "If you'll be seated, I will see that your dinner is as pleasant as possible."

Rachel and I took our seats and looked at each other, wrinkling our noses at his adorable manners. Arie went out through a doorway and into the kitchen beyond where we heard the clatter of utensils and the squeaking and bumping noises of an oven door being opened and shut. Arie returned in a few minutes and dished out his enchiladas. The food steamed invitingly, smothered with red sauce and topped with lightly browned cheddar cheese.

Muy bien, I thought, realizing that I was actually feeling a bit weak from hunger.

It was a simple meal with simple ingredients, but marvelous for that very aspect because it really was delicious. Arie poured us lemonade from a pitcher tinkling with ice cubes and dripping with cool condensation.

"Arie, this is fantastic," I said between mouthfuls.

"Yes," said Rachel. "Very good. So glad I stayed."

"Where'd you learn to cook like this?" I asked.

"Well, uh, from you, I assume," he quipped.

We all chuckled.

Rachel pointed to a shelf in the living room. "Is that like a transmitter, Arie? Like a, whaddyacallit? Ham?"

Arie glanced in that direction and nodded.

"Yep, it's a ham radio—when it works, that is. It's more of a decoration at the moment. Needs some work."

"A hobby of yours?"

"Yeah, I dabble," he said. "It turns out the real hobby is tracking down replacement parts for it. There's not much traffic on the airwaves around here, anyway, but I have a few acquaintances in the Agency that I keep up with."

"I had no idea we had anyone here who used ham radios," said Rachel. "Where would you even get a unit like that?"

Arie shrugged and said, "I bought this one from a guy who left a note on the bulletin board in the pool house."

"There's a pool?" I said.

"Olympic size," said Rachel and Arie together.

"Big hot tub, too," said Arie.

"Jeeze," I said. "This place just gets better and better."

I felt very happy, and by the time Arie had offered me a third enchilada, I felt myself beginning to feel at home in the place. But there was something underneath it all, something that kept me from relaxing completely. Maybe it was our over-eager laughter and the constantly pattered compliments. Or the way we couldn't move past the small talk, couldn't proceed into topics any deeper than how best to avoid long waits at the gym or what the neighbors were like. I suppose I should have been content with it—I'd arrived only a couple hours before, and neither I nor Arie had any memories or any connection to one another aside from our genetic relationship.

And indeed the three of us chatted very pleasantly even after we could eat no more. But there was something underneath it all.

I tried to tell Arie about myself, but I quickly realized there wasn't much to say. It's not very exciting to say that the only things that you can ever remember doing in your life are cleaning a small and not very cozy apartment and cooking mediocre meals from cans and boxed food. And Arie somehow very politely avoided asking any follow-up questions anyway, and he had an almost sly way of avoiding my gaze when there were pauses in the conversation.

"You have a job here, I guess," I said to Arie.

"Yeah, a good one," he answered.

He said it to me but he nodded at Rachel as he said it. She looked pleased. Arie continued.

"There are some education courses you can enroll in. I got a few technical certificates and got a production job."

"Mm, sounds cool. What do you do there?"

He glanced at me as though I'd made some error in my etiquette. "Well, like I said, I work in production."

I frowned and looked at Rachel.

"Arie is not being impolite," she said. "He is actually following one of our more recent guidelines."

Arie smiled sheepishly.

"We don't discuss our occupations in very great detail," explained Rachel.

"It's called the 'shop-talk directive'," said Arie.

"Yes," said Rachel.

"Oh," I said. "Because—" but I couldn't think of why such a rule might be needed.

Rachel assumed the public relations tone of voice she'd used when she first began to explain the workings of Lotus to me.

"Maybe you noticed last year," she began, "when security problems kind of got a little out of hand?"

"Oh, sure," I said. "For a while there I was getting woken up by gun shots outside every other night."

"Mm." Rachel closed her eyes and nodded. "Well, here at Lotus we really weren't affected, and—"

Arie cut in. "There were a few incidents in the West Tens," he said.

"Right, of course," said Rachel, her voice now suddenly firm and businesslike. "But we weren't getting woken up by gunfire every other night in any event."

Arie conceded with a head tilt.

"As I was saying," she continued, "we have not been overly affected by the uprisings and security problems here in Lotus, and we like it that way, want to keep it that way, so we implemented some firmer guidelines. A bit of confidentiality, you might say, so that those who cause trouble don't have an easy time obtaining information that can be used against us. Our security experts say that terrorists take the most innocuous pieces of information and compile them to make plans for disruption and attacks."

"I see," said.

"So," said Rachel, "that's where the shop-talk directive comes in—we don't talk about what we do at work, and any terrorists who are listening get less useful information from us. Besides, who wants to talk about work over a delicious dinner like this anyway?"

"You'll be told about this at orientation," said Arie.

"That's right," Rachel added. "Don't worry about it. It's just nitpicky rule stuff. You're gonna love it here."

Soon Rachel told us she really had to be moving on, and while Arie took the dishes into the kitchen, I walked out to Rachel's SUV with her.

"Are you all right?" she asked.

"Yeah, sure. Why?"

"I don't know. You seem a bit subdued."

"Oh, I don't know," I said. "It's been a really long day. I was up so early and hardly slept at all last night. Then all this excitement. Still taking it all in, I guess."

"Mm. Well, these big changes can rattle you," said Rachel, "even if the changes are good. Lotus can be a big shock to the system, and on top of that you've just met your almost-grown-up son for what is for all intents the very first time."

"Yeah. Gosh. I should probably get some rest."

"Great idea. It was a really nice dinner, though. Can you believe that kid?"

"Oh, I know," I said, laughing. "The table all set just so and waiting on us and everything."

"The candles on the table! So considerate," said Rachel.

"Yeah, wow. I really can't believe how nice he is."

"You deserve it. You deserve this. I'm sure it's overwhelming, but try to enjoy it."

I nodded.

"All right," said Rachel. She set her hand on my shoulder. "You're really okay?"

"Yeah."

"Then I'm off. We will talk again soon."

She got into the SUV and drove away. I watched the red tail lights recede from my view. They were the only vehicle lights I could see, but the window lights and street lamps of the neighborhood were twinkling on. In the air there was still a little warmth from the day. I looked around. I heard music from somewhere far off, and some voices. But otherwise all was quiet and very peaceful.

Maybe I was traumatized in a way, I thought before going into the cottage. Could that be it? Could Gary's neglect and my grim, featureless year in the Agency housing campus have turned me suspicious, untrusting? Maybe that was what I felt underneath it all.

"Relax," I said aloud. "Just—relax."

I took a few deep breaths. The sun was down and the remaining light was draining from the western sky. A chill crept into the air. I shoved my hands into my pockets and went inside.

"Hey, Arie," I said. "Let me help you with those dishes. I can dry and put away. I'm one of the all-time great dish dryers and putters-away."

But there were no sounds from the kitchen. Arie was not around and the lights in the house had been turned off except for the light in the entryway. I looked in the kitchen. The dishes had been cleaned and put away and Arie wasn't there. I checked the other rooms. All dark, and no Arie. The door to the room I assumed belonged to him was shut. I stole up to it and put my ear close to it, but I heard nothing.

CHAPTER 11

When I awoke the next morning, I couldn't remember where I was. The bed was comfortable and warm, and the house was very quiet. Gary's apartment was very noisy—there were sounds from above, below, left, and right. Sounds of people coming and going, sounds of doors and water pipes and drains, but most hatefully the sounds of the armored vehicles and bullhorns used by the guards and yes, occasionally there was gunfire. Compared to my old neighborhood, Lotus was like a tomb.

After being so tired the day before, I had surprisingly fallen into a restless sleep, but one without dreams. What would it take to have a night of deep and satisfying sleep? I awoke that morning and lay in the bed with my eyes open, dozing fitfully, and trying to recall what had happened over the last twenty-four hours. There was not enough light yet to make out anything in the room. My eyes and mind worked to make sense of the unfamiliar shapes and the calm that hung in the air.

And then it was as if every moment from the previous day flashed simultaneously into my mind. The little rest area with the dirty banks of snow, Rachel in her ball cap and sunglasses, the long drive across those abandoned open places, talking and laughing like roommates on a road trip, the man in the little guard shack, the streets and cottages and bicycles of Lotus, the appearance of Arie like some character from a legend, his dinnertime manners and enchiladas, our semi-awkward conversation, the odd tension that seemed to run beneath it all, and, finally, Arie's curt disappearance after Rachel went away.

"Relax," I whispered.

There was an alarm clock on the nightstand next to the bed, one with hands and a round face and two little tin bells on top with a clapper between them. I picked it up, but it had no lights or luminous paint and I couldn't make it out in the darkness.

I guess that means it's really early, I thought.

I got out of the bed and turned on the light. There were a few clothes in the closet and drawers, as Rachel had said there would be—simple clothes that she said would have to do until I could order more. I got dressed and headed for the kitchen.

The door to Arie's room was still closed, which I hoped meant that he was still home and asleep. The sun was coming up now. After a few minutes of opening and shutting the cupboards and fumbling around, I found a drip coffee pot and some coffee grounds, and even cans of evaporated milk. I brewed up a strong pot of coffee and in ten minutes or so I was feeling energized. The fridge and cupboard were decently stocked and so I rounded up the makings of a hearty breakfast—there were eggs, bread, a little bacon, and even berries.

I worked fast but kept poking my head out of the kitchen doorway so that I wouldn't miss Arie when he got up. Food smells filled the house.

The bacon was almost perfectly crisp—did I know what Arie liked to eat without actually remembering? In other words, would the few cooking skills I had but did not remember acquiring be satisfactory to the tastes he'd developed without remembering when? What an odd situation, I thought. I cooked slice after slice of French toast, piling it up on a plate—in case he was a big eater. I poured two glasses of orange juice. I sliced the berries and sprinkled them with some sugar. If Arie didn't emerge soon from his room, I'd have to go and wake him or let the food get cold. I started feeling slightly nervous.

At last he appeared. He was dressed already, with a jacket and ball cap. He came to the doorway kitchen and looked around with a cool brevity, and then he continued toward the front door.

"Arie!" I cried. "Hey! Good morning!"

He stopped and looked back. There was a strange look on his face, one I couldn't read.

"Hey, give me a hand here. Help me get this stuff to the table. And come sit down to eat."

He didn't say anything, didn't move.

"Come on," I said. "Sit, sit. Breakfast. French toast, bacon, the works. C'mon."

He made a small head shake. "No thanks."

And he walked out the door.

***

When Rachel asked about my first evening in Lotus and how things were going with Arie, I debated internally for a second or two about what to tell her.

She had left instructions on where I should report for work. Even after cleaning up the unwanted breakfast (how I kept getting myself into the situation of making special homemade meals for people who didn't want them was a question I didn't take time to ponder), I still had plenty of time to make it there with fifteen minutes to spare.

My red bike had been stored in a small utility shed behind the cottage, and the ride to East Ten Administrative Office was a very pleasant ten-minute ride away. I was assigned to a small office and shown around the building, and I'd met a few people. Then Rachel found me and it was time for our meeting.

"And how was the rest of your night at home with Arie?" she asked.

I turned the question over in my head. Did I want her to know the truth? Or did I want to keep the truth from her? The last thing I wanted was anything that put me on awkward footing with either Lotus or Arie.

"It was very nice," I said. "Just a nice, quiet evening."

"Sounds great," she replied. "He seems like a really sweet kid."

"Yeah," I said. "Really, really sweet."

"I'm glad to hear it's going well," said Rachel. She had no office in this building, so she ushered me into a small meeting room. "I think you two will get along famously."

Again, I debated in my mind about whether I should tell her what had really happened. There seemed to be no point in that. What if I had read the situation wrong? What if Arie were simply a little nervous about suddenly living with a woman he'd never met before? What if he were just shy? Not a breakfast lover—or maybe it was just French toast he didn't love, or the bacon looked too crisp? Maybe he was a pancakes man.

Or scrambled eggs? Why had I settled on French toast? Everyone loves scrambled eggs.

None of it mattered anyway, because what help could I expect from Rachel? She couldn't tell him to behave or eat his breakfast, and I felt like I couldn't burden her with every little misgiving or concern. I was a newcomer—I'd been in Lotus for less than one entire day, and I wasn't at all eager to mark myself as easily injured or a complainer.

Then again, I didn't want to be a liar, either.

"I think so, too," I said.

Rachel began the meeting. Thoughts of French toast and degrees of crispiness in breakfast meats were tripping and tumbling through my head, and I was just telling myself that I should probably be paying more attention when I heard Rachel say something about being selected to be "an officer in the Lotus administrative corps."

"I'm sorry," I said, "did you say, 'officer'?" I stammered.

She nodded, but added, "An administrative officer. But yes. An officer. Are you okay with that?"

"I—well, yes. I mean, I guess so. I just—well, I thought I'd be doing something else. You know?"

"What did you think you'd be doing?"

"I—I don't know. I just didn't picture myself as an *officer*. I thought maybe I'd be, well, maybe working in a factory? Maybe working with Arie."

"Arie is doing an excellent job right now," said Rachel, "but we're not going to have him running machinery and manufacturing doo-dads for very long. He's too smart for that. And so are you. I can't afford to put someone like you into production or landscaping or anything like that."

"I'm flattered," I said, "and I want to help however I can."

"Good. The way you can help is by being in the administrative corps," she said with a laugh. "I want you to start out as a case manager."

"Case manager," I said, more to feel the words on my tongue than anything else.

"Admin officers, and case officers in particular, are people who can think on their feet, see things from lots of angles. Someone who is sharp and analytical but also open-minded and compassionate. Do any of these things sound like you, Alison?"

I actually thought they did, but rather than admit that, I said, "Wow, I'm just kind of blown away that you would trust me—"

"And humble, fine," said Rachel, "but I suspect that you agree that you fit this description. You seem to have a sense of what's fair, and fairness is a value that you hold. And yet you're complex enough to consider and evaluate extenuating conditions, nuances. You value fairness but you realize sometimes things aren't cut and dried. Am I right?"

"Yeah," I said, with no little surprise. "Yeah, I actually do feel that way."

"I thought so. I meant what I said when I told you that I'm looking forward to seeing what you can contribute. I want you to start as a case manager and we'll see where you go from there. I suspect you won't stay in this job long before you're onto bigger things."

"What kind of cases will I be managing?"

"Well, like I said before, we are trying to build something here. And when I say 'we,' I really mean that. You and me, you and everyone else. Me and all of you," she gestured to include everyone in the building.

"Ask any of the people here. What we do is cooperative and we all contribute. This isn't me telling you what to do and you 'cooperating' by doing it. I need your ideas, your honest effort. That's how we will create a community that is stable, productive. Something that will last, something that will continue to grow and improve."

When Rachel spoke about Lotus, about its inner workings and its grandiose objectives, I couldn't help but be inspired. What she said honestly sounded right and good. But doubts crept in, especially when I recalled sitting in Gary's sad little apartment, and how it seemed that everything related to the Agency was broken down, behind schedule, corrupt, or simply just bleak.

"Do you bake, Alison?" said Rachel.

"Do I bake? You mean like cakes and bread and things?"

"Yes, do you like baking?"

I shrugged. "I'm no good at it, but I've tried."

"Perfect. Have you ever tried to bake a cake with substandard ingredients? Coarse flour? Powdered eggs?"

"Oh, yes. I can't remember using anything but substandard ingredients."

"Then you'll take my point. If you want to bake a very special cake, a high-quality cake, you will want the very best ingredients, yes?"

"Sure, yeah."

"The best chocolate, baker's flour, fresh eggs, real butter, and so on."

"You're making me hungry. Sounds delicious."

"Precisely," said Rachel with a smile. "And to make Lotus into the most delicious society it can be, we are likewise in search of the best ingredients. You'll be on the front lines here, looking out for those who can best contribute to this effort, to this cake. I sometimes handle cases myself—like yours. Technically, I'm your case manager. But I can't vet and evaluate everyone. And that's where case managers come in."

"I'm not sure what to say to all this."

"Well, say yes, first of all. Unless you really do want a job landscaping."

"No, no," I said, my face heating a little. "I'll take the job."

"Excellent," said Rachel. "I have some reading for you—more about the Lotus philosophy, mission statements, guidelines. You dig into that and we'll talk some more tomorrow."

She produced a notebook filled with printed pages.

"I'll get started right away."

"Got any questions?" she said as she rose from the table.

"I'm sure I'll have lots," I said.

We walked through a hallway and outside where a driver was waiting at the door of another SUV. He opened the door.

"I'll see you soon," said Rachel. "Don't get overwhelmed. Call a staff member here if you do think of any questions you need answered. If it's something they can't answer, they'll pass it off to me."

"This is going to be so different," I said.

"Different is good."

"That's true. So, just to be clear, I'll be, well, evaluating people who are being recruited into Lotus? Like deciding whether they can join or not?"

"Yes, you will," said Rachel. "And you'll deal with people who might need to be reassigned, too."

I furrowed my brow.

"Mm, maybe I rushed through this. You'll evaluate Lotus candidates, of course, and that's a big responsibility, but you'll do the same for people who have, well, made mistakes, or aren't committed to their work. Some cases, hopefully rare, may require memory suspension and reassignment to the Starting Zones."

I looked at her.

"Don't sweat it," she said. "We're gonna make the most delicious cake you've ever had. Read the notebook. We'll talk soon."

CHAPTER 12

With a chubby round face, white beard, and a stout build, the man who sat across my desk from me could have been a department store Santa Claus, if things like Christmas were still celebrated. He even had slightly rosy cheeks and a nose like a cherry.

His name was Archie, one of the first cases I'd been assigned, and certainly the first challenging case—he had a drinking problem. Alcohol was not a contraband substance in Lotus, but neither was it freely available. Still, gray-market supplies were available, and I'd talked to Archie several times over the past few weeks about his reported excesses. Public drunkenness was one of the milder of the charges he'd accumulated. He'd been found multiple times urinating in public, and there were other infractions, mostly related to disorderly conduct and failing to report for work.

"Archie, my recommendation is for you to return to the Starting Zones," I told him.

I hated saying it. It was the only part of the job I hated at all.

Archie's eyes widened, and his mouth opened, but he said nothing. He just sat there, his face frozen like a mask or photo of someone who's been slugged hard in the gut. Archie had been warned many times that his indiscretions might become a real problem for him—perhaps he'd thought they never would.

"For our society to reach its highest potential, we have to hold its citizens to the highest standards," Rachel had told me, repeatedly, phrased in different ways, using a dozen different analogies and examples. "We simply don't have room for those who are not living up to their potential."

"For our society to reach its highest potential," I recited, "we have to hold everyone to the highest standards."

Archie's face remained frozen. "Please," Archie said at last, with a sort of dry squawk. "Don't do this. I have a problem, I know. I'm working on it. I am. But you can't do this. The punishment doesn't fit the crime."

He went on, speaking faster and faster. I shook my head and held up my hands.

"Archie, Archie—no. We've been over this. This isn't a punishment and you haven't committed a crime. You have potential. The Lotus admin board saw it, and they recognized it and that is why you are in Lotus in the first place."

"Then let me stay, please. Don't send me down. I promise I'll—"

"Archie, stop. We've talked and talked about this. You've been in here to see me four times in the past five weeks, and you were working with—" I checked his case file "—Bernadette before I got here."

"Okay, I know, but—"

"Listen," I said. I held up my hand again, raised my voice a little. "Nothing we can do will eliminate your potential. I've spoken to several people at your branch and they all say you're a gifted programmer and you get along great with everyone. It's just—look, I'm almost sure that after a cycle in the Starting Zones you'll be right back here to try again. There's no prejudice against you, Archie. No bad record or reputation to dog you, no fines, no jail. You just need a fresh start."

His face had reddened and now contrasted angrily against his white whiskers. "You don't know what it's like down there. You wouldn't be saying any of this if you did. They starve you. There's never enough. Old guys like me get the shit knocked out of us. You're never safe."

I'd heard this from more than a few of my cases.

"The Zones are definitely no picnic," Rachel had told me. "I don't think they should be that way, but I kind of have my hands full trying to re-build society, so there's not much I can do."

"The Zones are definitely no picnic," I said to Archie. "But starvation? Let's not exaggerate."

"Ah, god, don't do this," said Archie. "You obviously don't know how it is. It's a nightmare. It's hell. I can't go—"

"Archie, I'm sorry. It's settled. The recommendation was filed on Monday and it's already been accepted. Keeping you in Lotus would be unfair to you. It's obvious that you're already burdened by your past mistakes and the odds are that you'll repeat them. It's a downward spiral. A fresh start will break the cycle and you can start again—hopefully soon."

He leaned forward, his hands reaching out to me in a pleading gesture.

"I'll do anything. I will do anything you say. Just don't send me back there."

I put my hand in the air and through the window of my office I caught the attention of the Agency handlers who were seated outside my door. They stood and came into my office.

"Archie, I have a lot of confidence in you. Like I said, I think you're going to be right back here before the year is out, but we will be in-processing you, not out. Now, Archie—look at me for a sec. Archie, will you please accept this? Don't make trouble?"

The man was shattered. His eyes were downcast, but they had a frenzied gleam in them. His breathing was shallow, almost asthmatic.

"Archie. No trouble, okay?"

He nodded very slowly. One of the Agency handlers placed a hand on Archie's shoulder. Archie looked up at him and then at the other. He stood from his chair and turned toward the door. The handler behind Archie caught my gaze and made a silent gesture by crossing his wrists to ask me if I thought Archie should be handcuffed. I thought about this for a moment and then nodded my head. The phrase, "For his own safety," came into my mind, which always made me cringe. We said again and again that we did not hand out punishments. That losing memory privileges was not a punishment. But how could it not feel like a punishment when two burly men cuffed you and drove you silently away?

The handler gave me a quick and subtle thumbs-up, produced a pair of cuffs from somewhere beneath his jacket, and said, "Hold up there, sir. We're gonna restrain you—just a precaution, as much for your own good as ours."

And then the handler placed his hand on Archie's back and pointed down the hall.

At least they don't remember being cuffed, I thought. They don't remember any of this.

I took my job very seriously. There was no way I couldn't—Rachel had preached the Lotus philosophy to me so fervently it had become very like a religion. When she explained our procedures and objectives, it all made so much sense, and I felt I had to do my best in service of the cause.

Also, of course, meeting with others living in Lotus had become, in a very short time, a very personal matter. Discussing their innermost fears and desires and problems could be exhilarating and rewarding but it also affected me deeply.

And so I tried to be as fair as my conscience allowed, and that usually meant being as lenient as I could possibly be without being reprimanded myself.

All the other case managers seemed very serious and very dedicated, too. Most of them who I'd spoken to recommended re-assignment only after repeated infractions and many warnings. We even utilized tools like counseling and probation and incentives. And we encouraged our cases to improve, advised them as though they were our own relations and close friends. It was only after our cases found themselves trapped in the familiar cycle of failure (as Rachel called it) that we reluctantly recommended re-assignment.

In-processing was much more pleasant, obviously. Telling a confused and cagey Zone dweller that her life was about to improve by about three hundred percent—there was nothing better than that.

Mostly we made minor adjustments, minor corrections, issuing friendly reminders and warnings to cases who had slipped a bit. We let people know when they were falling behind, when they were failing themselves. We let them know when it was time for them to remember the trust Rachel had placed in them.

Almost all of them responded immediately and favorably. We told our cases that we were proud of them for remembering and reaching for their potential, but if I looked at things in a more cynical way, it sure looked like they were simply afraid of being sent down.

There were other kinds of work, like long-term follow-ups and evaluations and training. Most of the time, I felt good about the job, and I got the impression that Rachel at least was pleased with me. It was difficult to know if I was "making a difference," but when I got home, it was sometimes difficult to stop thinking about a certain problem or case, and that at least made me feel like the job meant something to me, and that I meant something to Lotus.

And then another Archie would walk through my door, and I'd carry him around in my mind for a few more days.

Out in the hallway, Archie began to shout. I couldn't make out exactly what, but I knew, and when I turned in that direction, I saw that he was resisting the handlers, too, jerking away from their grasping hands.

He won't remember any of it, I thought to myself. I turned away and lifted the receiver of my phone to tell Lloyd to send in my next case.

***

That afternoon I rolled home on my bike and parked it in the shed, as always. I came in through the side door and shrugged off my backpack, and then my coat, and I threw these on the sofa—again, as I almost always did. But when I got to the kitchen to make my usual cup of tea, Arie was sitting at the kitchen table. I flinched a little and stopped in my tracks.

111

He wore a dark scowl and his arms were folded across his chest.

"Hey there," I said brightly. "I'm surprised to see you. You're hardly ever here when I get home."

I tried to keep my voice cheery but not overly so. Arie only glowered back at me.

"What is it?" I asked, hoping that I was misreading his expression but knowing otherwise. "Is there something wrong? Hey, since you're here, and we've hardly even seen each other, wanna make some dinner together? You know what they had in the produce distribution yesterday? Avocados!"

Arie maintained his angry gaze and chewed his upper lip, as though trying to avoid screaming at me.

"Real avocados," I said, my voice growing smaller. "Two of 'em. A whole one each. I guess I don't even really know if you like avocados."

Arie took a deep breath and then let it out with a huff.

"What is it, Arie? What's wrong? What did I do?"

"Is it true you sentenced Archie to have his memory erased?"

I tried to absorb the question without looking too stunned. There were so many problems with his raising such a question.

"Well?" he said.

"Well," I said, "first of all, that is confidential information. So, whoever told you that or however you found out is kinda shady, from an Administrative Services standpoint."

"So it's true."

"Hang on," I continued, holding up a hand and keeping my voice steady. "We both know that A.S. doesn't give out punishments, so this isn't a 'sentence.'

You've been here longer than me—you know this. It's an administrative move. I make recommendations based on long and sometimes very in-depth interviews with the cases who are assigned to me. This isn't a court. This isn't a punishment. It's a change of status."

Arie scoffed. "There's no way you really believe that. Those bureaucratic double-speak words."

"This is my job. I don't know where you're getting your information, but I'm pretty sure you don't know all of the—"

"He was my friend," said Arie, his voice raised. "We worked together. Did you know that?"

"As a matter of fact, I did know he was employed at the same facility that you—"

"These reassignments are basically death, Alison," he shouted back. "I know you've been brainwashed to believe they're something else—that you're being compassionate or looking out for everyone's best interest, but it's a death sentence. Without memories, the person you are just goes away!"

"It was his third major offense, Arie," I said, and my voice was growing louder, too.

"Ah. So. It is a sentence. A sentence for an offense. So kind of you to give him three chances—three strikes and you're dead."

"You would over-dramatize it. There's no cruelty, no jail, no punishment. It's a chance to start over. That's all it is. We have a unique technology that allows us to—"

"—kill people without having to bury them! Yes! It's brilliant! When they do things you don't like, kill them and bring them back so they can keep working. You're gonna erase him for getting drunk? Having too much fun? Missing a little work? You can't really believe this horse shit you say every day, can you? Do you really believe it?"

"Arie, you're not thinking clearly about this. You're taking it personally. I'm sorry if he was your friend, but we are building a new society here. Friends are nice to have, but there are some things higher than personal satisfaction and having friends. You know? This isn't the back before. The human race is on a knife edge here. We have to be better; we have to have higher standards. That's how we're going to survive—no, thrive."

As he stood to go, he rolled his eyes with a deeply disgusted aspect.

"Why are you doing this? I mean, I know you're basically an adult, but I am still your mother, you know."

"No. I can't believe that. I can't believe that someone I'm supposedly related to would ever even attempt to set themselves above everyone else this way. I refuse to accept that we're related. And if we are—" here he waved his hand dismissively "—I don't want anything to do with you."

"Arie, stop. Don't say things like that. These aren't my rules. I didn't ask for this job."

"No, but you've taken quite a liking to it all, haven't you? Does it make you feel powerful? Does it make you feel special?"

"As a matter of fact, I happen to think that Rachel's system makes us all special and useful. She's made it possible to feel like we really are part of something wonderful."

He stabbed a finger at me. "You're part of the problem."

He may as well have stabbed me with a dagger. In fact that would have been less painful.

"I'm your mother!"

"No!" he shouted hoarsely. "I *had* a mother! And Rachel and your goddamn Administrative Services took her away!"

I took a faltering step back. "What are you talking about?"

"They took my mother when some stupid test showed that you and me share some stupid genetic material. I had a mother. And she understood what's going on in the world, and we were working to set things right. She was smart, and she was actually compassionate. She actually cared about people."

"You're not making any sense. How could you have another mother?"

Arie stomped over to me. From his pocket he produced a small color photograph and held it up for me to see. It was careworn and frowzy at the edges. In it, Arie had his arms around a woman of about my age, but she was taller and had red hair.

"You think I was just living here by myself before you came? No! I lived with her," he said, tapping the photo with his finger, "my mother. My real mother. I don't care what some stupid fake test says. This is my mother and your people took her."

He stormed out of the house and slammed the door.

CHAPTER 13

I didn't sleep much for the next few days, by which I guess I mean didn't sleep at all.

I would have liked to have had a more civil conversation with Arie about what he said about Lotus and my job and our relationship, but I hadn't seen him for almost two days. This was the source of some worry about where he might be and if he were okay, but his angry shouts and arguments about the core of Lotus philosophy told me that there was probably even more to Arie than I'd first reckoned, and that he was more than capable of taking care of himself.

And so all the things he had said just swirled in my head and for a few days there were several things I found I couldn't do very effectively—eat, sleep, work, sit quietly.

There had not been a lot of communication between Arie and I for weeks, and no familial affection whatsoever, but in my mind I doggedly maintained that the unquestionably bad state of affairs might really be due to some combination of his personality, my personality, and the situation we found ourselves in. I'd never been re-united with a son I didn't remember. The experience might actually have been familiar to Arie, but I hadn't known that and the change in his life arrangements must have been jarring, nonetheless. In any case, I also considered the possibility that he might be suffering from something like culture shock. Family relationship shock? Something. I had trouble accepting that he didn't like me and never would.

Rachel would be visiting my Administrative Services branch in just a couple days, as she did several times every month. We met to discuss policy changes, escalated cases, and other matters. Sometimes she just came to make sure we were in good spirits.

In actuality, I could have reached out to her at any time to talk about my problems with Arie—as busy as Rachel was, she almost never failed to take a phone call from me, and she seemed pleased at the chance to give me advice or listen to me when a particular case made me feel bad.

"We're in this together," she'd tell me. "Your problems are my problems. You call me anytime."

Despite how Arie seemed to despise me, I found that I loved him fiercely in spite of it all. This came as something of a surprise to me. I was fond of Arie from the moment we met there on the front yard that night we ate enchiladas, but after he'd treated me coldly, and especially after our confrontation about Archie and my position in Lotus, in a weird way I felt even closer to him.

It was maybe just a way to soothe the hurt I felt that night, but I reasoned with myself that something like caring or affection toward me had prompted Arie to talk about Archie with me that day. If he had absolutely no care for me at all, would he have said anything? Can someone let you down if you don't care about them?

And, I told myself, perhaps grabbing at a straw that was the very farthest from me, Arie was at least very passionate about what he believed and quite able to put forward a solid argument.

But clearly we could never build any kind of family bond on the basis of shouting at each other. So, after my meeting with Rachel I would ask her what she thought of it. But first, I had to know about this other lady who apparently Arie thought of as his mother.

During Rachel's visit to our department meeting, I couldn't concentrate on anything that was discussed. There was something about a member of Lotus suspected of visiting A.S. just for attention, but I don't remember how such a case was to be handled. There was a policy shift about the timing of recommendations, but I didn't listen to what it meant for managers. Rachel warned us that there might be more in-processing cases, but I missed the reasons why. My co-worker Andre had some questions about cross-referencing cases to get better information for interviews, but Rachel's answers went into my head without staying in my memory.

And so I listened with one ear, with half my brain, waiting for the clock on the wall to count down an hour or so, which is typically how long Rachel spared for such meetings. All I really thought about was Arie and the person he said was his mother.

When the meeting finally did adjourn, after more than ninety minutes, Rachel remained in her chair making some notes while the others filed out of the room. I stayed seated, too. Without looking up from her work, Rachel dispensed encouragement and little inter-office reminders as the room emptied.

I'd planned to wait until everyone was gone and then ask Rachel if she could give me a few minutes more, but before I could say anything to her, Rachel said, "You okay, Alison? You seem a little out of it."

"I am," I said. "Or maybe not. I'm sorry. Something's come up, something that's upsetting me a little."

"Close that door," she said. "Let's chat."

I swung the door closed and sat down again.

"What is it?" asked Rachel, putting her pen and pad away.

I had intended to ease into the matter, but instead I cut right to it. "Arie told me last night that he already had a mother before I came."

She blinked, made a little head-nod, and said, "Arie had a caregiver, yes. I'm almost sure he was told not to discuss that, but he did have a caregiver before you joined Lotus."

"Why?"

"Even though he's nearly an adult and very capable of looking after himself, there are policies about people under eighteen years old. He's technically still a child. She was a caretaker."

"Arie seems to think of her as his mother."

Rachel shook her head again. "Well, that makes sense. They were together for more than a year. Makes sense that they'd grow close. Why is this a concern?"

"Well, where is she now? His—caretaker?"

"She was re-assigned. I'm not deeply familiar with the case, but I'm sure it was handled in a routine way. When these kinds of familial connections are uncovered, there are policies regarding the re-uniting or re-arrangement of the people involved. We have found that family members tend to harbor their connection to

119

one another even after their memories have been revoked. Would you rather not be with him?"

"No," I said. "It's not that."

"Then I'm still not sure I understand how this presents a problem for you or Arie." Her voice may have taken a colder tone.

"Oh, it is apparently a huge problem for Arie," I said. "For one thing, he is furious with me. I haven't told you this, but I think he resents me for replacing her. We've barely spoken since that first night when I arrived."

"Why didn't you tell me this earlier?" asked Rachel, placing her elbows on the table and leaning in my direction.

"I don't know. I guess I thought I was being over-sensitive. I thought I was over-reacting. I wanted to see if things got better. But now they're a lot worse."

"Why now? What happened?"

I drew a big breath and let it out. "He confronted me about one of my cases. The man with the drinking problem—I guess he and Arie worked together and were friends."

"You told Arie about one of your cases?"

"No, no," I protested. "Arie knew about it. I'd recommended the guy for re-assignment, and that evening, Arie knew about it."

"Did Arie say how he'd found out about this?"

"No, he didn't," I said, putting my palm on my brow. "But he was beyond angry. He shouted for a while at me and ran out of the house and I haven't seen him since."

"Did he say anything else?" asked Rachel.

"What do you mean?"

"Well, you say he didn't tell you how he knew about the re-assignment of his friend, but did he say anything that might clue you in as to how he knew? Or anything else that was curious?"

"Curious? No, nothing else aside from the fact that he'd had some other mother before me—that was curious."

"I'm sorry you had to find out about it like that."

"Well, then he ranted about how re-assignment to the Starting Zones is like a death sentence. That's what he said—death sentence. And he ranted about how cruel it was. I guess I kind of get it. I mean, having your memories—revoked—is a fairly drastic life change for someone who—"

"Alison, do we need to go over the grounding of this system? You know how it works. We are leveraging an opportunity that no one in the history of humanity has ever held."

And she went on from there and I nodded and I even agreed, as I usually did.

When she stopped, I asked, "Did you know her? Arie's mother? Or—caretaker?"

"No, I didn't."

"Can I speak with her? Maybe get together with her and Arie? Maybe we can iron things out. I mean, I feel connected with Arie, but he's obviously very shaken up about the change, and it's obvious they've not had contact—he's carrying around a tattered little picture of them together. I just think maybe if we could all get together in the same room? Do you think that might help out?"

"Well, I'm not sure, but it doesn't matter because that's just not possible, Alison," she said.

"Why?" I asked.

"I told you. She's been re-assigned. To the Zones. If my memory of the case serves, there were certain shortcomings in her participation at Lotus, too. In a way, it was fortuitous that we found you at that time. It was good that you could step in."

"Shortcomings?"

"I don't have the case in front of me and it's been a while since I reviewed it. But yes, she's been re-assigned and as you know, it wouldn't be helpful or productive to know the reasons anyway. We've put those things behind not just for her but ourselves, too, and besides all of that—she wouldn't know Arie now, obviously. She's had her memories revoked. It would just be confusing for everyone."

I sighed and nodded. "I just don't know what to do. Arie clearly doesn't need me to take care of him, which is fine, I mean that's what any parent wants, but I'm terrified that he doesn't want anything to do with me anymore. He seems to hate me, and it just hurts so much."

"Let's give him some time," Rachel said as she patted my knee reassuringly. "Let's see if he'll come around."

"I hope he will," I said.

"I really think he will," she said. "I still have a good feeling about you two. He's a really smart guy and very mature for a teenager in his position, but don't forget that he's also still a kid. And this situation we're in—it's not easy for everyone."

"Do you really think that's all there is to it?" I asked hopefully.

"I think chances are good that's all there is to it," said Rachel. "And I'm awfully sorry you're struggling right now, but I need to talk to you about one of your cases. Do you remember the case of Megan Williams?"

I did. Mostly because the case was so heartbreaking, especially given my situation with Arie. Megan was a young mother with a two-year-old boy named Sam. She'd been cooking something on the stove and left the handle of the pot extending out over the edge of the stove top. When she left the kitchen for just a moment, Sam had toddled over and grabbed the handle, and the pan of boiling-hot food had spilled onto his face and down his body. He'd gotten prompt medical care, but he developed an infection and had almost died.

Rachel and I discussed it for a while. The boy had apparently survived, though no one knew how. He was badly disfigured, however, was blind in one eye, and suffered from mobility problems. I thought of Gary, his face shiny with scar tissue.

The mother, Megan, had been assigned to me as a case manager and I'd been told a recommendation of re-assignment would almost certainly be accepted. The case looked like it should go that way to me, too. Megan had made other lapses in her parenting. Sam had gotten away from her once and had spent several hours outside, wandering, which had led to a nasty case of bronchitis. In severe cases like Megan's, there were almost never counseling or warnings. In the most severe cases, we did not give warnings. I never saw little Sam with his burns or bandages, but I could only imagine the small child, slathered in sticky antibiotic creams, oozing fluid, and wrapped in gauzy dressings. The thought of this tiny creature defenseless against his own mistakes and with such bleak recovery prospects troubled me to my core. I could only imagine what Megan was going through. Others involved with her case told me that she cried all the time—for the child, surely, but also for her negligence.

After the stove incident, however, Megan never left the little boy's side. She stayed with him every second until he was released, ignoring the nurses' urgings to leave to go get rest or at least a change of clothes.

"I remember," I said.

"You recommended taking no action on this case," Rachel said.

"I recommended further counseling and follow-ups."

"You upheld her behavior as acceptable?"

"I guess that's true," I said. "Megan's actions may have been neglectful, but I didn't see them as negligent or deviant in any big way. She would never hurt that little boy purposely. It looked to me like she had learned her lesson."

"Alison, we've gone over this. We're not here to teach lessons. We offer encouragement, we offer counseling, but we don't have the capacity to carry people who'd shirk their duties that way. We could have lost that little boy, and as it is, he'll never be the same."

"I know, I know," I said. "And Megan knows too. I doubt that anything remotely similar will ever happen again. She feels just awful about the whole thing."

"Exactly. She would have been burdened by this careless incident for the rest of their lives. Every time she looked at him. It was just too big a mistake to let pass."

"What do you mean?" I asked. "Are you saying you want me to look at the case again? Change my recommendation?"

"No, I already did," said Rachel. "It's been taken care of. The reason I wanted to speak to you about it is to make sure you understood your role. When Megan was referred to you, I thought we were all in agreement that she needed re-assignment. I was very surprised to see your recommendation. I don't second-guess my managers often, but in this case, it was called for."

"Wait, she's been re-assigned already? She's been wiped?"

"You know I don't care for that term. Wiped. Megan has been re-assigned and so has little Sam."

I sat dumbstruck for a few moments. Rachel put her hand on my shoulder.

"Like I said, Alison, I try not to micromanage or reverse recommendations very often. This was an exception. But I need you to know that your track record is somewhat on the lenient side, and there's nothing technically wrong with that, but please don't let it turn into a problem."

"I'm just shocked. I would have liked to have talked to her again. To make sure she understood. I mean, I don't agree with this. It was a mistake."

"It was a series of mistakes," Rachel reminded.

"Okay, it was a series of mistakes," I said. "She didn't deserve the Starting Zones."

"Alison, I know you're new, but re-assignment is not a matter of 'deserving'," said Rachel. "These aren't punishments. Megan will be better for the re-assignment. We gave her what she needed, not what she deserved."

All I could think about was poor Sam wondering where his mother was, spending his life in someone else's keeping with little chance of knowing his mother. Would Megan simply be replaced? Like I had been? For all Rachel's talk of placing priority on keeping families together, I found this decision hurtful.

"They were accidents, oversights," I said, more to myself than to anyone else. The case was shut. There wasn't a point to debating it any further.

"It was a pattern of behavior," said Rachel. "If she has the excellence we're looking for, she'll be re-instated. You know that. But listen—I didn't inform you of this to get your opinion about it. It was just a courtesy. And I know you're having trouble at home, and I know you think you're doing people like Megan a favor by showing leniency. I'm not reprimanding you right now, but I need you to be more careful from now on or you might find you don't have a position here anymore."

There was a growing iciness in Rachel's voice that I'd never detected before. She'd always been warm and positive to me before. Was it all an act? Were we friends or was she just a boss who was friendly until the first moment of disagreement? At first I was slightly frightened by this—the woman did after all have complete control over my life. But all at once, the combination of all of it—Arie's behavior, the overriding of my case recommendation, and even the odd undercurrent of uneasiness I felt on that first evening I arrived at Lotus—seemed to focus now like sunbeams through a magnifying glass. I almost felt that if there were any dry leaves nearby, my sudden hot anger might set them alight. It was perfection Rachel was after, and there is no warmth in perfectionism.

"Do you mean," I asked, my tone more acid than I intended, "that I won't have a position as case manager, or that I'll be re-assigned to the Zones, too?"

Rachel stood and placed her fingertips on my shoulder. She looked down at me for a second or two longer and said, "Just promise me it's not going to be an issue."

CHAPTER 14

When I'd gotten out of the building and down to the bike racks, I discovered that my bicycle had a flat tire. And I laughed at my rotten luck, though if I knew where that flat tire would lead me, I might not have.

"Can this day possibly get any worse?" I muttered.

Of course, I thought, replying to myself. It can always get worse. It's fine, it's fine. I'll walk, I thought. But I turned my face heavenward and flipped the bird.

Despite everything that had happened and everything I knew was yet to unfold, I couldn't deny that it actually was a beautiful evening. The days were growing longer now and everything was green and warm with the full expression of springtime and hints of the fast-approaching summer. The sun was dipping down, and the sky was indigo turning to purple and red.

Along my way home there stood a small food-processing plant, and its grounds were lined with a tall row of cottonwood trees that hissed softly against the breeze.

In the warm evening air, the ancient trees cast away their downy seeds, which fell like snow and were carried along on the gentle wind. The setting sun illuminated the white puffs, making them glow like giant sparks blown free from a fire. When these wisps of flame reached the ground, they collected and swirled on the lazy currents of air, spinning slowly. One after another the wispy whirlwinds approached me, whirled around me, and then dissipated.

It took much longer to make the trip to my house on foot than on the bike. I began to feel so tired that I thought I might just go home and sleep instead of making any food or reading a book.

I mused that when I awoke, maybe Arie would have forgiven me for replacing his former caretaker and for working with Lotus and their system of maintaining order. How lovely it would be to wake up and find things with Arie improving, to find my work at Lotus was rewarding and productive.

But the thing that lurked underneath it all was making itself known again, and in stronger terms. Something didn't sit right, though I couldn't quite say what, nor could I think of how to fix it. How can you fix something when you don't even know what is wrong?

Mostly, of course, it was Arie. Despite my attempts to explain it all away with justifications and excuses, Arie wanted nothing to do with me, and apparently he didn't have much confidence in Lotus, either. I had no good way to change that—might he show up in my office one day for acts against the community?

I thought of the two other mothers I had learned about at Lotus—Arie's caretaker and Sam's mom, Megan—who'd been cut off from the children they loved and had cared for. I was beginning to know the misery they must have felt. Or what they were still feeling.

The fiery cottonseeds rode the breeze in the coppery light, falling around me like a slow, warm blizzard.

Rachel had told me that people in families consistently out-performed those who were on their own in Lotus, even those who didn't remember each other at first. This made perfect sense, of course. I was overcome with an almost instant sensation of connection and belonging the moment I learned that I had a son who had survived—I hadn't even met him and I felt it. Even the presence of Gary in the apartment at the Agency campus was a mild reassurance against complete isolation.

Rachel said that Lotus had been designed such that our collective actions would lead to more family units, more belonging, more connectedness. Not necessarily moms and dads and kids. Not necessarily nuclear families, but units where people in various roles lived together, cared for each other, and could help cope with the pressures and difficulties of these days of rebuilding after the back before.

So what about Megan and the woman who'd been assigned to Arie? Where were they now? How were they getting along with these pieces missing from their hearts? And which was worse: to remember the bad things we have done or to forget everything that was good?

The buildings and landmarks that I saw each day on my bicycle commute passed by me that evening at walking speed, giving the impression that time had slowed down. The cottonwood castings fell slowly around me.

I had fallen into a kind of trance, the half-drowse of the long walk, when I noticed something unusual. I don't mean I noticed something and then evaluated it as unusual, like if I'd seen a hot-air balloon float by or a penguin wobbling along the sidewalk. I mean that in my hazy state of mind, I determined that something unusual was happening and was then left to say what it was.

It was a sound.

And it wasn't the kind of sound that put me instantly on alert. It was just unusual.

I approached the final landmark on my homeward trip—a cluster of metal sheds that seemed always to be closed, but that I assumed stored some useful goods or industry. My house was now just a mile off, and it was then that I puzzled out the sound and why it was unusual.

It was a vehicle. Approaching me. From behind.

There weren't many motor-vehicles in Lotus, so you got used to marking their presence. And I probably would have caught on sooner had I not been wandering in my slow-motion thoughts as I walked home.

I turned and saw that it was a van. But again, it was unusual. Most of the very thin vehicle traffic in Lotus took place in the morning and early afternoon—business deliveries and pick-ups. You hardly ever saw vehicles roaming around at this time of day.

Also, this van was rugged-looking, with big gnarly tires, and it was covered in mud and dust. The vehicles that drove around Lotus were, by and large, well-kept and clean.

I stopped, and the van slowed. It passed by me but stopped about fifty feet ahead of me. A door on the side swung open and three men jumped out onto the sidewalk.

And now, the situation no longer seemed just unusual but mildly threatening, and my nerves began to tingle as though I'd suddenly picked up a static charge from a balloon or deep carpet.

All three men were lean, athletic. They moved like they were preparing to take the court for some vigorous sport. I was about to make a rapid turnabout when I realized they were looking intently at me.

There is so much that we communicate and understand without words or other explicit signals. There's so much material that our minds can use to figure out when someone means us harm or when there is danger. A look in the eye. A firmness of step. Body language that is hostile. I don't know what details made me all at once ready for action. Only my subconscious knew, but that was enough.

One of the men waved at me, beckoning me to come to the van.

"Hey, Alison, come over here," he said—his voice was calm but heavy, serious.

"No," I said. "Who are you guys? What do you want?"

Two of them looked at the other guy, the one who'd waved at me. He made a quick, almost imperceptible nod, and then the other two men bolted in my direction.

They were fast. I had almost no time to decide what to do before they crossed most of the distance between me and them. I swung the bicycle in front of me so that it stood cross-ways between us, and then I let it go, shuffle-stepping furiously backward. The bike stood there for a split-second, balanced on its flat tire, then began to slowly fall. I was now practically within reach of the faster of the two men. He leaped to hurdle the bike, and his form looked terrifyingly perfect to me, but one of his feet struck the seat or handlebars and both he and the bike went flipping and sprawling onto the concrete.

I turned to run but the other man took hold of me and stopped me short, pulling me back by my backpack as I strained to keep running. It felt like I was suddenly tied to a tree, but I let my arms slip free of the straps and he too staggered back and down onto the pavement.

I fled into the easement between two of the metal buildings, but I heard their footsteps not far behind me.

"Hey," one of them said, "stop!"

Despite my slowness to react at first, I was fast, too, and now there was some distance between us again.

"Stop! Alison! We just wanna talk!" he shouted, his voice jagged with his running.

I didn't look back but he couldn't have been more than four or five long strides from catching me. Between the buildings I turned first one corner and then another before I came to a chain-link fence that barred the way.

For an instant I slowed my pace and thought, this is it. I'm trapped and there's nothing to do but turn and fight. But then, to my surprise certainly as much as anyone's, some kind of muscle-memory-impulse took over, and I hurled myself onto the fence. My hands caught the top edge and my feet landed high up on the chain-link and in another instant I'd clawed up the fence and vaulted over to the far side.

This gave me a moment to look back. One of the men was close behind and he made the fence ring as he too leapt upon it. The other man was running too, but he was much farther behind and favoring one leg, probably the result of his involvement with my bike.

I sprinted on, and with what must have been an entire pint of adrenaline dumping into my bloodstream I felt very light and fast. The metal buildings were of various sizes, a makeshift storage yard. I zigged and zagged between them and around corners, and when I chanced a glance behind me, I didn't see anyone there. If I could get out of their sight, they'd eventually run down the wrong alley and I could gain more ground on them and get out of reach.

Beyond the complex of buildings stood a wooded area, and I made for that, hoping to lose myself in the trees and undergrowth. After that and perhaps when it got dark, I could circle around quietly to my neighborhood and get to a phone. I ran harder.

As I turned another corner and was about to make for the trees, a figured stepped in front of me and swung his elbow into my face. The impact made me see a split-second of the most celestial white, and I was knocked hard to the ground like a big sack of oranges.

And then there was only blackness.

CHAPTER 15

The touch of something icy on my arm woke me, not from sleep but from a kind of stunned stupor, a fog of pain. Everything around me was black; I couldn't see a thing. I wondered how much time had passed since I'd been cracked in the face. I was sure that had really happened because my nose felt broken. My entire face felt caved in.

That's a swab of alcohol on my arm, I thought. Someone is getting ready to stick me with a needle. And my nose is broken, I thought.

These were the only coherent thoughts I could put together at first, but a few moments later it occurred to me with a cruel, too-late clarity that I'd been consigned to return to the Starting Zones, and that in a few seconds more, or probably less, I'd be injected with the memory serum and my mind would be scrubbed clean again. My past, my identity would be gone, just like that day in the hospital room with the big nurse and Gary.

So this is how a case manager's recommendation are enacted, I thought. A crew of guys jumps out of a scratched-up old van and bashes you on the head while you're going home from work, and then they jab a needle in your arm.

It didn't fit.

It didn't seem to square with everything else I knew about Lotus. However, to my mild surprise, it really did seem exactly like meeting death. What little I had done and the few memories I had accumulated were not particularly happy or compelling, but those thoughts and memories were mine, and they were basically who I was. Arie was there. My new start was there. They weren't just "my" memories; the memories were me. And like anyone who had contemplated this kind of memory loss—which included everyone involved with Lotus and surely all of those in the Starting Zones—I knew that the person who awoke afterward would not be me. More accurately, the person I was now, in the present moment, would lose all future influence over the future of the person who would awaken.

Was that not exactly the same as having no future events to influence? Was that not death?

I wondered if this had been the way it was when I'd met this memory-death before, this prick-in-the-arm death. As they took Gary away burned and dying, did they hood me and inject me to flush away whatever memories I'd made to that point? Was it the same squad of guys maybe even? The memory-death squad? Did they hold me and press down on me this way? Break my nose?

I waited for the needle to puncture the skin of my arm, just below my shoulder, the spot that long ago someone had decided was the place hypodermic needles should go.

Was this really for my own good? I asked myself the question. Were they justified in taking away my memories of Arie? I'd sided with the wrong people and apparently there was a deadly explosion and, yes, that sounded terrible, but what other memories had been taken from me? What knowledge might I have had that could have helped with the effort of rebuilding? What other people were in my life and my past that I might never be reminded of?

No, I thought. Not again.

I drew my knees up to my ribs to mule kick whomever was holding that needle, but I then felt additional hands hold me in place—there were at least the three of them holding me now.

"Three against one, you cowards," I said, only I quickly figured out that I didn't really say it, or, if I did, no one heard. In any case no one replied. I really was out of it—head spinning, hardly able to tell which direction was up. "Get off me, you slimy goddam cowards," I repeated without speaking.

I twisted and squirmed and bucked, but I was also bound at the ankles and wrists. I pulled at the restraints. It was duct tape.

"Get off me!" is what I wanted to (but did not) shout.

And then the needle stung me.

Not painful, I thought. Well done, memory-death squad. A quick sting. Like a flu shot.

This was followed by another touch of icy wetness.

I wondered how the memories would go away. Would I sense their departure or would I black out first? Would it be painful? Would it be sad?

A new layer of grogginess seeped into my senses. My limbs suddenly felt like they were made of lead.

Wait, I thought. No, this can't be right. This thuggish treatment. This cannot be right.

This was not Lotus, I thought. No, Lotus is about order, safety, dignity. So, they're not from Lotus, and this is not a memory wipe. They're drugging me. Taking me somewhere. They've bound me and thrown me into their van, and now they have to drug me so I don't flail around.

Yeah, I thought, good idea, you pathetic creeps. Clobber me, sit on me, tie me up, and then, just to be sure the hundred-and-thirty-pound office worker doesn't kick all of your asses, drug me up. Because I'm just that threatening. Well done, you jerks.

But I didn't think any of that, I spoke it aloud.

"Oh, quiet down," said a man's voice. "You're worse than they said you'd be."

The hands let me go, and I was lowered on my side onto the hard, cool floor of the van.

As a drowsy warmth spread from my chest and into my extremities, I noticed that my surroundings were not dark, but that there was some loose covering over my head, a sack of some kind. I could see light through the weave of the fabric. It had an unpleasant smell, like old motor oil or engine parts. I drifted down and away from consciousness. I heard quiet voices, and I heard the sound of the van's doors slamming shut. Then the engine started. Then the springy jostling of driving.

I thought: it really can always get worse. But I said that out loud, too.

"Very true," said the male voice. He chuckled bleakly. "Sorry about your nose."

"Where are you taking me?" I demanded. At least I thought I demanded that. But there was no answer. As I drifted off, I realized that I was at least no longer feeling any pain.

CHAPTER 16

When I awoke, again, I was still bound at the hands and wrists, still lying on my side, still shrouded in darkness.

But not in a vehicle.

Everything was still. I moved a little. I ached all over. The floor was of cool concrete, I decided, and it was gritty. I tried to sit up but couldn't.

My head was pounding like a hangover now, my nose throbbed miserably again, and I felt a little sick to my stomach. I was dying for a drink of water. I struggled to sit up again, but this time I heard footsteps approaching me from a short distance. Then hands beneath my arms hoisted me up and into a chair with my wrists taped together behind me, sitting wasn't much more comfortable than lying on the floor. I felt woozy and everything from my neck up ached and throbbed.

"Sorry about leaving you on the floor." It was a gravelly male voice, one I hadn't heard before. "I put you in the chair when you got here, but you almost fell over."

"Where am I?" I demanded. This time I was pretty sure I got the words out, but they were slurred.

"Don't worry about that right now," said the man. His voice was gruff and baritone, but it wasn't unkind.

"There'll be people looking for me, you know," I said. "I'm a Lotus officer."

"Mm, yeah, an *admin* officer."

"They'll come for me."

"I'm sure someone is out looking for you right now," said the man. "But they're not going to find you anytime soon, so maybe just chill out for now." His voice was modulated not for scorn but for comfort, and he was oddly reassuring.

"Easy for you to say," I spat back.

"Also, we're not going to hurt you."

I scoffed at this. "A little late to say that," I said. I sniffed and swallowed the clot of blood that slid down the back of my throat.

"Please just relax."

"Why am I tied up?" I growled. "You afraid of me? Why is this bag on my head?"

"Orders," he said.

"Whose orders?"

"Ruby's."

"Who's Ruby? Who are you? Where am I?"

"Still so stubborn," he muttered. "My name's Woolly. I can't tell ya where you are. Just wait. You're safe."

"Can you at least take this bag off my head? It's making me sick. It stinks."

The man sighed. "I'm not real sure what I'm allowed to do or not do here. I didn't think you'd wake up so quickly. So, if it's all right, I'd rather we wait until Ruby gets here and let her explain everything."

"Please," I said. "Please, *Woolly*?" I tried playing to his evidently compassionate nature. "I was having a really shitty day before you thugs chased me down and punched me in the face."

"Someone punched you in the face? Who punched you?"

"How should I know? Probably you!"

I heard the man get up from the chair and I heard his quick, heavy footsteps approach. He snatched the sack from my head and threw it aside.

We were in a small room, probably a basement, judging from the concrete floor and the heavy beams above. It was cluttered with debris and dusty, and the only light came from the yellow kerosene flame of a lantern that hung from a nail on the wall behind my captor.

The man who'd called himself Woolly glared in disbelief at my face, which I assumed was caked with blood from my nose. Woolly was probably in his late twenties and massively built. His arms hung at his sides like enormous cables. His legs were like young oak trees. He wore a black t-shirt and denim cargo shorts. His bushy, faintly red hair was cropped short, and his round face was fringed by a beard of coarse and curly whiskers. He examined my face for a couple seconds more with his appalled expression, and then he stormed off behind me. I craned my head around and saw him pass through a dark doorway.

"Henderson!" he barked, his voice flat and harsh in the small space.

Someone far off answered.

"Get down here!"

I heard someone descending stairs, and then there was a scuffling of strong men and not a little bit of cursing.

Woolly returned, dragging another man, presumably Henderson, into the room by the arm like a misbehaving toddler.

"Apologize," growled Woolly.

"I'm sorry," said the man. "Really. I didn't mean to be so rough."

Had I not been tied up, I'd have socked him in the nose, but I also knew he really meant it.

"All right," said Woolly. "Get back to work. This isn't over. You better stay away from Ruby."

The man shrugged at me and said, "Really. I am sorry. I've heard you're really nice." And then he scuttled from the room.

"I apologize, too, Al," said the big man with a long, heavy sigh. "I hate violence." He went and sat spraddle-legged on a chair about ten feet from me.

Who were these thugs, so apologetic and reassuring?

"It's okay, I guess," I said. "I don't think it's broken."

"Oh, I'm glad," said Woolly.

With the oily sack taken from my face, I felt a little better, and my head had cleared some. It now seemed less likely that I'd been abducted for some summary execution, and I felt safe enough for the moment, but I didn't need any of my original memories to know I was still in a dicey situation. And although the man who watched over me seemed at least decent, if not actually quite civil, I really just wanted to be at my home in Lotus. I thought of Arie, and then I bowed my head to cry.

"Oh boy," Woolly groaned. He stood, holding up his hands and shaking them. "Oh, don't do that. We're not gonna hurt—I mean they're not gonna—I mean no one's gonna hurt you. I promise. We—they—just want to talk to you is all."

"I want to go home," I half-sobbed.

He stood by my side. "I know. But you can't. I'm sorry. How 'bout a drink of water instead?"

I nodded. He went back to his chair and picked up a steel canteen. He came close and gently set the spout to my lips so that I could drink.

"Thanks," I said.

"No problem," he said, patting me on the shoulder with a massive paw. Then, he pulled a handkerchief from his pocket and wetted it with the water and gently dabbed at the blood on my face.

"Would it help if we talked?" he asked. "Let's talk."

I didn't answer.

"I'm going to get in a lot of trouble for all of this. The talking. The letting you see me. God help Henderson when Ruby sees your nose. Anyway, I toldja who I am. I'm Woolly." He placed his big hand on his chest. "And you are Alison. We used to know each other. We were friends, if you can believe that, and then you were—well, you left."

I blinked at him and then attempted to wipe my eyes with my shoulder.

"You know me, too, huh?"

"Yeah. It's a weird feeling, isn't it?"

"I'm getting used to it," I said. "Seems like everyone I run into lately says they know me and I don't know them."

He shrugged and nodded glumly. "Well, believe it or not, we knew each other before we knew each other the last time. Does that make any sense? It's all still very bizarre to me."

"How did we know each other?"

143

"Well, I had only just taken the serum and reawakened myself about a month before you and Chase took off, so there's not much about you that I remember. But you and me sort of had this same conversation when I came to. But that time it was you telling me that we were friends before, and it was me deciding if I believed it."

Chase. I stiffened in the chair. I took the mention of his name to mean that this Woolly person and possibly the person named Ruby to be players in my past life, the criminals who'd somehow ensnared me, and had eventually led me to somehow setting off a bomb that almost killed a person who may or may not have been my husband.

"Well," I said in an acid tone, "I can tell you right now I don't want to have anything to do with you or Chase or this Ruby person. Thank you for not hurting me—anymore—but I have nothing to say to any of you."

"Suit yourself," said Woolly, "but they are gonna wanna talk to you."

"So, why not just come to my house? Knock on the door? Ever heard of that?"

Woolly smiled. "Believe it or not, Lotus isn't that easy to get into. We only just discovered this place existed a few weeks ago. The place is crawling with plain-clothes guards, and the uniformed guards you see around town aren't carrying water pistols. Plus, word on the street is that a lot of spying goes on in Lotus. It's hard to know who to trust."

"So, you're criminals, terrorists. I'm telling you, I don't want to have anything to do with you. I won't cooperate."

Woolly shrugged his big shoulders, rolled his eyes with pure exasperation, and said nothing.

I stopped talking, equal parts frightened and angry. What would Arie think when I didn't come home? He probably wouldn't even notice. Would anybody miss me? I supposed I'd be reported for not showing up at work, but I wasn't scheduled to work for three days, and the truth was I had no one in the world to actually care for me. Not Gary. Not Arie. Not Rachel. Nobody.

Woolly had crossed his thick arms over his chest and was looking at the floor with a meditative gaze.

I sat in the chair with my limbs bound, growing more uncomfortable.

"How long before they get here?" I asked, thinking that I might at least be untied.

"There's really no telling," said Woolly. "But hey, do you like chess?"

"Do I like Chase?"

Woolly scoffed merrily. "I already know the answer to that. No, I said *chess*. The medieval game of kings." From a knapsack at his side he produced a miniature magnetic chessboard.

"Oh. *Chess*. Do I like chess? I don't know. Yeah?"

"How 'bout a game?"

"What did you mean you already know the answer to—"

"Black or white?"

I glared at him.

He stood and placed his chair across from me, then he unfolded the beat-up little board and began setting up the pieces.

"Black or white?" said Woolly. "Do you have a preference?"

I shrugged and nodded vaguely to my hands, which were bound behind me. "No, but I don't think I can move the pieces. Not like this."

"Right," said Woolly, "I thought you could just tell me where you want to move and I'll move the pieces."

"Psh. How? I don't know what they're *called*."

"I thought you said you liked chess."

"Well, yeah, I mean, who doesn't love the medieval game of kings after getting clubbed and drugged and abducted?"

Woolly looked at me with a hurt expression. "You weren't supposed to be treated rough. That wasn't supposed to happen."

"And yet here I am with a broken nose and tied up with duct tape."

"You don't know any of the pieces?"

"Well, I know the queen. And the king. Horse. And what are those little guys called?"

"These? Pawns. Look, how 'bout you just point at a piece and I'll move them."

"Point with what? My broken nose? Listen. Forget the game. It would really just feel good if you could just undo my hands. It's awkward like this. My shoulders are killing me. If you could undo my hands and tape them in the front, that'd be wonderful."

Woolly pressed his lips together and gave me a stern look. He sat quietly for a few more moments, then leaned forward. "If I cut the ties, you won't make any trouble for me will you? Because the Alison I know probably would."

I stared back at him. What did he know about me that I didn't? What kind of trouble could I make? We were miles from anywhere, it was dark out, and he was a human bulldozer.

Woolly shook his head. "On second thought, I don't think you will." He reached into a pocket, pulled out a pocket knife, and flicked it open. I twisted around and he cut the wraps of tape from my wrists.

"Now," he said. "White or black?"

***

By the time Woolly's boss finally appeared, it was very late—maybe near morning. Woolly had checkmated me six times. He'd tried to offer me pointers, and once he even tried to let me win, but apparently I was something of a hopeless case when it came to the game of kings.

After that, Woolly cut away the tape on my ankles, made us some hot tea on a tiny alcohol-burning stove he carried in his knapsack, given me two tablets of ibuprofen for my aches, fed me some strangely tasty cakes made from coarse grains and molasses, and then loaned me his enormous jacket to curl up into. And when at last I sighed contentedly, and did as he'd first told me and relaxed a little, Woolly smiled at me as if I were a stray sick kitten he'd rescued from a rain storm. I slept a little and was beginning to feel almost human again when I heard a woman barking orders outside.

"Keep a watch, you knuckleheads!" Her voice was a brassy squawk. "Stand up. Put them cards away. Stand your post. Criminy, you people."

Woolly stiffened in his chair, and though he'd turned down the kerosene flame, in the dim yellow light I thought I saw his Adam's apple bob in a nervous swallow.

He looked over at me. I caught his eye, and he said, "Let me do the talking. At least at first."

"By all means," I said. "Be my guest."

Woolly stood up, but I only sat up a little straighter. Woolly turned up the lamp's flame and faced the door.

Although she walked with a limp, the woman descended on the room like she owned it and everything inside it, including the people, and everything outside, too. She was short and stocky, and while her gray hair was cropped short like a man's, it stood up on her head at wild angles. She noisily chewed a piece of gum, and from behind a pair of scratched and filmy plastic eyeglasses she peered keenly at me and then Woolly.

"Well, shit," she said, gesturing at me and shaking her head sadly.

Woolly shrugged sheepishly.

"Why ain't she secured like I said? And why's her eyes black? Who hit her?"

"Sorry, boss," said Woolly.

"Ah, jeeze, wha'd I tell you not twenty-four hours ago?" she griped at him. "We don't identify each other in front 'a prisoners! An' she's s'posed t'be blindfolded!"

"Sorry, Rube," said Woolly in a quiet voice.

"An' no names!" she shouted. Then she turned to me and held out her arms in exasperation. "Hopeless!" she said to me, shaking her head. "You—you would not believe how hard it is to find good help anymore."

She turned to Woolly. "I don't suppose you checked her for weapons."

Woolly cringed. "They might have. I forgot to ask. I didn't." Then he looked at me and said, "You got any weapons, Al?"

"Kinda late for that now, ain't it, seein' how she's untied and all."

"It's just I thought you'd get here sooner," said Woolly. "Seemed kinda mean to keep her all tied up that whole time when she didn't really do anything to deserve it. Did you want to keep her blindfolded this whole time? Even when we get up *there*? Anyway, we played a little chess, and it's fine." He trailed off.

The woman swept the glasses from her face, pinched the bridge of her nose, and squeezed her eyes shut.

"S'alright," she said. "Ya done good bringin' her here. And I don't even wanna know who her hit her in the nose."

"I took care of it," muttered Woolly.

"Was it Henderson?"

"Yeah."

"I'll kill him."

"I'll keep him away from you."

"Yeah. Do that. Sorry for snappin' at ya, Wool. You all done good grabbin' her and gettin' her here."

Woolly gave me a quick glance and I could see the relief in his big round face. He pantomimed a motion like stabbing with a knife and mouthed, "Do you have any weapons?"

I rolled my eyes.

The woman took a deep breath and let it out in a quick, heavy sigh. Then she turned to me and leaned over, resting her hands on her knees.

"Well. It's real good to see ya, Al," she said with a weary smile.

It was strange again to hear in her voice the tone of sincere compassion I'd heard with the others—Chase back at the Agency apartment and now this one they called Woolly. As I looked into Ruby's eyes, no one had to tell me that she knew me, and that she'd cared for me at some earlier time.

I said nothing to her in reply.

"I know ya don't remember me," she continued, "and you're probably real mad at me right now, but you and me used t'be good friends and we went through some things. I'm Ruby, like this big dumb fella here probably already toldja." She held her hand out to me.

I ignored her cordiality. "Why'd you bring me here?" I snarled. "You can't just abduct people. Ever hear of law and order? Let me go. Take me home."

She blinked and there was a flash of disappointment or injury in her eyes before her expression changed and she peered at me again as she had before, with a look of grim determination. Her jaw made a circling, rotary motion as she slowly and loudly chewed the gum.

"Cuttin' right straight to it, huh? Well, okay. Tie her back up, Wool, and lock her in here and let's get some sleep. In the mornin' we'll go on up."

And she limped out.

Without saying much, Woolly locked me in the black and dusty basement room, but he didn't tape my wrists or ankles again, and he tried to make me as comfortable as possible. He made us another cup of tea and he gave me some crude bedding to sleep with. I made a bed of flattened-out cardboard boxes, and when I managed to get comfortable, I fell into a deep and exhausted sleep.

CHAPTER 17

Early the next morning, before sunrise, Woolly wrapped my wrists in duct tape—in front of me this time, not behind my back. He blindfolded me, too, but this time with a strip of cloth tied loosely around my head instead of the smelly burlap sack.

Then he guided me to the van and helped me into the passenger seat.

"Not gonna throw me in the back today, huh?" I said.

"Get comfy now," he replied. "It's a long drive."

And we were off.

Despite the blindfold, I could tell we went slowly and on rough, unfinished roads, and we were somewhere with trees—I could tell that the sunlight was peeking and flickering through trees alongside the road. The blindfold left me feeling carsick at first, but I slept awhile and when I snapped awake again, Woolly had opened his window and the air whipping in felt cool and refreshing.

"We've got to be hundreds of miles from Lotus now," I said, "so, I assume I won't be returning home? Ever?"

"If I understand right, that's kind of up to you," said Woolly. "Who knows? Maybe you'll like it where we're going."

"I like my home back at Lotus. That's where I want to go."

"Ah, Al, where's home, really? What is home?"

"Well, I have a house, for one thing. A nice house—that's my home. I have electricity and a bicycle and a coffee machine."

"Sounds lovely."

"It is. My son is also there."

"Mm. Right. But I've heard he's not too happy with how things are going. Is that true?"

"What do you mean? How do you know anything about it?"

"We don't have to talk about it, if you don't want to."

"I don't."

I got the feeling that our drive took us gradually and steadily upward in elevation. Along with the steeply pitched parts of the drive, there were many downhill parts and parts where I couldn't tell if we were going uphill or down, but the main thing was the air seemed to be growing cooler and keener as we went along, and there were often the fragrances of pine and juniper, which added to the impression that we were heading mile by mile deeper into forested lands.

The final leg of the drive was definitely a mountain road that went up and up without turning down. It was very bumpy and dusty and winding, and we drove slowly.

"How ya feeling?" Woolly asked.

"What difference does it make?" I replied.

"Good point," he chuckled.

After what seemed like hours, I felt the van slow and turn into a tight circle, and then we stopped. I heard the brake squeal and the crackle of gravel under the tires of another vehicle slowing and stopping nearby.

"We're here," said Woolly. He patted me on the shoulder.

The van jostled noticeably as Woolly hopped out of it. He came around to my side and opened the door, and with his knife he cut away my duct tape restraints. I stood up and got out.

"It's okay to take off the blindfold now," he said.

So I did.

My eyes twinged momentarily as they adjusted to the brightness. All around me were pine and fir trees under a blue blazing sky. We were encompassed by mountainsides and peaks. There were valleys and meadows of mountain grass and wildflowers. A breeze touched my face, so clean and fair that I thought for a moment that I might begin to float away like a kite.

We had parked at the edge of a vast, tremendous gorge that stretched for miles to my left and right. I looked over the edge to the bottom. The huge ravine was hundreds of feet deep, lined with tall pine trees, and at the bottom I saw a line of frothy white and blue—a river gleaming in the early afternoon sunshine.

The granite peaks rose above us, shining in the sun. Patches of snow clung to their south-facing shoulders. Between the impressive peaks, I saw a series of distant stony mountain ridgelines marching to the horizon. The sky above was speckless, and the blueness of it was almost mesmerizing.

I was definitely angry and resentful at the people who'd taken me—even Woolly, who seemed to be doing everything he could to comfort me or at least make me less angry. I was also somewhat afraid for my overall safety, and I was very worried that I might never see Arie again. I was weary and cranky from the coarse living and being knocked around.

And yet, my mouth fell open as I spun slowly in circles to take in this seemingly endlessly grand mountain wilderness, the gorgeous forested hillsides, and the towering cliffs and peaks.

"Beautiful," I said. I hadn't meant to say it aloud. The word came out in spite of me.

"Yep," said Woolly, gazing out over the gorge. "My new favorite place."

Ruby rocked herself awkwardly up out of the passenger seat of the other car. She was accompanied by the three henchmen who'd chased me down back in Lotus. Ruby limped over to me at the edge of the cliff where Woolly and I stood gawking.

"How do ya like this?" she said, grinning.

"Beautiful," I said again.

"Yeah, thought you'd think so. Howd'ya like ta' live up here? With us?"

I scoffed, the spell broken like a popped soap bubble. "I said it was beautiful, but this isn't where I live and this isn't where my son is. I'm still a prisoner, aren't I?"

"Hey, Wool. Notice she's still as stubborn as she was before?"

Woolly smiled and nodded.

"Gettin' yer memory wiped 'parently don't make ya less contrary."

I glared at her.

"Well, c'mon," said Ruby, "let's keep a'goin'."

The henchmen led the way. The rest of us fell into a single file and hiked down a trail that headed away from the cliff at the edge of the enormous gorge and wound a way downhill between the trees. The sunlight streamed down between the branches and undergrowth, dappling the trail. Little blue damsel flies darted among the trees, and little birds twittered and flew after them.

We hiked for more than an hour. Ruby's face was slick with sweat.

She must be a tough old bird, I thought, to limp along all this way without complaining.

Woolly was sweating, too. His face was red and I could hear him breathing. The henchman had outdistanced us and were out of sight.

"Not too much farther," Ruby panted.

We entered a clearing where bumblebees and small butterflies flitted over a low carpet of wildflowers, visiting each bloom and then buzzing on. The sun shone down and warmed my face.

Then I heard voices ahead. Not just the henchmen. I thought I heard children and women. And then I smelled the smoke of a campfire. We crossed the wildflower meadow and then proceeded onto a wider footpath, and I saw people coming our way along the trail. It was a few men and women with shallow baskets woven from reeds or willow shoots. They greeted us and passed by, apparently off to collect food of some kind.

"Here we are," said Ruby with a wide smile.

We stopped, and I looked up from the trail and realized that we had walked into the middle of a large camp. I almost hadn't noticed it. Tucked between the trees at wide intervals, and nestled among the forest undergrowth, there stood tents and shelters and small log cabins. Had it not been so sunny, and had there not been people here and there occupied with chores like woodcutting and rinsing clothes, I might not have noticed the camp at all.

Also among the trees were small cook fires, clothes lines, fish-drying racks, and water stations. Many of the people had dogs, and I even saw chickens scratching in the underbrush.

There were ladies and men and kids dressed in a motley collection of clothes—some in colorful but weathered outdoor clothing, some in heavy flannels and work clothes, some in costumes that looked quite rustic and probably handmade—like colorful and loose cotton dresses and buckskin pants.

The men had long hair and bristly beards. The women had long, braided hair. The kids wore their hair long, too. All of them were tanned and wild-looking, but they didn't look grim or desperate. They looked relaxed, contented.

Most of the tents were the large, heavy-canvas kind that looked to be military surplus, but there were red and blue and yellow camping tents, too, and I saw makeshift shelters of canvas tarps draped over cables strung between trees. Near the middle of the camp were a few cabins or lodges made from stacked logs with sod roofs so thick that grass and flowers grew there.

A low, pleasant murmur of voices ran throughout the camp, and there was in the air the gentle energy of industry. From somewhere not too far off, I heard singing and laughing.

Woolly led the way to a place on the uphill edge of the camp where a large canvas tent stood, held up by stout wooden poles. The tent was a dark olive color and was perhaps sixty feet long and twenty feet wide. Woolly pushed aside the large sheet of canvas that evidently served as the front door, and we all went inside.

The only light in the tent came from a few window openings with their coverings rolled-up. Inside I saw a man with his back to us. He turned around when we entered.

It was Chase. He smiled at me.

"Hey," he said with a little chuckle. "You don't happen to have my gun, do ya?"

My hands were trembling a little, so I folded them in front of me. A nervous tingle raced up my back, though whether it was because I felt danger or something else, I wasn't sure.

In the tent there was a large table with chairs around it, and there were a couple smaller tables that seemed to be used as desks. There were maps and other papers pinned to the canvas walls. A canvas curtain hung down from the center of the tent and divided it into two large rooms. The curtain was drawn aside and beyond it I saw crates and supplies and food and even a few rifles.

Alongside the nearer of the two main support poles sat a small wood-burning stove that appeared to have been made from an old steel barrel. A chimney pipe climbed up out of it and ascended to an opening in the roof.

A tea kettle steamed on the stove's top. Chase picked it up, and from it he filled three metal cups. Ruby and Woolly each took one.

"Here you go," said Chase, handing me the third cup. "Mountain tea. Careful, it's hot."

157

"Go on and have a seat why don't you?" Ruby said to me.

She motioned to a folding chair at the table, and I sat down.

"I think I'll get going," said Woolly. "I have some things to take care of."

"Thanks for getting her up here, Wool," said Chase. "It was more than I was able to do." He grinned at me.

"I couldn't help but notice that you're not dead," I said to Chase in reply.

"No, not yet," he said, chuckling, "although you came as close to doing the job as anyone else has." He lifted his shirt to reveal a livid, sunburst-shaped scar at the edge of his abdomen, just above his belt. He turned around and there was another similar disfigurement on his back. "Bullet went in and out without causing too much chaos. I appreciate that. Five inches to the left and you'd've hit me in the spine. That woulda been a little harder to walk off."

"Now listen, Al," said Ruby, setting her cup on the table. "We ain't your enemies, you understand. We all used to be friends before you ran off and got yourself pinched and they wiped your—"

"Ruby," Chase interrupted, his voice suddenly stern.

"Right," said Ruby, holding up a hand in surrender. "That's all in the past."

She went on to explain our previous associations, how we'd met, but I knew who they were. Of course I did. These were the terrorists that had somehow gotten to me before. The ones who had tricked me into joining their side, which led to my involvement in the explosion that nearly killed Gary. I almost asked for their version of that story, but I'd told myself I

158

wouldn't talk to them—not in any meaningful way. And here they were trying to get to me again.

I stared at the ground as Ruby spoke and Chase added the odd detail or perspective. Whoever I was in the past was weak, but I would not let them get to me this time.

"I can't make you stop talking to me, but I won't talk to you," I said. "I won't answer your questions. I won't help you."

Ruby leaned back in her chair. "Hell, ya don't even know what we want."

"Doesn't matter," I said, clenching my teeth. "I just want you to take me back home."

Ruby exhaled heavily and leaned back in here chair to study me. "Chase," she said. "Talk some sense into her, will ya?"

"Al, I don't know what you think or how you feel about it, but Lotus isn't some kind of magic utopian societal reboot. It's an evolution of the Agency, which was basically a gestapo system that kept us down and helpless and mindless with fake medicine and memory control. Am I telling you anything you don't already know?"

"There was a pandemic," I said.

"That's true," he said. "We saw the bones, you and me together, though I suppose you've forgotten that. But the serum is a fake. The pandemic passed over some small proportion of us, and we survived, but that was years and years ago and we're no longer even sure if the original serum had any real effect on us apart from the amnesia. Now the serum and the threat of infection are just measures of control, ways to keep the world's survivors under their management."

"I already know that," I said.

159

Chase and Ruby looked at one another.

I went on, my voice edged with anger. "The Agency and the people of Lotus have been upfront and honest with me from the very beginning—unlike you. Lotus works with the Agency Starting Zones for their own benefit. They—we—are trying to rebuild, not just survive. And to rebuild better. The serum is a gift that can make the new world better."

A disappointed expression clouded Chase's face. Ruby rubbed her brow.

"And do you know what else?" I said. "They treat everyone with respect and dignity and they certainly don't go around kidnapping people."

"Are you sure about that?" Chase asked smugly.

I clamped my mouth shut, determined not to say another word.

"Now listen here," said Ruby. "You say 'dignity' and 'respect,' but what about them in the Starting Zones starving and living like animals? Like zombies? The memory serum is just another form of death penalty—they kill the person and then brainwash the poor sucker who wakes up in their place. And now, in this Lotus place, you brainwash 'em into this new society where everyone's supposedly perfect, but you send them down to the ghettos when they don't behave."

"You don't know what you're talking about. We make assignments based on ability and adaptation and, yes, based on mistakes. But everyone benefits—every time someone returns from the Starting Zones, they're strong, and the society is stronger," I said.

I was basically regurgitating what Rachel had told me so many times.

"People make mistakes. We unburden them of the guilt and shame and stigma, and we allow them to return as new people. Eventually, we'll have a society where crime and violence and other societal ills are practically non-existent, and the problems that remain are handled without cruelty."

"Mm," said Ruby. "So, in this Lotus, there's no cruelty or unfairness, ya say."

"Don't patronize me," I said. "You obviously don't want to understand any of it."

"No, no," said Ruby, her tone conciliatory. "I do want to understand. It's just that there's a woman I know. Her name's Sandy. She used to be in the Lotus Project. Fact, she had a son, like you. She was living her life and doing her duty in Lotus, but someone else came along, someone who was maybe more important, so one day she gets taken away—for no reason at all—and gets her mind erased. And this other person got moved in and assigned as Arie's mother."

"I don't believe you," I said, but my blood pressure seemed to be in free-fall. "If that were true, she wouldn't remember."

"She doesn't," said Ruby.

"Then how would you know about any of this?"

"We pieced it together. Not everyone in Lotus is perfect. People talk, Al. People who ain't happy."

A cloud of dread had moved into the tent and settled around me. I knew what was coming next. I knew what Ruby was going to do next.

"Hey, Chase," she sneered, "do you know if Sandy happens to be around right now?"

"Yeah, Rube," said Chase, his voice quiet and sad. He looked at me and sighed. "I think she might be around."

161

"Why don'tcha go fetch her?" said Ruby. Her smile was cold and hard. "Alison here might want to make her acquaintance."

Chase left the tent. Ruby finished her tea with a gulp and then rose to refill her cup.

"Can I get ya a refill?" she said with a smile.

I shook my head.

"You may not remember me, Al," she said quietly, "but I know you, and I know you know what I'm sayin' is right. You know alla this Lotus business is just a way to keep people down, keep 'em dumb, keep 'em slaves."

She sat down and watched me as she blew on her tea.

"We're the good guys, Al. And you're one of us."

"Do good guys blow people up?"

"Whaddya talking about?"

"I'm talking about the explosion that almost killed my husband."

"You had a husband? That's news to me, and you oughta listen t'me because I was there when they took Arie away from you and you came to me for help. You didn't have no husband."

"So, what about the killings? What about the bomb?"

"You don't know anything about it," she said. "Alls you know is what they told you. I'll tell you what happened, and when I do, you'll know it's true. Because you're a mother, and a mother knows things."

Her words landed on me like physical blows. I swallowed hard.

"You set off that explosion to save Arie. To make sure he got away someday. You meant yourself to die in that explosion and to take out as many of the bad guys as possible. It was only blind, dumb luck that any of you made it through."

I shook my head. "No. You tricked me somehow. You set me up. Blackmailed me or something else, and then you sent me on a suicide mission."

She smiled a warm, sad smile. She reached over and gave my forearm a squeeze.

"Tell yourself both stories, kiddo. The one I'm tellin' ya, and the one they toldja. Then let your heart tell ya which one is right."

No, I thought. No, I won't.

"The whole reason your memory was erased was because you wouldn't tell them what you knew and they couldn't let you keep those memories. But we can help ya. Up here you don't have to forget. Up here it's just people living. We got problems here, too, sure. But there's no mind control, no death by memory wipe. We can help you, Alison. We can make it so you never have to forget again."

"So that's why I'm here? Huh? Just so you can help me? There's nothing you want in return?"

"Well," she said with a sheepish laugh. "This society up here is based on mutual assistance. Each of us bring what we can to the table. So. It wouldn't hurt if you were able to also help us some, now would it?"

I wanted to hit her in the nose. I could see the deceit so clearly in her face—the false pretenses. Just like when Chase had shown up at my apartment to rescue me. Even as I tried to understand how I myself felt about Lotus, my strongest impulse was to not give into these terrorists, these criminals who crept around trying to subvert what I knew was the only serious and coherent attempt to raise the pandemic survivors from the ashes.

I sipped at my tea and tried to pretend Ruby wasn't there.

Chase returned a few minutes later with a person I recognized at once as the woman in the picture that Arie had shown me. Chase came with her into the tent but didn't stay.

The woman nodded at Ruby and said, "Hello." Then she turned to me and likewise smiled and nodded.

Ruby struggled up from her seat. She put her arm around the woman.

"Sandy, I wanted you to meet Alison. Alison, Sandy. Sandy, Alison has never been to the Zones. At least she can't remember bein' there. You were there for a while, weren'tcha? Think you could tell her a little bit about what it's like?"

Sandy sat down and Ruby got her a cup of the mountain tea. Then Ruby sat down again.

"Why do you want to know?" Sandy asked, but before I could answer she said, "It's awful. There's never enough to eat, not enough fuel, no electricity. It's a nightmare. You never knew if you were going to be robbed or attacked."

Out of habit I opened my mouth to repeat the lines I'd been coached to say—lines about how the Zones met the "basic needs of the residents," lines about "let's not exaggerate," about surely the conditions described were a result of "terror attacks and security problems," and were not general to all of the Starting Zones. I had many answers to Sandy's grim assessments, but she didn't pause long enough for me to say a word.

"I saw a gang of teenagers attack a man just a few blocks from the depot. They beat him with baseball bats and took his rations and his shoes. I almost wish someone would erase my memories so I could forget the place. I just—I couldn't believe it. Neighbors and strangers would turn on each other in just for a few extra rations. There were guards everywhere but they wouldn't actually help you if something went wrong. Honestly, we were more afraid of them than anyone else—they had the guns, and they could haul you in for any stupid excuse. They could make you do whatever they wanted. If they found a woman attractive, they just took her. I hated the way they looked at me, but I guess my luck held out until I came here."

Then she was quiet. She sipped her tea, her eyes wide and blank.

"Sandy," said Ruby, "you got any family? Any kids?"

She looked at Ruby and then at me, as though weighing her answer. The hint of a smile was on her lips.

"No," she said. "Technically, I don't. My records in the Zones said that I'm alone, no kids or known relations, and I don't remember anything from the back before of course. But—"

She trailed off.

"But what?" said Ruby quietly. "Go ahead."

"I don't know. I feel like I'm a mother. Maybe my family was wiped out back before, or maybe we were separated. But I feel like I am a mother. Or maybe I just want to be."

"I think a lot of us miss people we don't remember," said Ruby, her eyes on me.

"Yeah," said Sandy, nodding. "That's a good way of putting it."

"You like it here, Sandy? Reason I ask is Alison here is thinking about joining us. Just wondering what you think of it."

Sandy took a gulp of tea and narrowed her eyes. "Yes. I do like it here. It's not easy. I don't think I was much of an outdoor person before. It's cold at night, and there's lots of hard work to do. Like the other day I was on rock patrol."

"Wassat?" said Ruby. "I don't think I've been on that detail yet."

"Oh, gosh," said Sandy. "Well, see, we need flagstones for cabin floors and walkways. They're building a winter lodge down in the gully," she jabbed her thumb in the vague direction of downhill.

"Yah," said Ruby. "I heard about that. It's big, huh?"

"Yeah, huge. It's for when this whole place is under fifteen feet of snow. And we need lots of flat rocks to sort of pave the floor and walls and build little brick furnaces. So, a group of us went down to the river and gathered up flat rocks. We had to haul them up out of the river bed and we put 'em on these sledges and pulled them back here. For three days it went on. It was exhausting. I smashed my thumb, split it open, which if funny because a few weeks ago I was on fish-cleaning duty and I cut the same thumb then with the fillet knife."

She laughed and held up her thumb. It was bound in a coarse dressing. Ruby and I frowned our sympathy.

"Seems like I'm just constantly wrapping up my thumb in bandages. Anyway, I'm off duty today, but I walked down to the gully to see how the lodge is coming and it's gonna be beautiful. That's kinda how it is here, I guess. It can be difficult and exhausting, but it's amazing what people can do when they work together. You feel like you're making a difference."

Ruby beamed. "Thanks, Sandy. Glad it's working out for ya. Sorry to hear about'cher thumb."

"Thanks for the tea," she said with a diffident laugh. "Guess I'll get going now. I was going to take a walk to the ravine with my roomies."

"Sure," said Ruby, her grin still wide and warm. "Come by anytime."

Sandy got up from her chair and looked to me. "It's good here. I shouldn't complain about the duties. Before the rock patrol, I was gathering wild greens. That was very nice. Peaceful, you know? I don't know how you feel about full-time camping, but it's peaceful here, at least. And you can trust people. It's safe."

She had a shy friendly way, and she seemed genuine and honest. She told us goodbye and then left the tent.

She'd make a good mom, I thought. Hell, she'd make a good friend.

But that's where I had to leave it. That's where I had to stop. She would make a good mom—nothing further, because I knew if I dwelt too long on who Sandy was, and where she'd been, and what had happened to her, I'd find myself in a very difficult emotional place.

"Nice lady, in't she?" said Ruby.

"You know, you might not have the whole story," I shot back. "She wasn't just dragged out of her house and stuck with a memory-wiping injection. She was making trouble in Lotus."

"Mm, yeah," said Ruby. "Seems like a real troublemaker, that one. We're keeping a close eye on her."

"What are you getting at?"

"Seems like she was given a death sentence so that they could make a little space for someone else."

"It's hardly a death sentence—she's going on a hike with her roommates."

"Yah," barked Ruby. "But who is 'she'? Is she the lady who took care of Arie? If Arie met her, that's not who she'd be. The lady who Arie knew is gone. Sure, they could get to know each other again, and maybe it'd be almost the same. But all them memories, all that time, and the person who was Sandy before is dead. Just like the Alison we knew is dead."

"It just doesn't make any sense," I said. "Why would they care who was with Arie? Why would they wipe her memory just for my sake?"

"Good question. Why would they push her aside and move you in? Why are you so important? Whaddya do in Lotus? Push papers? Make 'recommendations'?"

I tried to come up with something that'd put Ruby in her place, but I couldn't.

Ruby leaned in my direction. "If I was trying to control a person, someone who might be useful to me in a bigger plan, I think telling her that they'd found her long-lost son might be a good start. That way she'd be happy to work for them, be loyal, and if things went south, they'd have something to hold over her head. Like say if someone might have connections to a group they wanted to knock outta commission."

"But I don't want anything to do with you," I said firmly. "And I don't remember any of you."

"Yeah. But maybe they got a way t'bring your memories back. And 'sides, *we* remember *you*. And you saved us all. So when Chase came and tried to grab you, maybe they realized they could put you right out on display, in Lotus, like bait. They're devious, Al. We've seen 'em pull shit like this before, and it don't surprise us a bit that they treat you and Arie this way to get at us."

I felt blood rushing to my face. "I am Arie's mother," I said. "That's why I'm with him. I'm his mother. We have DNA test results."

"Sure ya do," Ruby said, nodding soberly. "But you'da believed he was your son without any old test, wouldn't ya? Like ya said to me before they took you— you knew he was yours."

"Maybe. I still don't see what is so bad about reuniting a mom and son."

"You're a pawn."

"How am I a pawn? Because I work for them?"

"They let us grab you this time. They let us get away with you."

"Who?"

"Your bosses. Your Lotus people. They were seeing if we'd come after you and we did."

"Oh, please," I groaned. "How could they possibly benefit from letting you kidnap me?"

"They thought they could follow us," said Ruby. "We don't think they did. Chase and Woolly saw to that. They've gotten good at throwing Agency bird dogs off the track."

"Then what?"

"Well, they know you want to be with Arie more'n anything. Right? You've probably told them that yourself, haven'tcha?"

I bit the inside of my cheek.

"So," Ruby said, "they didn't follow us, but now they figure you'll be back for him—whether or not you wanna join us—and they'll hold Arie over your head until you lead them to us."

"You people are full of conspiracies, aren't you?"

Ruby pressed her lips together and took in a great lungful of air through her nostrils. Then she exhaled it in a huff. "Chase?"

"Yeah," said Chase. He'd slipped back into the tent and was standing behind me. He sat in the seat next to me.

"You wanna jump back in here?" Ruby said to him. "I think I'm just pissin' her off at this point."

"Sure," he said. "Listen, Al, I refuse to believe that someone as smart as you isn't making sense of at least some of this. We really think they want to get to us through you."

"Fine," I said. "So what if you never let me go back or I never got away? Then what?"

"Well, like Rube said, you're *a* pawn, Al," said Chase. "Not the *only* pawn. They're a crafty crew. Arie's a pawn, too. We've always thought we have too easy a time contacting him."

"You've been in contact with Arie?" I cried, half raising out of my chair. "Is he here?"

"No, no," said Chase hastily. "I've never even met the kid. I've only ever talked to him a coupla times, and only by radio."

He motioned warily with his hands for me to lower myself back into the chair. His mention of radio communication agreed with what I knew of Arie, so I sat down again.

"I'm sure you've noticed he's not exactly satisfied with Lotus. He doesn't share your feelings about the way things are there."

"Yeah," I said. "I know."

"He's part of some kind of grassroots thing in Lotus," said Chase. "I'm not even sure they have any

170

organization at all. We've reached out to them a few times. Nothing has ever come of it though."

"So, you're saying you can't ever let me go because I'll go back to Lotus and sell you out? Is that it? Or are you going to erase my memories here and then let me go? Hm? You going to give me the death sentence?"

"Absolutely not," said Chase, his eyes suddenly bright. "Just the opposite, really."

"I don't understand."

Chase looked at Ruby, and she nodded at him. My glance darted between them. Then Chase reached over and cautiously touched me on the arm. The tingle of his touch swam upstream against my anger and resentment.

"Let's go on a hike," he said.

CHAPTER 18

The day had gotten warmer, and I had to admit a part of me wanted to stay at Ruby's mountain sanctuary for a week or so just to take the place in. The air was cheery with laughter and talk and birdsong. Someone was cooking meat somewhere, and its tantalizing odor made my mouth water.

Chase took me back to his tent where he grabbed a small backpack. Into it he stuffed a water bottle and a sweater and some other items.

There was a dark blue hooded jacket hanging from a hook on one wall of the tent. Chase took it from the hook and held it up.

"This is yours," he said, with a smile. "From before. I'll bring it along. It'll be chilly before we're back. Just let me know if you get cold." He rolled it up and stuffed it into the pack.

"How long have you been living here?" I asked as Chase fastened up the backpack and slipped into the harness.

"About a year," he said. "There'd been a smaller group of survivors up here since year one, but they were barely hanging on. We joined with them and things got better—for both groups. We've been bringing more people here every month."

We left the tent and went back through the camp. Chase waved and greeted people as we passed by them.

"And this is better than living in a real community? Living in the dirt? Eating nuts and berries?"

"Hey, you ever had fresh buffalo berries?" he asked.

"I think you know the answer to that."

Chase stopped on the trail and faced me. "They're tiny," he said, indicating the size with his fingers. "Maybe half the size of a green pea. Some of them are the size of BBs. Bright red and delicious. But buffalo berry bushes have thorns on them about an inch long. Sharp as needles. You kind of have to get the hang of getting at 'em without getting too punctured up. A quart of them could keep you alive for a week. We make wine with them."

"You make wine up here?"

"We make all kinds of things."

We made our way through the camp. At the tree-line, there was a fork in the trail. Chase stopped again and gestured to the spread of tents and people and fire pits.

"Look around, Al. This isn't just some refugee camp," said Chase. "It's a community. We have a schedule of duties. We cooperate to gather in food, to maintain security, to build and maintain our shelter. We stay busy, but it's a good place. We eat well. We're healthy. We have some livestock down in the valleys, and we make runs down into the real world to scavenge the things we can't make or grow or raise. We're getting a band together—do you play an instrument?"

"You can't just live up here like cavemen."

"Oh, I think I might could do. And sure, there are those who want to go back to the way it was in the back before, with cars and houses and offices. I suppose

173

that's the long-term goal of all this, but nothing like that can happen while the Agency exists. They've taken the most dangerous technology to come along since nuclear fusion, and they're using it to enslave anyone they encounter. Don't tell me this doesn't seem like a good alternative to you."

"I'm not a slave. What I have at Lotus looks good, too. To me. Running water, electricity, books, coffee."

"Mm. I do miss a good strong cup of coffee," said Chase. "I'm working on getting coffee beans in a more-steady supply, but UPS doesn't deliver out here. Not every day, anyhow." He pointed to the fork in the trail ahead which turned and climbed steeply. "Let's go up this way."

We left the trees and climbed a series of switchbacks that took us up the mountain's bare face. With the sun low over the surrounding peaks, the views were stunning. I saw broad, lush valleys in every direction, rivers twinkling in the afternoon, and a broad lake that glimmered in the distance. The high peaks were turning golden. Again, I felt the impulse to exclaim how beautiful it all was.

Instead, I said, "So, you're saying I should just forget Lotus and join alla you hippie campers up here in the woods."

"Well, you will never have to worry about having your memories wiped up here," he said over his shoulder. "That'd be the worst thing that could happen to one of us—once you get trained on how to find and harvest buffalo berries, we want you to remember that, and show other people."

"How many people are here?"

"At this camp? Just two hundred. Don't tell Ruby I told you that. A little shy of two hundred, actually. The

174

land will only support small groups. We have to kill game and forage from the surrounding mountains, which means we can't camp up here too densely. When we get too many people, a group leaves to start a new camp."

"How many camps are there?"

"That's what I want to show you."

The trail became even more steep, like a rocky staircase. At times the hiking was more like climbing a ladder. A few times Chase helped me up an escarpment, and when we touched, I'd again feel the thrill I felt the night he broke into Gary's apartment.

"I'm getting a bit tired," I told Chase. "Where are we going, and how much longer?"

Chase looked upward. I followed his gaze. The trail zigged and zagged up the face of the hill and above that there was a craggy mountain peak. Chase pointed at the spire.

"All the way up there?" I whined. "Seriously?"

"It's not as far as it seems. But let's refresh ourselves," he said, unshouldering his backpack.

The water from Chase's steel bottle was icy and had a mineral sweetness, a few gulps of which seemed to revive all of my senses. Then we ate a few grain cakes like those that Woolly had shared with me the night before. Suddenly I felt as though I could hike all night, and so we went on. And Chase had been right. We came to the top of the mountain more quickly than I thought we would. There were still a couple hours of daylight left and the gold-tinted mountainous wilderness stretched out in stony convolutions in all directions.

"It really is beautiful up here."

"Just a little further." Chase pointed to a copse of trees just below the very peak of the mountain.

We went there and found a man sitting on a large, flat rock. In front of him was what looked like the remains of a large campfire.

"Hey, Miguel," said Chase.

"Chase," the man said with a wave. He stood up and clapped the dust from his butt.

The two clasped hands, and then Chase gestured at me.

"This is Alison," said Chase.

"Did we know each other before, too?" I asked, shaking the man's hand.

Miguel laughed. "No, but I have heard about you. What you did for us."

"Well, I'm sure the good parts are true," I said.

"I think I can see that, now that I've met you in person."

"Miguel's been here as long as me. He's a good friend."

"Now that's true," he said. "But there is supposedly fresh trout tonight, and I'm not missing out, so, you two enjoy the view."

He gathered up a backpack and walking stick, and then he went down the trail we'd just ascended.

"Happy trails, Miguel," said Chase.

Miguel waved without looking back at us. Chase and I stood there looking over the vastness of the landscape.

"Well, let's get to work," said Chase.

"Why are we here?"

The rock we stood on was large and flat, like a shelf jutting out over the steeper ground below. Beneath it lay a large cache of firewood, brush, and green tree branches.

"Help me out," said Chase. He began collecting arm-sized branches and a few bigger logs. He tossed them up onto the rock shelf, into the black and gray ashes there. Soon he had a sizable fuel stack, and he stacked them tee-pee-like to make a new fire.

"We came all the way up here to make a fire? Why's it so big? It's not even cold out. Are we staying the night up here or something?"

"Nah, we'll be back before dark."

"Then what?"

Chase took what looked like a small flint and tinder kit from the pack and set the great stack of wood on fire. It blazed hotly for some time with only a little gray smoke.

"Will you tell me what we're doing?" I said again.

"There," said Chase. He pointed to a far distant peak.

I looked where he indicated, and for a moment I saw nothing, just a faraway mountain. But then I realized that what I'd thought was a tiny cloud was a puff of smoke arising from the peak or somewhere near it.

"Smoke signals?" I said, an involuntary smile hiking up one side of my mouth.

"Yep," said Chase. Then, from under the flat rock he took a large rolled-up canvas. "Now grab those branches, those green ones, and throw them on the fire."

I did what he said and the green lumber sizzled and began to steam on the fire. Chase hastily tossed the canvas across it. A cloud of whitish smoke accumulated quickly, and soon it was roiling out around the edges.

Chase waited a few seconds more and then whipped the canvas into the air, and with that a massive plume of the white smoke rose into the air like a balloon.

"Look over there," he said.

From another peak there was another white plume.

"And there," he said, pointing. "One cloud means everything's okay."

And with that, he kicked at the center logs of the fire. With the fuel separated, the fire burned low, and he smothered the remaining flames with the tarp.

"So, you just send smoke signals to each other all day?"

"No, it's just one way to keep in touch. We have a mail system, too, people who ride horses between the camps on a circuit. We've got other ways, too, like message-drop points."

"And the point of showing me this is what?"

"I wanted you to see what we're about. This isn't just some silly camping trip or escaped Zone dwellers hiding in the woods. There are a series of camps, loosely affiliated, and we know of others, too. There are probably tribes like this all across the world. The camps you see here are off-shoots of this one, but they're independent, too. We try not to be too connected. It's a resilient network because we're connected but not dependent on each other. Just trying to show you there are alternatives to a system that controls people by wiping their memories."

"If you're so comfy and secure," I asked, "why do you care about the Agency or Lotus?"

"They'd take us if they could find us, if they could overpower us. You know that. They'd take us, wipe us, and stick us into the Zones. And we'd either be ground down and left in the Zones permanently, or we'd be promoted to Lotus—and they'd grow. They have to grow to be successful, see. I'd love to ignore them, but they'd never return the favor."

"Why do you care about me, then?"

"You're in Lotus," he answered, "which means you're at least somewhat trusted by the Agency. Plus, you're married to an Agency officer, which means you could access a lot of information that could be helpful to us."

"Helpful how? I don't understand why you care about any of that down there. In all the time I've been there and even in the Zones, no one ever said they were looking for mountain hippies to take into the Zones. The only taking that I've ever seen is you taking me."

"We can't just sit here and wait to see if they come. At the very least we need to let them know we will defend our independence, and at the best, we need to shut them down."

"So, it's really so bad, huh? You have to go to war with them?"

"There's no way to say no to them, there's no opting out. Lotus collects the people they want and sticks everyone else into the Zones. They'll use your family and friends to keep you in, and if you don't comply, poof, you're gone. I won't join them, I won't let anyone I know be sucked in, and I plan to do everything I can to take them down and free those who are already in. And that's where you come in—maybe. You're an officer in Lotus. You're married to an Agency officer."

If you only knew, I thought. I could barely get Gary to say "good morning" to me when we lived together. How was I supposed to gain Agency secrets?

"I would never do that," I said. "I believe in Lotus. They've given me a life with my son. I can't betray that. I can't walk away from it. Let's just stop this. Take me home. Or just let me go, and I'll find my own way there."

"I wish I could show you what you've lost at Lotus," he said. "You know the whole reason your memories are gone is because you cared for your son so much that you would have done anything to protect him. That included risking forgetting him completely. I feel like I failed you."

"What do you mean? What happened after the explosion? After Gary?"

"We were doing what we did back then. We were breaking into a depot again to find their network or an officer so we could find Arie."

"I was breaking into an Agency facility."

"You wouldn't stop trying to find Arie. You'd have done it on your own if we didn't help. You're a stubborn little donkey, Al. So, we worked on it together."

"So then what?"

"Bad luck."

"We got caught?"

"A security patrol literally stumbled onto us. We got out of the building all right, but we got separated. I thought you were right behind me. Honest, I did. I never would have left you behind."

"I was captured?" I asked.

"Yeah, of course. Why?"

"I guess I always assumed I had turned myself in."

"I don't think anyone's ever done that," Chase snorted.

"Well, when I think about it, it doesn't make a lot of sense. But I guess I'd always thought I had just gone back to be with Gary," I said.

"Let's get one thing straight," Chase said sternly. "I tried telling you this before, but that guy is not your husband. Before the explosion you were in the Starting Zones with Arie. Gary was your area supervisor, not your husband. Do a DNA test with Gary—see what that tells you. He's not Arie's father."

I folded my arms and stared at him. He folded the tarp in thirds and began rolling it up.

"And if he was your husband, you had a funny way of showing your love for him. You nearly killed yourself and him—presumably so that he wouldn't have any further influence on Arie."

"Why would he have my memories wiped and then tell me we were husband and wife?"

Chase paused from stowing the tarp and exhaled roughly. "God knows. The guy always seemed a little twisted to me. But this is kinda the whole point, Al. People shouldn't forget who they're married to or who their kids are. Ever."

I opened my mouth to answer, but I didn't know what I was going to say.

"No," said Chase, pointing an accusing finger at me. "Don't answer. Because I know it'll just be more of your Lotus propaganda horseshit, and to be honest with you, I can tell that of the two of us, you're maybe more fed up with it than I am."

Chase put the rolled-up tarp under the rock. The sun was setting, and a chill had crept into the breeze. I sat on the shelf rock and hugged my knees. Chase opened his backpack and withdrew the jacket he said was mine. He handed it to me.

"Thanks," I said.

The jacket was a little weathered and needed a good washing, but it fit me perfectly, and it kept the chill away.

"They can erase minds," Chase said, "clear out memories, but do you think people really forget everything? Every single day a part of me aches for something missing and I don't even know what it is."

I thought about the way just knowing about Arie seemed to fit into and fill up an empty place in my heart that had nothing to do with what I did or didn't remember.

Chase continued. "And here's something else for you to think about—you know that the Agency is using the serum as a way to enforce rules and govern. But do you know that people in the Starting Zones are being told they have to take the serum every year to fight off the virus? The virus from the pandemic?"

"Every year?"

"Yeah, Al. Every year. Lotus claims to use 'memory management' as a means to improve society, but those poor bastards in the Starting Zones are getting dosed just because January has come around again. What kind of life is that?"

I couldn't look up at him, couldn't let him lock eyes with me, or he'd see the doubt that was collecting in me like a plume of acrid smoke. He'd evidently formed some good guesses about how I felt about it all, but I couldn't help him make his case.

"Tell me something, Al, when was the last time you saw someone in a wheelchair in your Lotus town? Or a person who wasn't able-bodied? How many old people live in your neighborhood?"

I'd noticed. I assumed people like that lived in Lotus and I just hadn't encountered them yet. But everyone in Lotus was healthy and if not educated, at least able-bodied and in possession of at least one valuable skill. Rachel had told me that Lotus was in search of the best, but I'd never thought of this as being any sort of societal fascism.

"So what," I said. "It's not me. I'm not making these decisions. It has nothing to do with me."

Chase gave me a hard look. "It absolutely has to do with you and any other person who looks the other way while the disadvantaged are trampled. It's not fair, and it's not right. It isn't the better world, and I'll put my life on the line to stop it."

"What would you have me do?" I yelled. "Huh? You have all the answers, what would you have me do?"

"We need information. You could go back into the system, supply us with intel."

"No, I can't! I'm literally the last person that would be able to get any information. I'm a no one."

"You're married to Gary Gosford—"

"—and he hates me," I interrupted.

Chase frowned.

"That's right," I said. "He hates me. I could no sooner get information from him than I could from this rock or that tree."

"Well, surely he's talking to other people, or he has files—"

"There's nothing," I said. "I have no special access, and if I tried to get it without authorization, I'd be detected and sent down to the Zones. I can't help you." My face burned with humiliation.

183

Chase bowed his head. "How could anyone hate you?" he asked.

"It's cold up here," I said. "Can we go back now?"

"Yeah," said Chase. "Let's go."

CHAPTER 19

As Chase had told me, we got back to the encampment just before dark. Lanterns and candles flickered here and there. People were clustering around the fires, and there were smells of cooking food everywhere. Chase first stopped at his tent.

"Wait here a sec. I gotta pick up our dinner reservations."

I raised an eyebrow at this, but he darted inside without explaining and in less than a minute he emerged holding something heavy wrapped in a rough canvas sack.

He made a little bow and held out his hand, saying "Your table awaits, if you'll come right this way."

I held out my hand and Chase clasped it gently and warmly. Then he led me through the camp to a circle of tents on the lower slope of the hill. There, in a small round clearing in the trees, twenty or so people stood gathering around a large dutch oven suspended from a crude tripod straddling a bed of red coals. At a distance from the fire pit, atop sticks driven into the ground, torches flamed merrily. I took them to be bundles of reeds dipped in oil or tallow, and their reddish flames cast a festive mood over the clearing.

A tall, slender woman with long silver hair stepped away from the others and came in our direction.

"Chase!" she cried. "Will you be joining us for supper?"

She was perhaps old enough to be my mother, and she practically shone with the easy, unforced beauty of maturity and wisdom. Around her shoulders she wore a vast shawl knitted from undyed wool, and beneath that she was wrapped in a sort of full-length sun dress of light-colored linen.

Chase grinned and reached into his canvas sack. He withdrew a large, corked bottle with dark glass and presented it like a sommelier. The woman smiled and nodded and beckoned us into the clearing.

"Everyone," she cried, raising a hand into the air. Her voice was silky and clear like that of a storyteller. "Everyone, Chase is here with his lady friend. Make them welcome, if you please."

The cheerful group gathered around us and there were several minutes of handshakes and back-pats. There were young people and old, but all appeared quite fit and very comfortable in their rustic surroundings. Something was steaming in the big black dutch oven over the fire, and its savor distracted me in the worst way. At last the tall woman appeared before Chase and me.

"Alison, this is Brigitta," said Chase.

I was not very surprised when Brigitta performed a dramatic, courtly curtsy.

"This is her tent circle," Chase added. "Her people excel in cultivating and gathering fresh herbs and wild greens. They have some of the best food in camp."

"I'm so pleased the two of you could join us," Brigitta said.

And then she approached me. She was taller than me, as tall as Chase. With her chin upthrust she looked down at me, and I might have taken this for stuffiness or arrogance, but it was hard to mistake the kindness in her eyes.

"Please get your supper," she said, looking at me and then at Chase. "And then we will talk."

We were given heavy clay crocks and spoons carved from hard, gnarled root wood. From the dutch oven Brigitta's people spooned out a thick, aromatic stew of venison and garlic and some kind of wild tubers. Slices of grainy and fire-scorched flat bread were passed around. Chase and I were given seats near the fire. I took a mouthful of the stew. It was richly flavored with spices I apparently had never tasted. I held the memory of Arie's enchiladas close to my heart, but I thought the stew might be the best meal I could ever remember eating, and I felt instantly warmer and more at ease. I wolfed down the stew and the bread, and I accepted eagerly when asked if I wanted more.

Brigitta appeared and gave Chase and me cups made from the same heavy clay, and then she filled them from the bottle Chase had brought.

"What shall we drink to?" said Brigitta.

"To hippie campers and cavemen," said Chase, raising his glass and winking at me.

"To hippie campers and cavemen!" cried Brigitta with a silky laugh.

The others laughed in kind and repeated the toast.

I hoped it was too dark for Chase to notice my face coloring, but I had to laugh, too. I raised my cup and took a deep draught. It was a sweet and rich wine, and it warmed me even more deeply than the stew.

"Buffaloberry," said Chase, with a grin. He clinked my clay cup with his.

A young man brought a chair and placed it near us, but it wasn't a folding camp chair or a chair of ax-hewn slats of pine. This chair appeared to be fashioned from twisted gray tree roots and planks of smoothly worn driftwood. Brigitta lowered herself into the chair—her hippie camper throne. Her long silver hair cascaded down her shoulders and spilled over the great shawl. She crossed her legs with a flourish that made her dress flag into the air momentarily, and then she reclined in regal repose, and there she sipped her wine while Chase and I ate more of the stew and sooty bread.

"So," said Brigitta after a few minutes, "you're the little lady who has the camp in such a dither," said Brigitta.

"Oh, I didn't mean to cause any dither," I said.

"You'll be joining us, then?" Brigitta asked me. "You'll become a hippie camper cavewoman?"

"Me? Um, I'm not sure. I guess I'm sort of here on a fact-finding mission."

Brigitta set aside her cup on the armrest of her throne and leaned forward. She looked at me again with that haughty but kind, evaluative gaze. Then she held out her hands to me. When I did not react, she fluttered her fingers impatiently to take my hands in hers.

I looked at Chase, my spoon halfway between my bowl and mouth. Chase only made a small shrug. I clumsily set aside the cup and food, and then let Brigitta take my hands.

"Alison. My child. What is your purpose?"

"My—my purpose?"

"Yes, dear."

"Well, I have a job, and I, you know, I'm assigned to—"

"You don't know, do you? Your purpose."

I had no answer.

Brigitta smiled at me. "Don't be embarrassed, child. You have one. Even if we don't know what our purpose is, we still have one. We all have one. I. You. Even him." She inclined her head in Chase's direction.

Chase chuckled and before I could stop myself, I did, too.

Then Brigitta said, "I walked the earth for more than sixty years before I knew what mine was."

I raised my eyebrows. She looked no older than about fifty.

"Then came the plague," she said, looking at me earnestly. "Plagues tend to serious you up pretty goddam quick. Don't they? You know what I mean."

"What's yours?" I asked.

"I'm a healer," she said without hesitation. "Before though? Who knows? Today I am a healer to people who have no one else. These people," she gestured with her chin to the faces and voices all around us, "and to others." She fixed me with a smiling gaze. "Now, tell me about you."

"I'm a mother," I said quietly.

She closed her eyes and nodded once. "I know. One mother knows another. Listen. Child. Gather your facts. Do whatever you have to do. But find your purpose. Because do you know what happens when you find your purpose?"

"What?" I said.

"You can stop looking and start living."

She arose, gave us a very formal goodnight salutation, and walked slowly to the edge of the clearing like some graceful, queenly phantom.

As the chill of night set in, they served us more of the ubiquitous mountain tea and the grain cakes, only now they were glazed with hot, sweet preserves.

"Wild blackberry," said Chase, munching and nodding approvingly.

As we sat watching the fire and listening to chatter of the others, Chase reached into his jacket and withdrew a silver flask. He held it up, offering. I was already feeling flushed and drowsy from the wine, but I shrugged and held out my cup of tea. Chase poured a little clear liquid into my cup and his.

Even with the buffering effect of the tea, it was obvious this was some kind of backwoods, high-test grain alcohol, and it landed hot and rough on my palette. I coughed and sputtered a little after gulping too much. Chase chuckled and shrugged.

It must have been closing in on midnight when, with the wine and liquor buzzing pleasantly in my head, Chase walked me to a tent not far from his. We stepped inside. There was a tiny candle lantern inside hanging from a cord fastened to the roof. Chase lit it with a small plastic lighter, and the tent was filled with a soft glow. Along one wall there was a cot piled with blankets. In the corner there was a plastic milk crate upon which sat a small bucket of water and what looked to be a towel and soap and other comforts.

It wasn't a large tent. It was tall enough to stand up in, but Chase's head brushed the roof, and he had to stand close to avoid bumping the cot and the tent walls.

"We got you bunking in this tent for now," said Chase.

"It's lovely," I said sleepily.

He nodded. "But if you need anything, knock on my door." He jabbed in the direction of his tent, but he was slightly tipsy and it was the wrong direction, so he pointed the other way.

"Thanks," I said.

He handed me the plastic lighter. "Hang on to this. For the candle."

"When do you think Ruby will let me go home?"

"I don't know. I think she thinks you'll cave in sooner or later."

"I won't."

"We all know you're stubborn, Al, famously, but if they hadn't wiped you, you'd know you're kind of out of your league when it comes to Ruby."

I shook my head and let out a sigh.

As Chase moved to the tent door he came yet closer to me and we stood there for a few moments, our thighs brushing together. His chest grazed against mine. Our faces were just inches apart, and the wobbling candle flame was reflected in Chase's kind, brown eyes. Neither of us spoke. We stood still and stared. There was comfort and kindness in the closeness.

I knew Chase had known me before, and I didn't need the token of a jacket for proof. He'd known me and, like Woolly and Ruby, I knew that Chase cared for me—then and now—and that he'd never hurt me. I didn't remember him, but in his eyes I could see a past, a history. He had feelings for me. I could sense it, and it drew me in. I wanted someone to care for me, and here he was. Ready and waiting. His arms were ready to embrace me and never let me go.

"Okay," I said at last, and I let my gaze fall from his. "Well, thank you for the hike and the wonderful dinner and—everything."

He nodded. "G'night, Alison."

He turned and went out of the tent.

I stripped to my underwear, blew out the candle, and got into the blankets on the cot. I must have been asleep before Chase ever reached his tent only twenty or so yards away.

But I awoke very early in the morning. Again, even though I fell asleep quite easily, a truly restful night would have to wait.

Nothing specific woke me. No sounds or disturbance. I woke very deliberately, and in the darkness of the tent I arose and put on my clothes and shoes and the jacket Chase had returned to me. I detached the little unlit candle lantern from its cord. And then I slipped into the cold and the dark.

CHAPTER 20

The night's chill clawed at my jacket and clothing. My breath condensed on the air. I wondered if it was always this cold in the mountains, and I hoped I would warm up after an hour or two of hiking. I worried about getting my bearings and finding my way in the darkness, but the moon had risen by then and the stars blazed brightly, and the entire encampment was awash in enough dim bluish light to see and walk, as long as I went slowly. I picked my way along the trail making almost no sound, and I heard nothing aside from the occasional chirp of a cricket or the tweet of a night bird.

The trail that ran down the camp's middle had many branches, and a couple times I strayed off, but I knew that I really just had to follow the upward incline of the campsite to the upper tree line, and there, somewhere, I'd find the big canvas tent.

I was still putting a plan together in my head, and it wasn't my best. It was rather bold, depended heavily on luck, and was probably more than a little stupid, but I knew I couldn't stay here with Ruby and Chase and the others.

After ten or fifteen minutes of moving slowly and stopping occasionally to ensure I hadn't alerted anyone,

I found the tent hulking among the trees. Before going in, I walked all the way around the tent, listening, looking for any signs of people. There were none, and so I crept to the front flap. It was tied shut with a series of strings along the seams. I fumbled in the deep blue of the night shadows and one by one untied them. Then, after taking a long last look and listening to make sure I hadn't been detected or followed, I entered the tent.

Utter blackness greeted me inside. I wouldn't have been able to see a full-grown man standing an inch away from me, but after creeping forward with my hands outstretched, I managed to locate the table without tripping over the chairs and crates. From inside my coat I produced the small candle-lantern, set it on the table, and lit it using the lighter Chase had given me earlier. It provided only a small halo of light in the large space, but I remembered the general layout well enough, and it was better that the flame was smaller, so as not to be easily noticed.

"Hey, Al."

I gasped and startled back violently.

It was Chase. He sat at the table.

"Dammit," I muttered. "You scared the hell out of me."

"Sorry," he said.

"How did you know?"

"I know you."

"I don't want to be here."

Across the dark space in the tent he tossed something in my direction. It arced across the table, jangling softly. A keyring. I caught it.

"Take the Subaru," he said. "The tank's full and there's almost a full refill in cans in the back. It's parked out there with the van."

I stood there for a few seconds, wondering if this were some trick.

"Oh, and it's a stick, too. I know you can drive one. Hey, did I tell you I learned? Guy here in camp showed me."

"You're letting me go?" I asked, my temper deflating as rapidly as it had flared. "You're letting me take one of your vehicles?"

"Doesn't seem like I can stop you. I thought maybe if I make things easy for you, you'll start trusting me—and the others, too. I know you know that we're not the enemy."

"You know, I know, huh?"

"Yeah."

"What else do you know I know?"

"I think you're really confused, Alison," he said. "I think you got re-united with your son and you were thinking that everything was gonna be great, but now your eyes have been opened and you're all churned up and you're responding to all this with fear and anger."

"Must be great to know everything about everyone."

"Not everyone. Just you. Al, you don't even know what you've lost."

"I can go back down the trail we came in on? And find this Subaru?"

He nodded, but in the dimness I could only just detect it.

"Thank you."

There was a backpack on the table. Chase gave it a shove, and it slid across the table to me.

"Take that with you."

I set the bag upright and opened it. There was a large plastic bottle of water, some food, a blanket, a flashlight. There was also what looked like magazines. I pulled them out to better see them.

"They're notebooks," said Chase. "Look at 'em later. I wouldn't let your Lotus friends see them, though."

"I have no idea how to get home from here," I said.

"It'd take too long to give you directions. Take the 'Ru, follow the dirt road until you come to a paved road. It's a state highway. Turn south. That's left. Keep driving south till you're outta gas."

"And that'll just take me straight to Lotus?"

"No. It won't take you anywhere near Lotus, but if you go far enough south, you'll start seeing Agency patrols—or rather they'll see you and pick you up. They'll take you home."

I put on the backpack. Chase stood up. I turned to go.

"Al, wait," he said.

I stopped and turned back to face him. He came around the table and stood in front of me. Again we stood almost nose-to-nose in the darkness.

"Is there any chance you'd stay?"

"No," I said. "Why'd you give me these keys if you thought I'd stay here?"

"Like I said, I know you," he said, shrugging his shoulders. "Or, I thought I did. Besides, Ruby's gonna kill me for this. If you really wanted to help me out, you could stick around."

"You're being serious?"

"About her getting pissed off about me letting you take one of our valuable automobiles? Yeah, of course."

"Then why go against her?"

"Ruby and I agree, well—broadly—about how to approach most problems. Sometimes we differ just as broadly in terms of specific execution."

"Then I better be good and gone before she wakes up."

"I guess so," replied Chase.

He reached under his coat and pulled out a pistol. It was much like the one I'd taken from him that night he'd come to Gary's apartment.

"Might as well take this," he said. "It's not safe out there. Don't stop unless you need to, and don't stop in any towns, and chances are you won't run into another soul until you hit Agency country. If you do run into anyone, blast 'em."

I nodded and stuffed the pistol into the backpack.

"You're getting really good at separating me from my sidearms."

"Thanks," I said. "Thanks again. Thanks for everything."

CHAPTER 21

According to the little LED clock in the Subaru's dashboard, I'd been driving for four hours by the time the sun came up, and I drove for another four before stopping for the first time to pee and stretch my legs. Assuming Ruby discovered my departure around dawn, I had at least a four-hour head-start on whomever she'd send after me, which was further assuming that the pursuers would know to follow me due south instead of turning off onto one of the many intersecting highways.

I'd made it down out of the mountains in only a couple of hours and now I drove through the sage-dotted and low-rolling open rangelands of what had been the very sparsely inhabited American West. I hadn't seen any other vehicles at all, let alone any Agency vehicles, but Chase had said I'd need to drive until I was out of gas before I started meeting patrols.

When the gas gauge light came on, I stopped on a featureless stretch of road and emptied the three plastic gas cans into the tank. Then I took another pee on the roadside and went on.

A few times I tried pushing my speed to eighty or ninety miles per hour, but the highway was pitted and rotting with disuse. Tall stalks of weeds and even sagebrush had invaded the road, too, and although I could drive over or around them without issue, the whipping sounds they made against the car were startling, so I slowed to fifty or sixty.

My supply of gasoline would last longer that way, too, I reasoned. But after driving a few more hours through that immense, empty landscape, fifty miles per hour began to feel like only a little faster than running speed, and I began to think I'd never get anywhere.

The inside of the car was quiet but for the thrum of the engine and the occasional banging and clatter of the weeds and rough road beneath the wheels. Inside my head, however, it was as though my mind became a passenger, a chatty one who wouldn't stop talking.

I thought about what I'd tell Rachel—if she or anyone noticed that I'd been gone.

I thought about what I'd say to Arie and how I might be able to connect with him.

And amid these thoughts of what might happen tomorrow, there were all the people and things I'd seen over the past couple days. I thought about Sandy and if it might be true that she'd been pushed down into the Zones simply to make way for me. I thought about what Ruby and Chase and Woolly had said. What did I really know about the Agency and Lotus? Ruby and Chase made a convincing case, but I knew that I'd been drawn to their side before, turned against the Agency, and for that to have happened they must have had convincing arguments then, too. How can you know if you can trust someone if you can't remember what you once knew about them?

Of course I already doubted almost everything Gary had told me, but what about Rachel? Was Lotus a bold experiment at the dawn of a new, promising age for humankind, or was it just a way to grab power from the ashes of the back before?

And I thought about Chase. Not that he'd come into Gary's apartment with a gun or that he'd orchestrated my kidnapping—I just thought about him. As a person, as a man.

I came to a large hill. When the car had climbed to the top of the mile-long grade, I could see a long way all around me, and I felt very insignificant. As I drove down the far side of the hill, I knew that if the Subaru broke down and I were stranded, I'd probably perish of hunger and thirst within a week, and it'd likely be a week or more after that before anyone discovered me—if anyone ever did at all.

According to some embedded memory from when I'd learned to drive, I'd been dutifully driving all day on the right side of the highway. Not even the Agency's memory-killing drug could suppress such habits—not just regarding driving, but how to hold a fork and knife, how to write, or how to throw a baseball. And so it suddenly occurred to me that I'd been obeying the long-dead traffic laws of a civilization now extinct.

I drifted into the middle of the road until the wheels straddled the centerline. I even felt the need to justify this violation, telling myself it was smoother and less sprouted with weeds in the center, and I felt the odd thrill one feels when willfully breaking well-established rules.

Out of the same set of deeply ingrained habits, I'd been checking my rearview mirror periodically, and for the first time that day, I saw something.

There was a vehicle on the road behind me.

At least I thought it was a vehicle. A dark object had crested the large hill I'd passed over minutes before, and I saw it for only a moment as it was silhouetted against the sky.

However, at first, I did not even register this as a threat. I'd fallen into a sort of driving daze, my senses dulled by hours of driving and fatigue. Nothing, evidently, could have seemed more natural to me than seeing a car in my rearview mirror.

It was a few seconds before it dawned on me just how much danger I faced, but the vehicle had disappeared into the folds of the land that lay between us. I kept my eyes on the mirror for so long, that my car kept creeping onto the shoulder, and I kept swerving back into the middle.

Chase told me there might be raiders out here, wild people, who'd slipped the Agency's grasp but took a wholly barbaric approach to survival. And so I looked forward and pressed the gas pedal.

I now had the speedometer at eighty-five miles per hour and it was fluttering up to the mark indicating ninety. Weed stalks whacked alarmingly against the bumper and the tires banged against the pot holes and the road's weathered surface. I worried about the tires, the suspension, the entire automobile, but I couldn't slow down.

According to the little LED dash clock, I'd driven fifteen minutes and therefore about twenty miles without seeing the dark spot behind me again. Was there really some murderous raiding party behind me, masked in the folds of the road, or had I simply imagined it? Had it been just a trick of the heat that was beginning to wobble and refract on the pavement as the day warmed?

Then it reappeared.

As I swerved around a long bend and onto a straight, flat section, the vehicle was in the mirror again, much closer now, maybe just a mile back. It was a pickup truck.

I sped up again. The car bumped and boomed horribly over the crumbling road. What could they want? I forced myself to think. It was definitely not an Agency or Lotus vehicle. Even from this distance I could tell it was a truck of significant age, and my gut told me I still hadn't driven far enough south to encounter any Agency personnel—I was only a little more than halfway through the gasoline.

Could it be someone from Ruby's camp? No, I'd seen all the vehicles in their small fleet, and they had no pickup like this one. And they could never have caught up to me so fast, anyway.

This narrowed the possibilities to two. It could be someone without ill intent, just another drifting survivor who'd happened upon the same stretch of highway. But what were the odds of that on so remote a road, and why would they want to overtake me?

A raider, then. Someone who meant to kill me.

After a few more minutes, I saw the truck more clearly. The rearview mirror vibrated violently, but I could tell the truck was a genuinely ancient model, perhaps older than me. Its panels and fenders were crumpled and so rusted and dirty, the truck was the same neutral gray-brown of the surrounding land.

It was also close enough that I could hear the growl of its motor, and I saw a blackish blue trail of exhaust pouring from the tailpipe.

And it was still gaining.

Between the jiggling mirror and the truck's hazy, cracked windshield, I could not clearly see the driver. It may have been an old woman or a young boy for all I could tell, hunching darkly behind the wheel.

But then a man rose up from the bed of the truck and stood behind the cab. The rags he wore and his long wild hair whipped crazily in the wind, and he had something in his hands, something long and black—a rifle, I supposed. I pressed the gas all the way down, waiting for the Subaru to shake into pieces. If not for the seatbelt, I might have bounced right out of the seat, and it was difficult to stay on the road.

Something struck the car with a thump. The man had started shooting. There was another thump, then a third, but we'd entered a series of bends in the road, and I couldn't look back long enough to see anything of use.

Together we hurtled down the road at sickening speeds. The loose pavement against the underside of the car made a fearsome racket that drowned out the sound of the engine. I chanced a glance in the mirror and saw the truck's headlights were now only a few feet from the Subaru's bumper. Then came a loud, hissing crash, and the back window shattered in a blizzard of pebbled safety glass.

Without another thought, I stomped as hard as I could on the brake.

Maybe it was panic or maybe it was some canny tactical impulse arising from my reptilian brain. I pressed my head into the seat back, locked my elbows to brace against the wheel, and practically stood up on the brake pedal.

The car shuddered and bounced as it slowed, and an instant later the truck rammed the rear of the Subaru with a dreadful crash. My eyes flicked to the mirror again, and I saw the man who'd been standing in the truck bed was now floundering there, his legs in the air.

I down-shifted and floored the gas, putting some yards between me and the truck. The truck accelerated, too, its back tires squalling on the loose road bed and the growling engine louder now through the gaping back window, but I spotted tendrils of white smoke coming from under its hood.

When I'd gained a few hundred feet, I fumbled furiously for the backpack Chase had sent with me. It had been on the seat but now was wedged upside-down into the floor-well of the passenger side. Keeping the gas pedal pinned, I grabbed the pack and hoisted it upright onto the seat, but the engine revved, demanding I shift into fourth gear. After clumsily shifting, I tore at the top of the pack to retrieve Chase's pistol.

Smoke billowed from the truck's engine, and I thought if I could just keep it behind me for a few minutes it might slow down or stop running altogether. Instead, it gained on me, engine roaring madly. This time it came alongside the Subaru on the passenger side. My head swiveled from the road to the truck and back as we thundered along.

The man in the bed of the truck was on his feet again. He was gaunt and spindly and filthy. His face was deeply tanned and lined with desperation. Woven into the tatters of his clothing and hair, I saw what must have been small bones—finger bones or toes or molars. They whipped and blew around him.

Then I saw that it was not a rifle he was shooting but a hunting bow, with heavy fiberglass limbs and pulleys and cables. Standing with his feet far apart, he drew the bow back, aimed at the Subaru, and let an arrow go. It came through the roof on the passenger side at a shallow angle and froze there, its sharp-bladed tip only a foot away and pointed directly at me.

The truck pulled slightly ahead of me now. The driver was likewise gaunt and wild-looking. She turned and leered at me savagely.

I leveled the pistol and fired at her through my passenger side window, which erupted into powdered glass and was gone. In the small space of the car, the gunshots deafened me, but there were finger-sized black dimples in the truck's driver's-side door. I fired a few more times and now the driver's-side window of the truck likewise vanished in a glittering spray of shattered glass, and the driver slumped out of view.

The truck slowed and careened away to the right, but in my peripheral vision I caught a flash of dark motion, and I knew the man had hurled himself from the truck bed. A half-second later there was a heavy, metallic *whump* as he landed on the Subaru's roof.

I stood on the brake again and braced against the wheel as the car practically stood up on its front end, tires squelching hotly against the pavement. The man flopped across the windshield and hood, but he avoided sliding off the front of the car by hanging onto the roof rack. His face was pressed against the windshield and I saw his eyes blaze with fiendish triumph, knowing the thin sheet of glass was all that remained between us.

As I tried to shift gears, I dropped the gun, and it fell between the seats. I down-shifted, hit the gas, and popped the clutch. The car bucked forward, but not only did the man not slide off the hood, he hauled himself to his feet. I floored the gas and felt around for the pistol.

Then, with his hands still on the roof rack, the man hopped into the air and stomped on the windshield. A

205

spiderweb of cracks appeared under his boots as the safety glass strained to hold together. I fumbled around for the gun. The man jumped again, and the windshield dished inward, raining jewels of glass into the car. My hand, wriggling between the seats found the gun just as the man jumped again and came bashing boots-first into the car.

I let go of the wheel and raised the pistol. In the close awkward space I gripped the gun in both hands, pointed the barrel at the man's chest, and pulled the trigger.

It only clicked.

CHAPTER 22

When I opened my eyes, I was treated to a rugged and sunny western vista. Small dark desert birds darted between the clumps of sage brush, which trembled in the light wind. The prairie stretched into the distance, specked with the dark dots of sage and occasional stands of dark-green juniper. Farther away rose the blackish-brown desert hills that formed a jagged horizon against the deepening blue of the sky, where far-off clouds might, with a little coaxing from the sun, become thunderstorms.

It was stark and beautiful.

It was also upside-down.

I don't know how long I hung in the seatbelt and shoulder harness of the Subaru, staring at the inverted desert. Perhaps I'd been knocked out or perhaps I was so exhausted I'd slept that way. Slowly I came to my senses again. I ached all over. My head throbbed. I reached down to my side and pressed the button to release the seatbelt and fell into a heap onto the Subaru's roof.

All the car windows were broken out, and the roof was partly crushed. I was covered with shattered safety glass. I wormed my way out of the car and into the powdery dirt of the desert. There was a thin, salty crust on top, and a flour-like dust beneath.

The Subaru lay on its roof like a stricken beast about a hundred yards out into the sage at the bottom of a slope at a bend in the road.

The last thing I remembered was the man crashing through the window and into the car with me. The marred floor of the desert told the rest of the tale. We'd left the road at the bend, rolled several times, and then came to rest upside-down. I'd been bashed around and my ears rang harshly, but I was apparently in otherwise decent working order. There was a cut at my brow but I wasn't bleeding from anywhere else. I shuffled and staggered along up the incline, backtracking along the car's disastrous trail.

About halfway back to the road, I found my backpack. I stopped in my tracks, picked up the backpack, grabbed the water, and then let the pack drop back into the dirt. The water held a trace of last night's cold, and it was marvelously refreshing. I knew I shouldn't, but I drank a good third of it, letting it run down my cheeks and neck. Then I put the pack on my back and continued.

Soon I spotted the tattered, dusty figure of the man from the truck. It looked as if the car had tossed him from a window and into its own tumbling path. The man lay tamped partway into the soil, a crushed and twisted tangle of unmoving, half-buried limbs and rags.

"Is he dead?" someone shouted.

"Oh, yeah," I said. "He's dead."

Then, over the ringing in my ears, I heard the idling of an automobile.

I felt around for the gun, but it was gone. I looked up, and there at the edge of the road above me was a clean, dark-colored semi-tractor with a white trailer. It grumbled quietly. A man in blue overalls was making his way down the hill in my direction.

"What about you?" he said.

"No," I answered. "I'm alive."

He came closer.

"Stop," I said. "I have a gun."

He stopped and raised a hand.

"It's here somewhere," I added, searching the surrounding ground.

"I won't hurt you. Just come to see if I could help."

"Come from where?"

He pointed. "The Interstate's over there. Saw that pickup smoking, and all the kicked-up dust."

I looked where he pointed and saw a straight white line cut into the desert. Then I saw the old pickup truck. It lay on its side, a thin column of black smoke rising from it and carrying on the wind.

"There's an exit ramp a mile or two further south," said the man in overalls. "I figured I'd come down to see if there were any survivors."

"That was nice of you," I said. "Did you find any?"

The man smiled grimly. He wore an ancient trucker's hat and a thick mustache. He was short and rotund, which lent him a friendly disposition, regardless of whether he really had one.

"Where were you headed?" he asked.

I thought about whether I could trust him. His clothing and the clean truck in good repair told me he was somehow connected to the Agency, and I was an officer of Lotus—in good standing as far as I knew. If he'd meant to harm me, he'd have done so already; I could barely stay on my feet. As far as I could tell he wasn't even armed.

"The Agency Depot," I said. "South of here. The Zone 1891."

He chuckled. "Well, you're in luck," he said. "That's not far from where I'll end up. After a few other stops."

The man introduced himself as Bill and told me that he trucked supplies between Agency installations. I asked him what he hauled and where the other installations were located, but he just shook his head.

"Oh, I can't tell you much. I'd get in an awful lotta trouble," he replied.

He didn't seem to know anything about Lotus, and I felt it was probably better that way.

Bill stood looking around at the wreckage.

"Someone else was driving the pickup?"

I nodded. He put his hands on his hips.

"Kind of a shame to leave 'em unburied this way," said Bill.

I scoffed. "They were trying to kill me. Or worse probably."

"Still," he said.

I got my backpack from the dusty ground and Bill helped me up the hill to his truck. He retrieved a shovel from somewhere.

"You don't gotta help," he said. "I just feel it's wrong to leave people to the coyotes and ravens like that. Wait here. I'll be quick."

I sat on the running board of Bill's truck and sipped at my water as he dug two shallow graves. It was comforting to see Bill observe the ritual on behalf of people who'd all but given away their humanity.

He did work quickly, and soon he brought the woman over from the pickup truck and dragged the man over to the graves. Then with a care and civility that seemed wildly out of place, he laid the two barbarians to rest.

When he'd covered them over with dirt, he began to cover the graves with rocks from the surrounding desert. I went down to help him. The stones were all alike—dark and rusty-looking and sharply jagged.

"Thanks for the hand," said Bill. "T'be a shame to bury them just to be dug up again by varmints."

I nodded.

When the graves were complete, Bill removed his hat, bowed his head, and stood quietly with his eyes shut. I bowed my head, too, but kept my eyes open.

After a minute, Bill stood straight again. He took a deep breath, let it out, and then looked at me.

"Well, shall we?" he said.

***

The interior of Bill's truck was tidy and comfortable and very warm. I immediately fell asleep in the passenger side seat. I must have slept for several hours, because when I woke up, the sun was setting. We were pulling away from some kind of storage facility. I should have paid more attention, watched for road signs or other info that might come in handy. We were so seldom allowed to travel around or know what was going on around us. Unfortunately, I was too warm and groggy for that level of discipline.

I did step out of the truck on our next stop, however, to stretch a little. It was another loading dock in a place I didn't know. I walked around the truck and then climbed the steps to the loading dock. It was a large facility, most of which looked abandoned.

As I strolled along the dock's enormous length, I saw Bill come out of the warehouse. He was looking at a sheaf of papers on a clipboard. He waved to me when he saw me, and I walked in his direction. We converged at the back of the semi trailer, the doors of which stood open.

"Well, let's get back on the road," Bill said cheerily.

But before he could get the doors swung closed, I saw that the semi trailer was almost completely full of wooden crates painted with labels indicating what I thought was ammunition. *5.56 BALL AMMUNITION 1000 RDS, 7.62 BELT AMMUNITION 500 CTRGS,* and more. Crate upon crate.

Bill didn't seem to feel sheepish about me seeing what was inside the trailer, but he shut the doors without another word.

When we got back in the truck, he said, "We'll be on the road for a while now. Seems like you been through the wringer. Feel free to go back to sleep. We won't get to 1891 until after midnight. You could even jump into the sleeper if you want. Just lay down and zonk out."

The height of the rig was impressive. We seemed to be flying through the air rather than driving on the road. The rig's suspension took almost all the roughness from the road.

"Maybe I'll do that," I said. "I am pretty tired."

"What happened to you out there?" Bill asked. "Where'd you come from and where were you going?"

As we bounced gently along, I told Bill that I, too, worked for the Agency. "I was on a, um, fact-finding mission," I said.

"And them two somehow hunted you down?" he asked.

"Yeah," I replied. "Just got lucky, I guess."

"Guess I probably shouldn't ask you too much about your job," he said, laying his index finger alongside his nose.

I laughed and nodded knowingly.

"I've run across folks like that," he said, jabbing a thumb at the road behind us. "That's why I use these small highways. I figure they're less traveled. But maybe not."

I nodded.

"This here outfit has armored panels," he said, "especially around the engine compartment. Not so many up here where the driver is. I guess they figure if I get shot up, they'll find someone else to drive it, but if the truck is shot dead, that'd be really bad. I got some guns hidden here'n there, so I feel pretty safe, but every time I see some other car or truck, I always start wondering if my number's up. I've had some close calls."

"Thanks again for helping me out, Bill," I told him. "I hate to think what would've happened if you hadn't seen me."

"Glad to help."

I climbed into the sleeper cab. There was a small sink there, and so I washed my face and hands and brushed my teeth.

And then I couldn't sleep.

The dark empty road unfolded in the intensely bright headlights of Bill's rig. I lay awake watching for a while. Bill played old music from back before on a sound system at low volume, singing along sometimes.

Then I remembered the backpack, and I felt around inside it for something to eat. Instead, however, the first thing I felt was the notebooks. I removed them and squinted at them in the darkness. There was a small reading lamp near the bed, and I switched it on.

Once I opened the first notebook, I knew I wouldn't sleep. They were diaries. Mine and Arie's. I recognized my handwriting. For the first time, things were finally making sense.

I cried when I read about my life with Arie. We'd ridden bikes everywhere, we ate together, worked together. I read of our adventures outside the Zone boundaries, searching the houses. We'd been attacked by wild dogs and we'd found a little girl in our backyard. We wrote down our memories so that we'd never lose them.

And then the Agency took him.

There were entries about meeting Ruby and Woolly, pleading with them for help. There were passages in which I told my future self how I'd felt about Chase. We searched for Arie, we broke into Agency buildings, we snuck around, and we stole. Little Gracie was killed, and they sent soldiers to kill us, and still we didn't find Arie. The Agency had told me he was dead. And I'd wondered if he had died.

But I saw no sign whatsoever of trickery or subterfuge or blackmail. I'd never been involved with the Agency, and Ruby's gang hadn't subverted me. Arie and I were just a couple starving Zone dwellers looking for a way out. I'd gone to Ruby, and she'd taken me in. The whole gang had taken me in and treated me like one of them.

There it all was, in my own handwriting, dated, annotated, and in my own words. I could of course never truly remember writing those stories, but I could hear myself speaking from the pages, and more than once I finished the written lines in my head before I'd finished reading them—not because I recalled what I'd written, but I knew how I would write it were I to write it again.

Chase's words came back to me like an indictment: "You don't even know what you've lost."

How right he'd been. I'd known nothing about what had been stolen from me and what I'd been fighting for. Even now, reading the journals from before my memories were erased, I probably couldn't even begin to comprehend what was lost. There were so many moments between the lines—little things like watching Arie repairing our bicycles or cooking cans of soup on a little burner. Had we really done that?

The journals comprised only one year of my life, but what a year it had been. A lifetime of living and learning and loving all in a year. A year of work to free myself and my son and my friends. A year of finding out who I really was. All of it had been taken from me—to say nothing of what might have been lost in the years before that.

I'd been murdered, brought back to life, and reprogrammed.

The journal also confirmed that Gary hadn't been my husband. He was mentioned in the journals a few times, but only as an acquaintance associated with the Agency.

There wasn't any writing about the explosion. My guess is that I was on the run and had been captured and that these journals had been left behind, and that is when the journals must have fallen into the hands of one of Ruby's people. But I'd pieced most of the rest of the details together from clues in the journal that led up to that day, and from things Chase and Ruby told me. I'd led Gary and his small army to Ruby's headquarters and then triggered the booby traps she'd laid there, fully intending to kill not only Gary but myself as well.

I knew why, too. I was still more or less the same person, I could map out my rationale without even trying very hard. It was for Arie. It was so that Arie could get free of Gary and the Agency.

And so the question that emerged was why on earth Gary had kept me with him, why he'd let me live at all. It could certainly have no relation to Gary's feelings for me. I'd left him ruined and pushed aside by the Agency. It had to be something much darker which had eventually resulted in my recruitment by Lotus to be a pawn in their game.

As the night wore on, I felt my eyelids drooping. It must have been close to midnight, and I struggled to stay awake. But the more I read, I realized that the notebooks and the contents of Bill's trailer were connected in a way that was immediate and terrible, and that the coming of Bill's truck was like a black storm cloud on the horizon.

CHAPTER 23

Bill dropped me off at the Agency Depot. I asked at the all-night office about finding a ride to Lotus. The on-duty guard looked at me warily but confirmed my identity and took me to a room where I could wait until a series of morning deliveries were headed to Lotus.

As we came to my neighborhood, I immediately noticed that there were official-looking vehicles parked at intersections and at certain buildings. They were security patrol cars and black SUVs without any markings. People in fatigues stood on the sidewalks by the vehicles. They weren't carrying rifles, but each had a sidearm in a holster. They waved at me as we passed by.

"What's all this?" I asked the delivery man. "Do you know?"

"No," he said. "I was just about to ask you. Been more and more security lately. I don't know why. I mean, I assume there's trouble."

The delivery man dropped me at my house, and I found a sheet of paper folded up and wedged into the crack between the front door and the frame. No doubt a note from Rachel or a co-worker noting my absence from the office. I took it inside and set it on the table. I checked to see if Arie was home, but he wasn't.

I went straight to my room and took off the clothes I'd been living in for three days, and then I took a long shower.

I had to admit that if I ever joined Ruby and Chase, it would be difficult to get over the loss of such luxuries. The refrigerator at least partially full of good food would likewise be missed. I made myself a little soup and had a cup of tea. Then I went straight to bed.

As I lay in bed, I thought about what I should do. Even before I'd gotten home I had decided not to report Ruby or what had happened, but I wasn't sure what to do with myself next. How could I continue working in Lotus, knowing how I now felt, and knowing how things stood before I'd gotten my memory erased? And what about Arie? He might find it suspicious if I told him I agreed with him about Lotus. He rarely spoke to me and seemed to regard me as an enemy. How could I speak to him about any of this without arousing his suspicion? I could never even be sure about when I'd next see him.

What would he say about the journals?

As I began to doze off, I remembered the note on the table. I got out of bed and opened it. It was written in shaky handwriting. I assumed it had been written by an adult, but there was something childlike about it. It definitely wasn't from Arie or Rachel. I'd seen their handwriting. I didn't think it was from anyone at the office. Could it be a note from one of Ruby's people? This seemed unlikely—how would any of them gotten to my house before me? I got back into bed, too tired to unravel the mystery just then, but I couldn't deny it: something about the note caused goosebumps to raise on my arms.

Alison, I've been looking for you. I'll come back later. —D

***

As I walked into my office the next morning, I was wary about what might be said of my absence. And though I had covered the bruises on my face with makeup, I also worried that it was still noticeable. I had excuses ready to fire if necessary, but aside from curt head-nods and "hellos," nothing was said.

Something was different, though. It apparently had nothing to do with me specifically, but I could feel it in the air—a heavy nervousness that hung in the air like a bad smell. Then Rachel showed up, and I knew something was definitely amiss. She wasn't scheduled to meet with any of us for several days.

I went to Cathy's office, next door to mine.

"What's going on?" I asked her.

Cathy waved me in and shut her door.

"I'm glad you're okay. Where were you yesterday?"

"Oh. I wasn't feeling well. What's wrong? What happened?"

"There's been some trouble."

"What kind of trouble?"

"Trouble at some of the manufacturing plants. Trouble with the younger people."

"I don't understand."

"The younger workers are grumbling, pushing back. I don't know. Like a—rebellion? Everyone keeps saying it's nothing to worry about but everyone's worried. I've heard some production lines are shut down completely. Worst thing, though, Henry got attacked."

Henry was another case manager, perhaps best known among us for always saying, "Howdy" instead of "hello" or "hi." He was admittedly a stern-looking guy.

He wore a perpetual frown, even when he was happy, and his large forehead seemed to squat down over his prodigious, grumpy eyebrows. Despite that, we all found him quite pleasant.

"Oh, no," I said. "Is he okay?"

"No one knows," said Cathy. "He was working with a case, a young guy, and he somehow got Henry down onto the floor and beat him with a shoe."

"My god."

"Yeah," repeated Cathy. "He was still unconscious when Andre and Terri found him. They took him to the infirmary. No one ever found the kid. He was getting recommended for reassignment. It's a group of young people making all the trouble. After everything Lotus has given them. They're not satisfied."

"Well Cathy," I said. "Let's not panic. I'm sure they're working on it."

The trouble Cathy spoke of seemed to be confirmed when an unscheduled meeting was announced.

Nearly everyone gathered into the large meeting room—case workers, supervisors, security people. Extra chairs were awkwardly carried in. Rachel spotted me filing into the room and seemed to single me out for a warm smile. She was the picture of calm and composure, with her hair in her trademark chignon and her immaculately applied lipstick and eyeliner. I searched her face for alarm or worry or doubt. If she felt any of those things, she wasn't showing it. She gave me an affectionate pat on the shoulder as I passed.

When we were seated, Rachel stood at the front of the room, leaning on a table there. She looked us over for what felt like a full minute. Her gaze went from face to face, and she gave each one of us a look of smiling approval.

"Before I get started," she said at last, "I'd just like to let you know how much confidence I have in each one of you, and really how much I think of you. We all suffered a terrible calamity when the human race was practically snuffed out by a deadly virus. Many people succumbed to the virus, and many people died in the aftermath. People die every day from effects that stem from that worldwide event. Some people die simply from the despair of it all."

Again I asked myself what it was about Rachel's oration that so moved me.

She continued: "But I want you to just take a quick look around at each other."

We did so, smiling and nodding diffidently, chuckling a little.

"You were all there," said Rachel in a grave tone. "Yes, you don't remember it, but you know you were there. As others were dying, as others were turning against each other, against you, as others lost hope— you survived. And now you're here, and you're not just surviving, you're laying the foundation of a new world. In a hundred years or a thousand, your names will be among the histories people study and celebrate. And I'm proud to know and work with each one of you."

Her voice didn't rise or crack at all.

"Now, I have some very good news," said Rachel. "As some of you may have heard, we have been facing some challenges. There are a few individuals at some of our production facilities who've been, shall we say, misbehaving, refusing to work, acting out."

Having the rumor promoted to an official bulletin, several people in the room murmured, nodded, and exchanged glances.

A supervisor named Angelo raised his hand.

"Angelo," said Rachel, pointing at him, "you're going to ask me why I said this was good news."

Angelo lowered his hand.

"I'll tell you," Rachel went on. "These 'troubles' are like growing pains. Anyone know what causes growing pains? You know, like when kids with growth spurts get all achy and sore?"

"Something about their muscles and bones," Cathy offered.

"Exactly," said Rachel. "The child's bones are lengthening. The child is running and playing hard all day. The musculoskeletal system is under stress, heavy use. So, it's not an illness, it's not a sign of danger. It's a sign of vigor, of success. Personally, I'm encouraged to see a little resistance out there. It means we're doing something right. It means we're growing, maturing, we're seeing success."

A few more nods.

"I've got more good news," she said. "I know that there has been some violence, and I apologize that something like this was allowed to happen. I visited Henry."

There were gasps and little exclamations.

"He's banged up, but he's doing fine," said Rachel. "I told him I'd tell you all 'howdy'."

A wave of quiet laughter at this.

Rachel went around to the other side of the table and leaned forward with her hands flat on the surface. "The good news is that Lotus cares deeply for all of its workers, for all of you, and this little hiccup will be cleared up shortly. And while we work on that, I'd like you to stay home from work so that those appointed to maintain order can do their jobs. Everything should be back on track within the next few days." She straightened. "Now, does anyone have any questions?"

Angelo raised his hand.

"Angelo," said Rachel. "Let me guess. You're wondering who these people are. These troublemakers."

Angelo nodded and lowered his hand.

"Great question, Angelo," she said. "I'm guessing you've heard it's young people. Teenagers and people in their twenties."

Nods all around.

"There are some members of that demographic," said Rachel, "but there are others, too. And more to the point, I think that many of these people are not troublemakers at all. That is, they wouldn't make trouble if left to their own devices. You'd be shocked if I told you who some of them were."

Were? I thought. What does she mean by *were*?

"Because these are some of our really great people," Rachel said with a frown, "and they've been misled. Someone has gotten to them. Someone with the worst intentions."

Rachel's glance landed on me for the briefest of moments, and a chill raced down my neck and spine.

Angelo raise his hand again.

"Who is instigating this?" asked Rachel on his behalf. "Another great question. I'll be very honest with you. We don't know exactly. But we have some good leads and I think, again, you'd be very shocked to discover who some of these people turn out to be."

She was looking from person to person as she spoke, but when she looked at me, I read something in her expression that made my face turn hot.

"That's why I want you to finish what you're doing and then head home. We've got the best people working on it, and it'll all be solved soon. And let me reassure you again—this is good news." She smiled her winning smile. "If we weren't doing something right, we wouldn't attract this kind of trouble."

Rachel dismissed us, and I headed for my desk. It wasn't that I loved my job or would ever miss doing it. After all that had happened, I wasn't sure what to think. I had just sat down at my desk when Rachel came in.

"Alison. Got a minute?"

***

"The majority of the problems we are having are coming from a few very specific facilities," Rachel told me. "A few specific groups."

She'd shut the door and sat in the seat where my cases normally sat. I hoped she couldn't tell that I'd started to sweat.

"Okay," I said.

"We have several production lines where we manufacture armaments," she said. "That's where most of the problems are centered, it seems."

"Armaments as in guns?" I asked.

"Right," said Rachel.

"I guess I didn't know we made that kind of thing. Why would we need so many guns to have entire factories?"

Rachel smiled at me like a parent smiling at a child who had asked an adorably naïve question.

"Alison," she said kindly, "we can't always expect to prevail on our strong ideas and work ethics alone. We often encounter resistance when we recruit. We sometimes encounter armed resistance. We have to be armed as well. For defense."

"We recruit people with guns?"

"That's not what I'm saying," she said. "I'm simply saying that we must be armed in order to be successful. To protect ourselves, to keep our operations safe."

"I'm not sure I understand where this is going," I said finally.

"Arie works at our main facility. Our munitions facility."

"You think Arie is involved in this?"

"I don't know. That's what I wanted to ask you about. Has he said or done anything you'd consider unusual? Have you noticed anything unusual about him at all?"

"To be honest, I don't see much of him."

Rachel tilted her head and narrowed her eyes.

"What I mean is," I hastily added "we don't spend a lot of time together. He does his thing; I do mine. I guess you might call him a moody teenager," I lied. "He's quiet. Spends a lot of time alone, in his room."

She looked into my eyes with a searching expression. My breath became suddenly shallow.

"Yes, teenagers," Rachel said with a smile that was somehow not a smile. "Luckily they don't stay at that stage forever."

I nodded.

"Keep an eye out, Alison, will you? If you see anything, let me know. Tell me directly. Even if it's something that might not be otherwise out-of-the-ordinary. Does that make sense? Dial up your sensors to super-sensitive and let me know."

"Do you think we're in serious danger?"

"It's nothing to worry too much about."

"What are you planning to do? I mean to resolve the problem?"

"Well," she said, "normally, Lotus doesn't work very closely with the Agency. They have their way of doing things and we have ours. We often disagree."

"I thought the Agency and Lotus were the same," I said.

"Hardly. We have formed a kind of symbiotic relationship, but it's an uneasy one."

"I didn't know."

"Recently, however," Rachel added, "we're both facing greater opposition. From inside, from outside. Various groups, individuals—people we usually refer to as 'terrorists,' but it's more than people simply trying to make trouble. They're getting sophisticated and organized to an extent we've never seen. It used to be people just trying to escape, to get away, trying to avoid treatment or reassignment. Now we're seeing what looks more and more like groups that are attacking us, subverting us, trying to bring us down. If that makes sense."

"Not everyone wants to rebuild the world your way, I guess?"

"Exactly," she said. "It's unbelievable. So, we're working together with the Agency's security forces. They're sending a large force. I hate to resort to such brute-force measures, but we can't allow these attacks to continue."

"A force?"

"They're sending an army. Working with the information we have, there's going to be a—" she stopped to think of the right word. "There's going to be a quick and vigorous clean-up. It won't be pleasant but it'll get us back on track."

"You're talking about a counter-attack," I said, and I thought about Bill's trailer packed with ammunition.

"A reckoning," she corrected. "There will be a reckoning." Then she clenched her jaw, and in her eye I detected the faintest glimpse of what I'd call desperation. She stood up and then looked me in the eyes.

"Keep watch, Alison. I mean it. One person can make a big difference."

"I will," I said. "I'll let you know if I see anything."

She nodded at me, and then she was gone.

I'd seen the military forces of the Agency. They were heavily armed, and they were not careful about how they used force. They shot first and asked questions later, if they asked questions at all. They would demolish an entire building to dislodge one or two armed malcontents. I'd often wondered where they'd gotten their guns, their supplies.

And then I thought of Arie. According to the journals, he'd been more than a little interested in subverting the Agency—not necessarily in acts of aggression or terrorism, but by simply finding out what had really happened and finding a way to keep our memories. Was he still fighting? Was he part of some kind of resistance or uprising?

I remembered the security forces positioning themselves on the streets of Lotus. Soon troop carriers and armed vehicles from the Agency would be rolling in as well. I pictured armed columns of the reckless and deadly Agency troops filing through the city. And then I remembered how Arie had spoken about Lotus' processing of members, memory treatments, and reassignments. If he spoke out or even said an untoward word—I might never see him again. And if he were, as Rachel seemed to suspect, part of some organized group—I wasn't sure I was ready to fully weigh those possibilities.

All I knew was I had to find him, and soon. I looked at the pile of filing and paperwork on my desk, but I didn't even think about touching it.

When I got home, I was winded and footsore. I'd run almost the entire distance to the house. I saw the Lotus security patrols. They'd smiled and waved as I jogged past.

I stood on the lawn bent over with my hands on my knees, breathing hard. I'm not sure what I'd been expecting to find—a Lotus security detail out front? Arie being dragged away in cuffs?

The house was as I'd left it, and when I'd caught my breath, I headed for the front door.

And I saw people inside.

CHAPTER 24

In the living room, chairs had been gathered into a rough circle—all the chairs in the house, I figured. A group of at least twenty people were seated there, and they were in the middle of some kind of meeting.

Though there may have been two or three people who looked to be twenty-five years old or a little older, almost all of them were Arie's age, eighteen to twenty-one.

When I'd thrown open the front door of the house, I'd heard their urgent voices, but when I came into the house and they saw me, they all went quiet. And then they sat looking at me.

Arie stood from his chair. He held up a hand to signal the group to remain quiet, and then he ushered me—also without saying anything—into the hallway and out of sight of the others.

"Shouldn't you be at work?" Arie asked me, his voice low and cold.

"We have to talk," I told him, keeping my voice quiet. "I think you need to get those people out of here and then we need to have a very serious talk. There's trouble."

"Why? Why are you here? Why now?" he hissed.

"In a way," I said, "I think we're here for the same reason. I work directly with Rachel, Arie. You know that. And so you know that if I tell you that these people have got to get out of here, you should believe me."

"They're my friends. There's no rule in Lotus saying someone can't get together with friends."

"Okay, but something tells me you guys aren't planning a game of kick-the-can. Tell them to go, Arie. I mean it."

He pressed his lips together until his mouth was just a taut, hard line, then he turned away in a huff and returned to the living room. I knew he wasn't obeying what I'd told him to do. It was simply that he knew he couldn't continue the meeting with me in the house. I followed him to the corner of the hallway but didn't show myself.

"We're going to have to leave this for another time," said Arie to the group, his voice quiet but quavering very slightly.

The group muttered their assent.

"Leave the regular way," said Arie. "One or two at a time. Three-minute intervals. Half on bikes, half walking. There're cops everywhere. Spread out and separate. They're watching us."

I stayed in the hallway. There were a few murmured exchanges, but for the most part, they all stayed very quiet. Then they began coming down the hallway where I stood. They passed by me without saying anything and continued on to the back door. They'd left their bikes in the backyard, I realized. Every few minutes, I heard the front and back doors opening and closing. I took two chairs from the living room and brought them to the kitchen table. No one said anything to me.

It took them a half-hour to disperse. I sat at the kitchen table. When it was just Arie and I, he joined me in the kitchen. He was wearing his coat and ballcap, as though he were going out.

"This was stuck in the door for you," he said, tossing a folded piece of paper onto the table.

On the outside of the folded paper was my name in the same childish scrawl as before. I unfolded it and inside it read, *Missed you again. I'll come back soon.* —D

I folded it up again and shoved the note into my pocket.

Arie didn't sit down. He stood at the window, watching the street through the cracks between the blinds.

"Okay," he said. "Start talking. But make it fast. I'm leaving."

"Tell me what's going on," I said.

"What does it look like?" he sneered. "We're getting organized."

"So, you're one of them?"

He laughed. "*Them?*"

"You know what I mean. I heard what you said to them. You know you're being watched. They're taking names, making lists, Arie."

"You might know what's going on with Lotus, but you don't know what we're doing. Other than not showing up at work, we haven't done anything wrong."

"What, you're just on strike? Like you want longer lunch breaks or something?"

"There's going to be changes," he said.

"Arie, this is a really dangerous little game," I said. "I don't think you understand."

"Don't talk to me that way. You think I'm some kid. You think I'm your little boy. I'm not."

"You are. You're my son. I'm your mother." I stood up and stood in front of Arie.

"I'm not a little boy. I'm a person, my own person. And I don't want to live like this."

"Live like what? In a comfortable house? With heat and running water and safety?"

"We're not safe here!" cried Arie. "No one here is safe. Every single one of us is one little mistake from death. One little case-worker recommendation from being executed. One little office form with your signature and any one of us could get the needle."

"Arie, I understand how you feel about Lotus, but you don't understand—"

"I understand that this so-called society of yours is a complete lie and a waking nightmare. I won't live in it, and I'm not alone. I'll die before I live in this vile *society*."

"You can't do that, Arie," I said, grabbing the front of his coat. "You can't die. You can't leave me again. Maybe there's something we can do from the inside. Maybe we can work with the system instead of working against it."

He pushed me away and scoffed harshly. "You know exactly how Lotus would react to that. Not even you can speak up against them. We'd both be brought into your own case-working office and they'd make very fine recommendations for us, wouldn't they? Reassignment, therapy, re-starting. It'd be so good for us, too. You'd be the recipient of your own recommendations, your own disgusting little memory-death sentences."

"Arie, you have to listen to me."

"No. Don't try to tell me that it's all just in the name of some goddam perfect society. I saw the notebooks."

"The notebooks?"

"Yeah, the notebooks. In the backpack. I read them all."

"Then you know I'm your mother. You know you're my son. We were together before."

"And I know you fought the Agency after they took me away," he said, raising his voice. "Did *you* actually read those notebooks? Because the Alison that wrote those journals would never put up with shit like this."

"I did those things to survive, Arie," I pleaded, "so that we could be together. And that's what I want now. I want us to survive this. To be together."

"How? By hiding? By rolling over? Don't you see what they took from us? It's all there in your handwriting. They took everything from us. They took our lives. And they'll do it again."

"Okay," I said. "I know. But I can't lose you again."

"Then help us. You could be a huge help to all of us."

"No!" I said. "I can't. You talk about doing what's right, but you're not thinking practically. You really think you can change things? They have the power, Arie. You and your little friends are just kids. Rachel and Lotus—they know things. I don't know what, but I think they're watching you. Rachel asked me today about you. Specifically. I think she knows you're involved. And she won't let you get away with this."

He quailed at this—just slightly. The set of his jaw softened and defiance relented. But then his resolve returned.

233

"Rachel has no idea what's waiting for her," he said. "There are too many of us. I know some of us won't make it, but that's just how it has to be sometimes when you want to make big changes. It's a sacrifice worth making."

"Arie, I am begging you to stop this."

"You should leave Lotus," he said. "Pack up your backpack there and go somewhere. Find somewhere to stay for a while. I'm warning you because I owe it to the Alison from those notebooks. I think I would have been proud to call her my mother."

"They're bringing in Agency troops," I said. "The real goons. Whatever you want to call them. I lived at the Agency Depot. I've seen them. You must have read about them in the notebooks. They're not like the Lotus cops. They're brutal. They shoot first and don't even bother to ask questions. They're coming. And there are a lot of them."

"It won't matter. We've got an army, too." He turned and went out of the house. He strode fast on his long legs down the walkway and out onto the sidewalk. I drew up the blinds and watched him go.

"It won't be enough," I said.

CHAPTER 25

Arie was right. I wasn't the person who'd written those journals. I had enough sense to know he was right about that. But having the sense to know what had changed between then and now wasn't so simple.

My memories had been wiped, of course, but was that enough to account for the differences? I could say it was, but it felt like an easy way out.

I'm simply not as bold as I was then, I thought, or as strong. After living with Gary and now in my beautiful little Lotus cottage, I'd gotten complacent and soft and sad.

When Arie had been gone for an hour or so, I removed the notebooks from the backpack and set them in my lap. I picked up one and then another, reading pages and entries at random. And just like when I'd read them in Bill's truck, my mind tingled at the risks we took—Arie and I. We'd risked our lives—not just for extra food or fuel (though we'd done that, too), but for knowledge, to find out if there was a way out of all this, to find a path to something better. We had no idea if we'd survive from week to week, and still we defied the Agency and its goons for nothing more than clues—clues to mysteries we didn't even understand.

And now, here I sat in my comfy little house on my comfy little couch knowing we had been lied to, knowing there was a better way but afraid to even dwell on it because the way I had chosen was at least better than where I'd come from.

The sun was getting low. I got my coat and went out.

It was cool that night. The day had been fair and warm, but now a cold breeze prevailed, and there were clouds piling up on the eastern horizon, as if preparing to work a night's worth of mischief while the sun wasn't watching.

Only a few lights shone in the cottages as I walked through my little Lotus neighborhood and on toward the town center. Word seemed to have gotten around that tonight might be a good night to stay indoors and go to bed early. I saw almost no one outside.

It was quiet, one would almost say peaceful. The streetlights winked on and glowed softly. The wind sighed in the trees. And yet, as the last light of the day drained into the west and the sky shone in shades of gold and burgundy, I knew it was a false calm.

Or maybe it was better to call it an anticipatory calm, because it was obvious the entire city was waiting for something to happen. It crackled in the air like the seeds of lightning forming in the gathering clouds overhead.

The security patrols appeared to have doubled. They were parked on the corners of main roads and they were now driving slowly through the streets, too. Somewhere far off I heard multiple sirens, and there was thunder in the distance, too.

I didn't know how I could find Arie and I didn't know what I'd say to him if I did. We'd said just about

236

everything we could to each other already without agreeing about anything. But I had to try.

And I laughed at myself—grimly. As angry and frustrated as I was at Arie, I had to laugh. I was secretly proud of him. Just as I had seen in the journals, he was bright and audacious. And with these qualities he had beckoned me out into the streets to search for answers, to seek the truth, to join in acts of subversion and rebellion. He was strong. He was smart. How could I be anything but proud?

When it was dark, and as I approached the town square, I saw small knots of young people here and there. They weren't strolling or socializing or laughing. They huddled in the shadows between the buildings and scuttled from one dark place to the next.

The wind was blowing harder now, and there were flashes of sheet lightning in the clouds overhead, creating snapshots of time along my way: three boys watching and pointing at a patrol car two blocks up the road, a Lotus cop leaning on the fender of his car, arms folded.

I knew that I'd never simply run into Arie walking around the town this way, but I also knew that one of these kids lurking in the shadows might lead me to him. And so I walked slowly and quietly toward a cluster of the young people standing at the back of a low office building where the street lamps cast a dark shadow. But as I crossed the street to reach them, they suddenly and conspicuously dispersed, each walking in a different direction.

"Wait," I said, breaking into a run. "I just want to ask you—" I stammered.

But they made no answers and fled.

There were two others not far away, walking at a determined pace toward the park, so I hustled over and fell in behind them. I walked fast, and after a block or so I was only fifty or so feet behind—almost close enough for them to hear me if I spoke. I redoubled my pace, but they suddenly veered into the park where there was a copse of closely spaced trees. I jogged up to find them, but they too had vanished into the blackness.

It was pointless, of course. Arie was too smart to be found unless he wanted to be, and the thunderstorm had grown so potent and heavy overhead.

And so I turned for home and saw no one else until a Lotus security car pulled up next to me on the street.

The driver lowered his window and hung his arm out the door. "Hey there, ma'am," he said.

"Hello," I answered.

"Everything okay?" said the driver. "Noticed you've been kinda crisscrossing the area here. Is there a problem?"

"No. No problem," I said, glancing at him. He wore a Lotus uniform. "I'm just walking."

"Well, I'm sure you've heard we're kind of on alert at the moment. We're getting reports about altercations, property damage, stuff like that."

"Yeah, I've heard," I said. "It's too bad."

"Right," said the officer, "but I guess my point is you might want to head home and stay in tonight. Gonna rain anyhow."

"Right. Sure. I'm on my way home now."

"Sounds good, ma'am." He tipped his cap. "Have a nice night."

I walked quickly home, noticing there were more sirens now. Thunder pealed and there was more lightning. The thunder boomed and rumbled and made me flinch. Waves of rain passed over. Two patrol cars raced past me in the darkness, obviously on their way to the scene of some new disturbance. It began to rain steadily as I returned to my house. As I approached the walkway, I saw immediately that something wasn't quite right.

Someone had broken out the front windows and kicked the door open. Across the front of the house, painted in blood-red letters two feet high, someone had scrawled expletives and epithets. On the front door were the words *FORGET THIS*.

I went in.

"Arie?" I yelled. "Arie, are you here?"

Inside it was all dark. I flipped a light switch, but it appeared that all the light fixtures had been broken. I went from switch to switch, trying to find one that worked. The floors were littered with broken glass and rubbish. Most of the furniture had been overturned. There were holes kicked into the walls, and there was more profanity and graffiti in red paint.

At last I found a reading lamp on the floor in the living room. It had been knocked over but the light bulb was intact. I set it upright and turned it on.

"Hello, Alison," said a voice.

A woman was sitting in the living room.

I yelped a little, startled. "Who are you?" I demanded.

"It's me, Donna," she said.

The woman wore large eyeglasses with thick lenses. This gave her the appearance of an owl in a frumpy cardigan. I judged her to be in her late fifties. She had a very petite frame, and she was even shorter than me. She stood up from the chair.

"What are you doing here?" I demanded as rain water dripped down my face.

"Did you get my notes?" she asked, sounding incredulous. "You're hurting my feelings, Alison. Why are you acting like you don't know me?"

"Because I don't," I said.

"So you didn't get my notes."

"Wait, you left me the notes?" I asked.

"Of course. Who else?"

"What did you say your name was?"

She harrumphed and blinked behind her big lenses. "Alison, I'm Donna."

"Donna!" I cried. "The notebooks. Donna! Yes! You have an RV. And cats. And books. You used to live at an abandoned drive-in movie theater."

"I still live there," she said with a little shrug. She looked at me curiously. "You remember now?"

"Well, in a way, yes. I wrote everything down—I mean, yes, of course I remember. Yes. You're Donna!"

She nodded and said, "Yes, I know that."

"Yes, yes," I cried. And before I knew what I was doing, I threw my arms around her.

She received the embrace rather stiffly, as though it were some ritual that she acknowledged but was not overly fond of. I kept it short and when I released her, she stepped back conspicuously to re-establish her personal space.

The notebooks didn't say whether I'd ever fully trusted Donna or not. It was hard to know if the Agency even knew about her. I never knew where she stood, and I'd even speculated that she was a little unstable, but it occurred to me that if I had mistrusted her I would have said so in my journals. Or at least I hoped that was the case.

240

"You stopped visiting," Donna complained.

"I'm sorry," I said. "There's been so much going on. And that was such a long time ago."

"I see you've had a little trouble here," she said, nodding her head at the room.

"Yeah," I said. "Trouble seems to follow me."

"I'll be quick, then," said Donna, "though I'm pleased to see you again, and to find out that we can still be friends."

"Wait, Donna, wait," I said holding up a hand. "Do you know Ruby? Or Chase?"

"The mountain people? Yes. I know lots of people."

"So, are you part of them? You don't live in Lotus?"

"I don't know what you mean by that."

"Well, how did you find me? How did you get here?"

"As I said, I know a lot of people. I asked around. It'd been so long since we'd spoken. I had to find you. I have something for you."

"What is it?"

From a canvas book bag at her side she produced a red notebook and handed it to me. On the front there was a rough, curious drawing of a skull with a compass or clock face, apparently scrawled white into the red cover with a pencil eraser, then traced with an ink pen.

"I think you lost this," she said.

"Another notebook?" I asked.

"You were always wanting notebooks."

I opened it up. It was filled with page after page of numbers. Every line was just a series of numbers. Perhaps Donna really was crazy.

She said, "I need to go now."

"Oh," I said. "Okay. Sure. Of course."

"You should come and visit me. The way you used to."

"Okay. I'll try."

She reached into the canvas book bag and withdrew a rain slicker and umbrella. She put on the slicker and made for the ruined door, which crookedly stood open by about a foot. Donna moved through the gap without the need to open it further. I followed her and saw her umbrella pop open.

"Thank you, Donna," I said, but she didn't answer. I watched her disappear into the cool, wet night.

The first thing I did was search among the overturned furniture and broken things to find the notebooks. They'd been stepped on and kicked aside, but I found them all and returned them along with the red notebook into the backpack. The house was equipped with a few spare light bulbs, so I replaced a few of the broken ones and turned on some lights. Then I began to pick up the broken glass and trash and demolished flower pots. I'd started in the kitchen and had been working for only fifteen or twenty minutes when there was a knock at the front door.

"I believe it's open," I yelled.

I went out to see who it was. A strobe of lightning framed her for an instant in the splintered doorway, standing cool and erect and perfect.

CHAPTER 26

"This is my fault more than yours," said Rachel.

Her voice was smooth and steady. Thunder boomed and the rain hissed as her guards calmly bound me to a kitchen chair.

"Every time someone in Lotus fails," she went on, "it's my fault. Well. That's not entirely true. I don't mean every single solitary little failure, obviously. It makes no sense, for example, for me to take responsibility if some new transfer from the Zones simply cannot master the supply depot software system, and she sends five cases of baby formula to our main dairy production farm, while sending five cases of bovine-grade antibiotics to the neo-natal care wing of the hospital. That happened, you know. Last week. And the two are not interchangeable. Powdered baby milk and livestock medications, I mean. Both are very much indispensable, but one can in no way be substituted for the other."

Rachel paced the living room floor, her high-heeled boots grinding the glass into powder. Her security guards stood by, watching impassively, not even blinking as the thunderstorm raged outside.

"But you see what I mean, don't you? If someone has overstated his skill as a bricklayer and the gymnasium he built collapses not ten minutes after forty-two second-grade volleyball players have left—which did also happen, two months ago—there is no advantage in me taking his blame. People let me down on a very nearly daily basis around here, and I simply can't be responsible in the strictest sense for all of them, can I? No. I can't." She laughed abruptly without smiling. "Do you understand where I'm going with this, Alison?"

I didn't. But I nodded anyway. Because of the zipties around my hands, my head was more or less the only part of my body I could move. The security guards blinked sleepily.

"However," said Rachel, "in this case, I feel a very real sense of my own culpability. Because I trusted you, Alison. Personally. That may have been the problem right there. It was personal. I don't know what they were doing with you over there at the Agency. Were you a political prisoner? Some kind of symbolic exile? Were you being used as bait? Or was it some perverted revenge thing? I didn't know, and I didn't care."

She ceased her pacing and stood directly in front of me. She looked at me. The stern but beautiful contours of her face were lit by a series of lightning strikes. I saw pity in her face contending with her anger.

"The only thing I knew about you, Alison, is what you'd done before they wiped your memory and stuck you with Gosford. What a creep, by the way. Gosford. Ugh. Never liked him. You know who got him put out to pasture after the whole amusement park thing, right?" She jabbed her thumb at herself. "Uh huh. I didn't know anything about you at the time, so I had no idea what was up with him sort of like almost purchasing you, like claiming you, like a stray cat. It wasn't until long after that that I saw what you were capable of, and I said, 'Yes. This is the kind of soldier I need.' Someone ready to sacrifice everything."

With her immaculate boot, Rachel kicked at the remains of a mangled lamp on the floor. The curtains were blowing into the room from the broken windows. A few wisps of hair had strayed from Rachel's severe up-do, and they swirled around her face in the breeze. She made a sour face at the shambles that lay around us.

"Loyalty," she scoffed.

There was a boom of thunder overhead that rattled the house. Rachel swept the tendrils of errant hair back behind her ear with her index finger, and she was perfect again.

"Loyalty was what I was looking for, and that is what I saw in you. Pure, unbreakable. Were you loyal to the Agency? When you were in the Zones? No. No one is, obviously. There's nothing to be loyal to, except maybe keeping your belly full and avoiding rape. They treat people like swine in the Zones. You know it, I guess. But this team of yours, that was a different matter, wasn't it? What do they even call themselves? Nobody knows. How many members are there? Five? Six? A hundred? No one knows that, either. They don't have a name or members; they just get things done, don't they? God. I'm impressed by that. That impresses me. And your loyalty to them was unbreakable, wasn't it? Wasn't it, Alison?"

"I don't—I really don't know. I don't rememb—"

"Of course you don't remember. It was a rhetorical question. Take my word for it—it was. Your loyalty, I mean. It was unbreakable. I saw the final report on what happened to Gosford and those men he took into the amusement park."

I could only blink up at her and listen. Lightning lit her from all angles like the firing of paparazzi camera flashes on the face of some superstar.

"And after you chased off that piece of garbage who broke into your apartment? I looked you up. You went to the mat for them, Alison, you gave them everything. Or you thought you did—it was pure luck that you weren't successful in killing yourself along with Gosford. Do you know what I'm talking about? Have you been told, reminded? Is that what he came to your apartment for? To remind you? Don't answer. I don't care. It doesn't matter. What matters is that I thought, ah, here is someone willing to give her life for a cause. Here is an opportunity to take some of that resistance DNA and splice it into Lotus. All I had to do was plug *you* into *my* cause. Because the cause wouldn't matter. How could it? You wouldn't remember which side you were on before. All I had to do was treat you right, let you make a real difference, and give you a purpose."

Although I was zip-tied to a chair, and although I was fairly certain my fate would be memory death, if not the actual kind, I couldn't help but be impressed by Rachel's rhetoric. I now knew how uncompromising and ruthless she really was, how she used people like building materials to be chopped up and pieced together and discarded if necessary. But I could never say she lacked the ability to inspire.

"Oh, and I would have treated you right," she said, her voice void of any sarcasm or irony. "This desk assignment was just your initiation. After that, you could have risen as far as you pleased."

Rachel stopped pacing again and rubbed her temples.

"But I was wrong," she said. "About your loyalty, I mean. There's something about your loyalty that shifts, and apparently it shifts in the same direction every time—to them. To whomever it is that is not *us*, if that makes sense. I counted on you when I shouldn't have, and that, Alison, is my responsibility. That redounds to my accounts payable, so to speak. So, you see, what I'm trying to say is that what will happen to you will not be a punishment, it will be, as you know, a re-purposing. You'll be re-purposed."

"No," I pleaded. "Rachel. I need another chance. It was just so much at once. Arie and the case worker assignment. I was overwhelmed. That's all. I was—"

"You're lying," she said. She purred the accusation, but she said it as there came another crushing peal of thunder. "Just like you were lying when I asked you about Arie. And just as you almost surely lied about the man who broke into Gosford's apartment. If you had come to me two weeks ago, we wouldn't be having this conversation. You've known about his leanings this entire time."

"No."

"You're being sent down, Alison. And you'll be flagged. You'll never come out of the Zones again. And I feel bad about that, not only because I will miss you personally but because things are getting worse in the Zones. You had the chance to work with me, with Lotus—to develop candidates, to rescue those who can make a difference. To shape society rather than being ground underfoot by it. I offered you a purpose—you declined. Now you'll spend the rest of your life down there in the sewers. You'll die there."

"Let me find Arie first," I shouted. "Please. I think I can find him and bring him to you."

Rachel sighed. "Why would you do that? And why would I let you try?"

"I don't want him to be killed in the fighting," I said. "They don't stand a chance. If I bring him to you, at least he'll be in your custody. And even if you wipe his memory, he'll be alive."

"See?" said Rachel. "This is one reason I had so much hope for you. You are smart. You see all the angles. Oh, how I would have liked to have had you on my team. My inner circle. I wouldn't mind having the boy back. Look at what he's accomplished. He could be useful. Ah, but here again, I can't trust you."

"Of course you can. Think about it."

"What do you mean?"

"Arie's all I care about. Even though I've forgotten everything at least twice and maybe more, he's all I've ever cared about. You can trust me to not just run away. You can trust that I won't stop until I find him. You may not be able to trust my loyalty to you, but you can trust my loyalty to my son. *He's* my purpose."

CHAPTER 27

Rachel gave me twenty-four hours. And she must have had supreme confidence in her own security forces and in the army she was borrowing from the Agency, because there were only two elements to the bargain she made with me.

"Bring me Arie before this time tomorrow, alive, or you're dead."

Rachel had a way with motivational speeches and philosophical discussions, but she was also very capable of reducing things to their essential components.

Without another word, she turned on her heel and left the house. Her security detail cut the zip-ties that held me to the chair, and they followed her out.

I rubbed at my wrists and promised myself that if I could find Arie, I'd also find a way to live that didn't involve so much getting tied to chairs.

When I heard Rachel's SUV drive away, I found the backpack with the notebooks inside, including the mysterious red one Donna had given me. Into the backpack I shoved some food, water, spare clothing, and a few other necessities.

The rain showed no signs of relenting. There were several bicycles left in the backyard of my house, stashed there I assumed by the young people who'd left on foot after their meeting with Arie. I walked a bike around to the front of my house, and for the second time that night, I headed for the center of town to search for my son. This time, however, I knew I'd find Arie. I knew exactly how I'd do it.

The rain continued to pelt down, and after only a mile or so, I was drenched. In the distance, among the flashing lightning, I saw the steady blaze of burning buildings near to the center of town. Above the sounds of the wind and the rain, I heard more sirens and gun fire. There were now even more people moving in the shadows, too, with their faces masked like old western bandits. Some of them carried baseball bats, tire irons, and other makeshift weapons. And we all seemed to be heading in the same direction.

I proceeded very slowly and carefully. I rode fast through the shadows when it would be difficult to see me, but I walked the bike to skirt open well-lighted areas. And I stopped and ducked into the dark places when anyone came near. The rain seemed to deepen the shadows, like all the world had been drenched in a thin layer of black paint.

As I approached the city square, I heard constant gunfire and booming noises that I was sure were not thunder. I ditched the bike and went on foot.

Even from a distance of several blocks, the city square now resembled a war zone. A small army of what I thought were Lotus cops were forming up in a line outside the sprawling city park. They were equipped with riot armor, clubs, and clear polycarbonate shields. A ragged force of young adults held the park from behind a chaotic barricade of overturned picnic tables, garbage bins, and flaming debris. Lotus patrol cars circled the park, their brilliant spotlights sweeping the rioters' battlements like the feelers of a giant insect. The kids hurled rocks and bricks and the occasional Molotov cocktail at the troops, who retaliated by firing teargas canisters. Lit by the glare of flames and the blinding spotlights, an oily black smoke roiled up from the park, and the acrid smells of aerosol mace and burning plastic carried on the cold, wet wind.

When the Lotus cops had formed up into a long rank with their shields and clubs, they charged into the park. Some of the rioters scattered, but most of them held their ground and clashed with the troops. There were shouts and screams and I searched the melee for Arie, but I was too far away to recognize anyone.

I crept away from the park, but everywhere I went it was the same—ragged bands of marauding young rioters wrecking buildings or huddling wretchedly behind thrown-together barricades, while Lotus riot troops attempted to dislodge and disperse them. In the alleyways and behind the dark, looming office blocks, the rioters gathered and regrouped and nursed their injured.

On a corner along one of the main roads that ran through the city center, there was a cluster of brick food shops. Two young women huddled on the sidewalk in the shadow of the buildings, while a third stood with her back to the bricks, watching the street. I took them to be lookouts, probably observing movement along the main through-way. I showed myself on the street and began walking toward them in long, fast strides.

The one who was standing watch signaled the two others. They stood. One of the women hefted an ax handle and another of them had a clumsy grasp on what looked like a large knife from someone's kitchen. The third, somewhat comically, wielded a garden shovel.

"Stop," said one of them. "That's close enough. Who are you?"

"Alison," I said, still walking. I was close enough to see their faces now. "Alison Gosford."

They hissed and muttered to each other as I approached, but I couldn't hear what they were saying.

"Who are you really?" barked the woman again. "Don't screw around. You could get seriously hurt."

By now I was only fifty or so feet from them. I kept walking. The one with the kitchen knife stepped off the sidewalk and took a few steps in my direction. I walked faster.

"You better stop," she said. "Stop and tell us who you are."

I punched her in the nose. She dropped the knife and fell on her butt. Then she rolled onto her side and cupped her nose in both hands. I picked up the knife and held it overhand. Then I continued to the sidewalk where the other two women held up their makeshift weapons, gripping them and re-gripping them nervously.

"Didn't anyone tell you to never bring a shovel to a knife-fight?" I asked.

The woman glanced at the shovel and looked slightly ashamed.

"You two know who Arie is?"

They locked eyes with each other for a brief moment, which I took as a yes.

"Who are you, lady?" said Ax Handle. "What do you want?"

"Take me to Arie. Right now." I pitched the knife into the blackness. It made a thin clatter on the pavement some distance away.

"Who are you?"

"I'm his mother."

CHAPTER 28

"What on earth are you doing here?" Arie demanded when he saw me. His face flushed hotly.

The three young and inadequately armed ladies I found on the streets of Lotus grudgingly but stealthily brought me to what appeared to be an inactive construction site at the center of town. It was a concrete office building four or five stories tall. The exterior appeared nearly complete, but the concrete interior was dusty and bare. The ground floor was tall and open and spacious, broken up by only a few concrete walls and pillars, but I was taken down a doorless staircase to the basement, where Arie and a dozen or so others had set up a secret command post in a complex of cramped utility rooms and hallways, lit by a few electric lights. A gas-powered generator puttered quietly somewhere not far off, and the cluster of rooms also served apparently as some kind of communication hub as well, because I heard radio chatter from one of the rooms.

"You're not glad to see me?" I said in a pained attempt to lighten the mood.

He sighed wearily. "Not especially, no."

"I had to find you," I said.

"I told you to leave."

"Well," I said, "I'm your mother. I don't take orders from you."

I could have been mistaken, but this time it looked like he tried to suppress a smile.

"All right," he said, "but I've got a lot going on here. What exactly did you think you were going to accomplish coming here? Make it quick. You know, technically, you're the enemy."

"Two things," I replied. "First, I want know if there's any chance at all of talking you out of this. This, this—revolt of yours. If there's anything I can do or help with to get you out of here."

"No," said Arie, without hesitation.

I sighed. "Okay. Well, you may not want to hear this, or you may not care, but I know somewhere we can go—somewhere full of people who feel the same way you do. The same way we do, Arie."

At this he raised an eyebrow.

"It's up in the mountains," I continued hastily. "They have camps. Hundreds of people. Maybe you and all of these, well, kids, can team up with them and do something more effective than setting things on fire and waiting for the Agency army to crush you."

"I think I know who you're talking about," said Arie. "I'm pretty sure I've been in contact with them, and it might be great to team up with them, but our plans here are already underway. This isn't *my* revolt. There are, well, I can't say how many, but there are more people involved with this than anyone knows, and if we don't go through with this plan, we won't get another chance."

"But you could be killed," I cried. "You could die. Here. Tonight. Another chance for what?"

He nodded. "To change things. To live the way we want to live."

"But if they kill you all, rebuild, and start over without you, will that be worth it?"

"We've all committed our lives to this," Arie said. "If one of us backs down, the entire effort collapses."

"What is 'this'?" I pleaded, gesturing indistinctly in all directions. "What are you trying to accomplish, specifically?"

Arie scrutinized my face. He certainly had no reason to trust me with an explanation of plans that had probably taken the better part of a year to lay, but as I looked back at him, I knew he was about to. He beckoned me and we stepped outside onto the sidewalk.

"Okay, look. It's the production," Arie said. "Tomorrow, every factory in Lotus will cease to exist. Everything's arranged. But we've got to hold on to the city center to make that happen."

"I don't understand."

"We've located and infiltrated just about every factory in Lotus, and we're going to destroy every goddam one of them. Barricading ourselves into the city center is just a distraction, a cover story. They're completely focused on us, sending all of their attacks here. Meanwhile, while we're on strike, every factory in their system is being rigged for demolition, and as far as we can tell, they've got no clue. But it's a slow process. The demo teams have to visit each production line, every factory. If we can gut Lotus logistically, they'll have no way to keep us as prisoners."

"Arie, this makes no sense. Blow up those factories and come with me to the mountains. You can't stay here. They're coming for you."

"No, you don't get it. We've got to provide cover until we can take them all down at once."

"Why? Why does it have to be at the same time?"

"Because if we execute the plan one or two or three facilities at a time, Lotus and the Agency will figure out what we're up to and short-circuit the plan. This distraction won't keep their attention, and they'll shift to securing the factories."

"Oh, so you're bait. That's just great. You're going to stay here and be overrun while your bomb people wire up the factories?"

"I think we can hold off an all-out attack on the city center until every thing's ready. Have you looked around? This place is a disaster area. They can't just roll through and sweep us aside. It shouldn't be much longer. A day or two at most. As soon as those explosives start going off, Lotus will peel off of us pretty quickly, and that will allow us to run for the hills. Then maybe we can visit those friends of yours."

"I think you're wrong, Arie. I think they're going to level this place with you inside it."

It was difficult to know if Arie thought I might be right, but it was simple to see that he wasn't backing down.

"I'm sorry, but I have to believe that in the end, we'll win, whether or not everyone survives," he said. "If we just surrender now, we're truly doomed. If, on the other hand, we stick together and go down swinging, someone will carry on for us. That's how revolutions work. They evolve. It's not necessarily the individuals who matter. It's the idea, the plans, the spirit."

"That's very noble," I said, "but you seem to be forgetting that they can wipe memories. They can make it so no one remembers you or what you did, and no one has a reason to keep fighting. They can erase your ideas, plans, and spirit."

Arie didn't have an answer to this. He took me back upstairs.

I thought about all the things mothers did to keep their children safe. It starts with keeping them wrapped in blankets as infants, I thought, then moves on to preventing them from falling down stairs or burning themselves on the stove. Later, mothers try to protect them from other children, from other people—bullies and bad influences and predators. And it continues into adulthood, wanting to protect them from life's disappointments and setbacks. It never stops. Mothers start out trying to child-proof their homes and back yards, and if they could, they would child-proof the entire world to keep their children safe.

All I wanted to do was to take Arie and get as far away from here as possible. I wanted to force him away from danger.

But I knew I couldn't.

Because he was trying to make the world safe, too. We really just wanted the same thing, Arie and I. And so the only choice was to fight with him.

"Listen," said Arie. "Mom." He looked sternly into my eyes, but the hostility and skepticism were gone. He put a hand on my shoulder. "I've really got to get back to work. People are depending on me, and I'm depending on them," he said. "What was the second thing you wanted to tell me?" Arie asked.

"I'm through with the Agency, Arie. Through with Lotus, with Rachel, with everything," I said.

"What do you mean?" asked Arie, his face darkening.

"I mean I want to help, but I'm a dead woman walking. I've been given twenty-four hours," I said. "If I don't bring you back to Rachel within that time, she'll have me killed. If I do bring you back, she won't kill me, but she'll wipe my mind and send me back to the Zones—permanently."

"That's insane," said Arie. "Why?"

"Treason, I guess. I didn't report the suspicious things you've said. Didn't turn you in when I found you meeting."

"Then you really do have to leave," Arie exclaimed. "You have to run."

"I can't do that," I said.

"I see," he said with a sarcastic grin. "You've just been lecturing me about how I need to get out of here, to run. So, are you gonna let Rachel kill you? Or send you down? Mom, you've got to get out of here."

"I can't run," I said. "I can't just run away."

"I get it," he said. "So, what are you going to do?"

There was someone I could turn to, I thought. Someone who might be able to help, if I could find him in time.

"I think I might have a way to help us all," I said, "but I need to borrow a car."

CHAPTER 29

It took all night and much of the next morning to sneak me out of Lotus and arrange for a vehicle. I'd read in the journals that Chase was known for his ability to scrounge up supplies and material such as vehicles. And he was apparently better than Arie's people because the best they could do was a decrepit old Honda. The odometer didn't turn but had frozen at 299,999 miles. The motor was just about whipped, and it chattered loudly even when I drove slowly.

I arrived at my destination just as the sun was going down. I made my way through the barricades with an unsettling lack of scrutiny, and when I reached the front door, I wasn't sure if I should knock first or just walk on in. One could argue that this was, technically, still my home.

I put my hand on the knob. It was unlocked. I opened it, and a moment later I was standing at the doorway of my old dining room.

"Hello, Gary," I said.

He was at the table with his dinner laid out before him. Lasagna, it looked like. He'd spread a checked tablecloth, and he sat with a napkin in his lap. He'd poured a glass of the cheap, vinegary wine the Agency circulated in its vain attempt at making its officers feel civilized. It was all so proper and formal, I almost laughed.

For the briefest moment, Gary looked at me in what could only be called unconcealed astonishment, a forkful of lasagna halfway between his plate and mouth. But then, in his sly and practiced way, Gary banished the surprised expression and replaced it in an instant with the smug, almost sleepy expression he always wore when he knew he had the upper hand.

"So," said Gary in what I knew was the very blandest tone he could manage, "you're back."

I opened my mouth to answer, but Gary looked away contemptuously and placed the bite of food in his mouth. He chewed deliberately, as if I wasn't standing in the room with him.

"Gary, this is going to sound crazy, but I need your help."

He said nothing. Instead, he swallowed, set his fork down, dabbed his lips with the napkin, and with a flourish placed it on his lap again. Then he lifted his glass and slowly drank what remained in it. All of this without speaking or even looking in my direction. He set the wine glass down, patted his lips again with the napkin, and took up the fork again.

In a mocking tone he said, "Oh, dear. How rude of me. Would you like to join me?" He gestured with the fork to the table. "There's plenty for us both."

"No. Gary, please. I don't have time for this."

"Time for what, Alison?"

"I don't have time to try to—I don't even know—reconcile?"

"I'm sorry," he said. "I didn't mean to keep you." He took another bite of his dinner, again chewing slowly and then setting the fork on the plate.

"Gary—"

He held up a prohibitive hand. He refreshed his glass from the wine bottle and took a drink. When the lasagna on his plate was gone, he carefully mopped up the remaining sauce with a hunk of bread and ate it. Then he washed it down with a final draining of his glass. He next emitted a satisfied, "Ahhh," and moved his napkin from his lap to the plate.

He faced me. "You were saying?"

"I need your—"

He raised his hand again to silence me. He'd furrowed his brow and tongued his teeth and cheek. After a moment, with his hand still raised, he stood and limped into the kitchen. He returned with a toothpick and made a show of working at his gumline to remove some particle of food. Finally satisfied, he sucked at his teeth and tossed the toothpick on the table. Then he poured himself more wine.

"Of course you need my help," he said, standing then limping toward me.

I made way and Gary shuffled into the living room.

"Won't you sit down?" he asked. "Unless you're in a hurry to go."

I sat on the couch. He remained standing.

"I knew you'd come running back here at the first sign of trouble," said Gary. He swirled the wine around in his glass.

My pulse felt a bit thready. This had been my home. The familiar sights and smells and even the way the light played on the walls and furniture brought me back to that time when I felt each day that I might simply fall over dead from Gary's treatment of me. How long ago it felt, and yet here I was, back again. But it wasn't my home any longer, and I grudged myself for ever letting Gary contain me here.

Still, there was no way to ask what I wanted to ask without enduring his gloating, his crow-plucking.

Gary finished his wine with a gulp and set his glass on the coffee table.

"Please make yourself at home," he said. "I'll be with you in a minute." He turned and limped into the hallway that led to his bedroom.

When he returned, Gary held a small steel box. He sat on the couch beside me and set the box on the coffee table. He opened it, and inside there was a pistol. He lifted it from the box and the barrel was pointed in my general direction. He must have seen me quail at the sight of it.

"Oh," said Gary. "This? Don't worry. It's just overdue for a cleaning. You don't mind if I work while we talk?"

"Gary, I—"

"Good. Now. I believe you were saying you need my help." He began to take the pistol apart, placing the pieces on the coffee table.

"It's Arie," I said. "He's gotten involved in an uprising in Lotus. And the Agency is sending troops to annihilate them."

Gary scratched his chin. "Yes," he said, "so I've heard. The troops have been massing for the past forty-eight hours. Maybe longer."

"Can it be stopped?" I asked. "Is there something you can do?"

He wiped each piece of the gun, holding them close to his face, as a thorough inspection was important.

"Not sure. What do you think I could do?"

263

"I don't know. There are lots of young people involved. Is there someone you could report it to? I know you're still in an advisory role of some sort."

Gary said nothing but took a metal rod tipped with a brass brush and contemplatively ran it down the unpieced barrel of the pistol.

"Gary, please—"

"Alison," he interrupted, "I'm flattered that you think I hold some kind of sway in these matters, but I have no real power in the Agency. Maybe before—" here he examined his withered hand with a forlorn expression "—but now? No. They don't ask me what they should do, and I don't presume to tell them."

"They'll listen to you. They still respect you. Wouldn't they listen to you? File a complaint. Or an injunction. Or simply tell the officers that it's kids they're going to be fighting. Maybe they'll refuse to mobilize, or maybe they'll stall or hesitate. I think Rachel is going to tell them to roll in there and shoot on sight, to just gun them all down. Isn't there something you could do? Someone you could contact?"

Gary shrugged. "Oh, perhaps. But the question then becomes, why? What's in it for me?"

"They're just kids, Gary. It's the right thing to do."

He rolled his eyes.

"My god, Gary. You Agency people sit up here and dose those poor phantoms down in the Zones. You act like gods and you treat them like cockroaches." I leveled this at Gary with the iciest tone I could summon, but the words made me cold, too. "If you have any humanity, think about several hundred kids over there in Lotus about to be slaughtered. You're telling me you won't lift a finger to stop it?"

"Maybe. Difficult to say."

"Would you do it for me?"

Gary snorted. "For you?"

"I'm your wife, aren't I?"

He gave me a hard look.

"Or am I? Why'd you do it, Gary? Why'd you say we were married when we weren't? Someone gave me my journals. I know everything about that year. I know about us, and I've figured out the rest. You nearly died after that explosion. Why on Earth would you bring me here and say we were married?"

Gary began to reassemble the pistol with obvious haste.

"You know," he said, pausing to lick his lips, "you have no right to question me. To question what I've done."

His voice was low but there was a tremble in it, a ragged edge. He gritted his teeth as, piece by piece, the dark metal components became a pistol again. When he was finished, he took an ammo clip from the box and slipped it into the magazine well in the handle.

"How dare you, Alison. How dare you come into my home demanding answers and telling me what to do."

"No," I said. "It's not that."

"You have no idea what I've gone through. The way I pushed myself. You're right. The explosion nearly killed me, but you don't know the agony I went through. When I woke up, the air was filled with the most putrid odor. I vomited, it made me so sick. Do you know what it was? It took me a while to realize it was the smell of my own burnt flesh and hair and the smell of my clothing melted to my skin."

"I understand that you suffered," I tried to say.

"You understand nothing!" he bellowed.

The gun was in his hand and his finger was on the trigger. I could only wait for him to pull the trigger.

"They didn't find me," he hissed. "Not at first. Not for several hours. I was thrown, see. A long way, Alison. Left for dead. I had to crawl I-don't-know-how-far to get noticed, dragged myself across that rubble and glass and weeds to get their attention."

I winced at this.

"And they found me," he jabbered on, "but that's not where the story ends, either. The skin grafts, the operations, the infections—I prayed for death. I still hurt all the time. All the time!"

He stood.

"Somewhere between the misery of wanting to live and the hope of death, I realized that I had to address the source. You." Here he pointed the pistol at my forehead as though it were an extension of his hand and finger. "Every time I wanted to give up, I pictured your face. Every time I fell down, I pictured you."

He pointed the gun at me again. But then he took a step toward me, bent down, and took my hand. Gently. He then turned my hand over and placed the gun in my palm. It sat there cold against my skin.

"I knew I was stronger than you, Alison. And I had to remember that," he growled barely contained rage. "That's why I brought you here. To make sure I never forgot that I am strong. I am stronger and I am better than you. And you didn't take anything from me. Do you understand? Answer me!"

He stood over me, leaning down and shouting into my face.

"Answer me!"

I shrank from him. He overturned the coffee table, swept the lamp from the table by the couch. Veins stood out on his face and neck, and spittle flew from his lips as he screamed at me to answer him.

I gripped the gun and pointed the muzzle at him. "No, I won't answer you!" I yelled back at him. "Because it doesn't make any sense! I did what I did to protect my son from *you*, and I'm *still* sorry that it had to happen! But *you*. You're twisted. You can't get over the fact that I beat you, that I won, that you got what was coming to you. You're so twisted with rage and revenge you're barely a person anymore. I'm sorry you were hurt, but you took my son from me!"

"No!" he screamed. "You're not sorry! You don't even remember it! How can someone who doesn't remember something feel remorse for it?"

He drew nearer until the gun jabbed into his chest.

"Do it," he growled. "Pull the trigger!"

I dropped the gun and shrank away until I was practically burrowing into the cushions of the couch. Gary remained there for a short while longer, bent over me, panting and trembling with fury. Then he stood upright. He lifted his chin and ran his good hand through his hair and over his face. He straightened his shirt.

"You see? You're not stronger than me. You're afraid of me," he said, still short of breath. "Me. A crippled-up, washed-up wretch." He scoffed at me.

I said nothing.

"You don't understand any of it, do you?" he spat. "Of course you don't. How could you? You don't have any idea what it's like to be humiliated, emasculated, thrown aside."

"Grow up, Gary," I said, getting up from the couch. "We all have pain. We all have scars. You use yours as an excuse for being dark and terrible. You blame me,

267

but the truth is you're weak and too afraid to face your own mistakes and shortcomings. You're a little man. I don't need my memories or journals to see that."

"Get out of here," Gary hissed. "Do your Lotus people know you're here? Does Rachel know? I bet she doesn't. I should call security and have them turn you over to her."

He couldn't have known I was living exclusively on borrowed time now, and that my contract with Rachel would expire within an hour or so. But the mere mention of Rachel chilled my blood, and I backed toward the door.

"You don't have to do that," I said. "I'll go."

"Then get out! Get out! Get out!" he pawed around in the cushions of the couch and found the gun.

I opened the door and fled down the hallway, gunshots ringing out behind me.

CHAPTER 30

I'd seen the armored vehicles and troop trucks moving around and gathering when I'd first driven the old Honda into the Agency apartment block, and Gary had confirmed my worst fears of an enormous military force assembling. But in the twilight, the scale of the troop movements could be seen even more clearly. I saw vehicle headlights everywhere. More than I'd ever seen. The sounds and odor of diesel engines were thick in the air. It had to be a collection of troops and vehicles from multiple Zones and Agency installations, and to me it looked like they needed only a signal to move out.

Oddly, with the gathering of so many troops and military vehicles, the checkpoints around the Agency facilities stood empty or were manned by soldiers who simply waved me through.

Without Gary's help, there was only one person left to contact. I had to find Donna.

Armored vehicles and trucks and troops lined the main roads, but they seemed to pay me no mind. They seemed eager to get on to their more important mission.

It turned out that the journals were of only a little help in finding Donna. My entries contained vague directions, but I didn't find the drive-in by following them. Driving out yet another abandoned and ruined road, I spotted the giant movie screens in the distance, tattered and falling apart.

I turned and drove there as quickly as the worn-out old Honda could carry me over the neglected roadways. At last I drove into the vast empty parking lot and stopped with a harsh, gravely skid.

The setting sun shone redly on the looming screens. Beneath them was parked the white and gold Winnebago. I had at least accurately described the old RV, for it was just as I had imagined it. I ran to the door and mounted the wooden steps. Then I pounded on the door as hard as I could.

No one answered.

A cat sat in front of the closed blinds in the window.

"Donna," I yelled. "Donna, it's me, Alison. Are you home?"

No answer. Where in the world could she be?

I ran back to the car and retrieved one of the notebooks. It had a blank page or two. In the rapidly dwindling daylight, using the Honda's hood for a desk, I wrote Donna a long letter. I folded it carefully and inserted it into her front door in a way I hoped wouldn't be missed.

Before I left, I stood on the rickety wooden stoop and shouted her name a few more times, in case she was close by. The cat in the window watched me, blinking serenely.

"Come home, Donna," I whispered. "Please come home soon."

CHAPTER 31

As I drove away from the Agency Zones, I saw the military vehicles were at last beginning to move. When I drove over a hill or into a long, straight section of road, I could see dozens of headlights formed into long twinkling chains behind me.

There must be hundreds of vehicles, I thought, carrying what must be a thousand troops, just miles behind me.

The invasion was underway.

I pushed the little Honda to its limits (which were not impressive), and soon the troops vanished out of sight. They would travel more slowly, I reasoned, but they could not fall much more than an hour behind me.

It was in the small cold hours when I approached Lotus. When I was still a few miles away from the first Lotus security gate, where I'd met the friendly guard on that first day with Rachel, I ditched the Honda, cinched on the backpack, and began walking.

If I hoofed it fast, I reasoned, I could be in the city limits in an hour, hopefully just ahead of the advancing Agency army. I could already see the flickering glare of the fires and police vehicles. I hurried through the pre-dawn darkness, along the edges of Lotus's tidy soy and sugar beet fields. From there I climbed into the low foothills so that I could drop down into town through the Lotus border fences, which I hoped would be unpatrolled at that moment of disorder. From the foothills, the town center looked like a smoldering crater left by some massive meteor impact. There were fires and clusters of strobing police vehicles, and a column of smoke rose into the pinkening sky. Somewhere in that disaster Arie was hunkered down.

I realized with a discouraging suddenness that I could not remember how long it had been since I had slept. When had it been? A day or two ago? When had I last slept happily? Contently? More than a week or so, I thought, when I was still kidding myself about Rachel's plan to rebuild society. But even then I was plagued by insomnia. And before that, when I was with Gary, I seldom slept at all.

I felt suddenly weary, as though somehow I just did not deserve the pleasure of deep, uninterrupted slumber, and would simply never know what it was like.

Arie must have passed around information about me, because when I was able to make my way far enough into Lotus to contact one of the young rioters, he knew exactly who I was and he immediately abandoned his post and spirited me through the barricades.

He said his name was Brady. He was older than Arie, perhaps in his mid-twenties. He had black hair cut very short, and large, brown eyes. I asked him what had happened in the past day.

"We've taken control of practically the whole city center," said Brady. "Some of the bigger teams demolished a few buildings, cut some of the roads completely. We're dug in pretty good now. Like an Alabama tick. The Lotus cops don't seem to know what to do, but we're hearing rumors that the Agency army is on its way."

"It is," I said. "They can't be more than an hour or so behind me."

"I don't know how we'll perform against real soldiers," said Brady. "Security forces are one thing, but if they bring in mechanized troops and armored vehicles, our barricades won't hold up for very long."

"What do you know about the demolition teams?"

He seemed surprised that I knew anything about that.

"Well, we'll know just as soon as they're done," said Brady. "There are I think nine factories right here close to the city—food processing plants, a textile mill, the water treatment plants, and of course the arms factory where this all started. As soon as the demo teams are ready, signal or no, the local factories and facilities will go off like World War Infinity."

We reached Arie's basement headquarters just as dawn broke. Arie was down there, cloistered in a small, dark room with a table stacked with a motley spread of radios and transmitters wired to a transmitter in a room with a window somewhere. Tiny lights winked red and green and gold. It looked like an electronic Christmas tree.

In the cold light of a fluorescent lantern, Arie sat on an old folding chair so rusted and broken down it looked like it might not hold his weight for another minute. He had his feet up on the table and his hands laced across his middle. As I approached, I saw that he was cat-napping. But he opened his eyes when I knocked on the door frame. He stood when he saw me and gave me a quick hug. It was only a simple gesture, but meant everything to me in that chilly, bone-tired morning.

"I didn't know if I'd ever see you again," he said.

Arie introduced himself to Brady and thanked him for helping me. Then Arie asked him to stay.

"We can use all the help here that I can get," said Arie.

Brady said, "I'd be honored. I already know some of your crew. I'll let them know I'm moving in. It was good to meet you both." He went out of the room and up the stairs.

Arie turned to me and said, "Part of me hoped you'd just go. Just go and get away to somewhere safe."

"As far as I'm concerned," I said, "you're stuck with me."

"I guess that's okay."

Arie explained that he and the other leaders of the Lotus revolt were scattered throughout the city and there were a few in hills nearby. He said he'd taken on the task of coordinating radio communication for as long as possible.

"When the real attack comes," Arie explained, "we might have to bug out of this building. Look at this—" he pointed at a red plastic toggle switch mounted to his main HAM transmitter "—this entire set-up is rigged to short out violently if I flip this switch."

"All that work, and you're just gonna melt it down with the flip of a switch, eh?"

"I hope I don't have to." The lantern cast deep, sullen shadows onto his face. "We'll stay as long as we can, but we can't just give them our comms net."

Arie went on to explain that he had twenty people in the building to defend his command post and the radios. Most of them were stationed in the upper floors, watching for the arrival of the Agency's forces. The rest of the rioters, he said, were spread across the city in small, autonomous bands.

"Basically," explained Arie, "we're each independently in charge of getting ourselves out of here alive."

I nodded approvingly, but a heavy, black stone was forming in my gut.

"So, what happened with you?" Arie asked.

"I spoke to Gary," I said. "He wasn't open to the idea of helping. It was a stupid idea to go to him. Waste of time."

Arie shrugged. "We have to leverage every resource. Have the Agency troops mobilized?"

"Oh, yes. Definitely," I said. "I saw them."

"Then it was good you went," he said. "I've gotten some second and third-hand reports, but nothing definite until now."

"They'll be here any time." I told Arie everything I'd seen as I was leaving Agency territory. Vehicle and weapon types and rough counts I'd made. He produced a pencil and wrote notes on a pad of paper.

"I think they've gathered troops and vehicles from more than one Agency Zone," I told him. "Maybe several. I lived there for a year and never saw that many vehicles. It really is an army."

"Well, I think we have more troops than they think. I have a lot of confidence in these people."

A series of conversations and reports began to crackle between the radios, different patrols and observation points checking in on the hour and reporting to each other. Arie put a finger to his lips and listened. He flipped his notebook to a clean page and made more notes. Several people gave reports directly

275

to him. There was a great deal of static and electronic noise. Arie acknowledged and answered the reports, all the while scribbling notes. He relayed information between teams who could not transmit to each other, then he disseminated the info I'd given him.

"Pass the word," he said into his mic. "Agency attack is imminent." Then he set down the mic and sighed.

"What do we do now?"

"Nothing," he replied. "It's just a waiting game, really. As soon as the demo teams report that all facilities are ready to blow, we'll give a signal and then disperse as best we can. Once the explosions start, I think they'll pull back pretty dramatically. Then we'll run like hell."

"I saw the convoys. It looked to me like they had plenty of firepower to keep the city surrounded even if they sent half their strength away to check on the already-destroyed factories. I really hate to be a Debbie-Downer here, but are you sure we can get out of here once the plan goes off? I mean you're armed with baseball bats and kitchen knives. I saw a girl with a shovel."

"You realize we've got guns, right?" asked Arie.

"What? Wait. You've got guns?" I struggled to decide if this made me feel more confident or less so.

Arie gave me an incredulous look. "Of course we have guns. We're armed to the teeth. What did you think we were planning to use? Harsh language and garden tools?"

"I just haven't seen anyone with a gun."

"Good," said Arie with a nod. "We thought it'd be best to stash them until the real fighting starts. The Lotus cops have not seemed interested in shooting at us because we're not shooting at them. There have been a few exceptions, some casualties. But right now we're keeping that ace up our sleeve."

My mouth opened, but then I realized that I was about to say: "I don't approve of you using guns, young man." It was just too absurd to say, so I shut up and we sat in silence.

I thought: we should be getting into disputes about whether you can borrow the car for the weekend, son, or what college you should go to. I'm your mom, I thought. You're my son. We shouldn't be having arguments about the use of deadly force. I kept this to myself.

Then I thought: we are together for now, at any rate, and maybe someday we can have a normal mom-son argument. I'm looking forward to that, I thought. Yes, maybe someday, when the world has rid itself of this darkness, and when it's no longer night, we'll be able to do the things moms and their kids are supposed to do.

The radios hissed and crackled, and there were occasional clipped conversations between teams. The lights winked green and red.

"You don't have to stay, you know," said Arie. "I could find someone who could get you away from here, though that will get a little more difficult when the Agency moves in."

"I'm not leaving."

"Yeah?" he said with a sleepy, sarcastic grin. "You gonna stick around?"

"Yeah," I said. "Is that all right?"

"Definitely."

Morning was breaking. Sunlight slanted in down the staircase and brightened the dark basement. We went upstairs to warm ourselves. It would have been a beautiful day, but the sky was marred by black columns of smoke.

"You read all the journals?" I asked.

"I did."

"We used to ride bikes through the empty neighborhoods, searching."

"Yeah, I saw that." Arie chuckled. "What were we looking for?"

"My journals say that was your idea, if I recall correctly."

"Yeah. That is my recollection as well."

"It sounds like it was a great mysterious adventure," I said wistfully. "Riding around, breaking in, looking. Sounds fun. I mean except for the part about almost getting shot by patrols."

"And mauled by wild dogs," added Arie, pulling back his sleeve and pointing at the scars that confirmed the stories.

"Sure," I said, chuckling, "that, too."

"What on earth could I have been searching for?" he said, looking more closely at the jagged, livid marks.

I shrugged. "Maybe someday we'll remember."

CHAPTER 32

The day passed slowly. The order had gone out to take up arms, and I watched with my heart in my throat as the people in Arie's command post produced their hidden cache of rifles and machineguns. Arie fetched himself a pistol with a small belt pouch of spare ammo magazines. He gave me one just like it. Most of the others had assault rifles and sub-machineguns, most of which were manufactured—in secret, Arie said—at the factory where he'd worked.

"These are ours," said Arie. "We built them."

Still, no one seemed sure about what to expect. Would the Agency swarm into the area with troops and vehicles? Would they wait until night and infiltrate quietly?

In the afternoon, spotters reported that Agency vehicles were moving into position, surrounding the city center and blocking any egress. An hour or so later we heard gunfire and received reports that small patrols of Agency soldiers were slipping through the perimeter, drawing fire and provoking skirmishes.

I slept a little but jerked awake at practically any noise louder than a footfall. Arie mostly stayed below by his radios, taking hourly reports and spreading information to the other teams and leaders. As the afternoon passed to evening, the reports of small-arms clashes increased. The sounds of gunfire and explosions both near and far were almost constant now.

"They're just probing us," said Arie, "trying to figure out how many of us there are, and where we are."

"No word from the demolition teams?"

He shook his head.

"Do you think something happened? Like they got captured or killed?"

Arie shook his head, but I knew he was weighing the same thought, and this chilled me. Without that part of the plan, I was sure that the Agency army would simply exterminate everyone inside the perimeter. We were nothing but a hoard of ragged rebels encircled by ten thousand tons of weaponry.

We languished in the command post until well past midnight. Guards were set and patrols were sent out, but whereas we were almost at the very center of town, Arie's people met no patrols, and there came no generalized or large-scale attacks.

Feeling that the night might pass without major trouble, I pulled my arms into my jacket, found a corner at the top of the stairs where I could sit and slouch, and dozed off.

I awoke to an explosion that seemed to heave the entire earth's surface ten feet into the air.

And there was another. I heard the Lotus kids shouting in panic. Then more explosions. Arie was bellowing orders from down the stairs, but they were lost in the cacophony.

***

When I'd gathered my wits, I joined Arie in the radio room. He stood in the stark buzzy light of the fluorescent lamp. His lantern had been knocked over and so had his chair, and together they cast a ghastly network of skeletal shadows across everything. Arie spoke into his mic in a frenzied voice, then strained to hear the replies over the din.

He turned to me between transmissions. "Mortars," he said. "They're softening us up with short-range artillery. They'll attack soon. Maybe at first light. Be ready for anything."

A mortar struck the building somewhere high above and shook us so violently that we were knocked from our feet. The tower of radios wobbled crazily. Several more shells impacted close by, followed by a terrific crashing sound from above, like a hailstorm of bricks. Cracks had formed in the concrete wall and floor of the small room. Dust rained down from the ceiling with each impact, as if the building were falling apart particle by particle. The dusty haze hung harshly illuminated in the air. Round after round struck. We staggered to keep on our feet and keep the radios from toppling.

Brady appeared. He was thoroughly coated in powdered concrete, and his nose and ears were bleeding. In the eerie electric light he looked like some horrific walking corpse.

"The whole west side of the building is gone," he stated frankly. "Stewart and Rodrigo are dead," he added, again impressively calm. "And I can't find Ignacia."

"Tell everyone to get to ground level and get behind cover," said Arie. "This won't last much longer. They'll lift their fire and then come after us on foot. We gotta be ready for that."

Brady nodded and darted away.

"We should get ready to move," I said.

"No, we're solid. I've got twenty people up there shooting from behind concrete."

"Well, twenty minus three, Arie."

He clenched his jaw and turned his attention back to the radios. Urgent reports flooded in. It felt as though everyone was simply waiting for death. And then, all at once, it was quiet. A few seconds ticked by. Then a few more.

"They've stopped," I said, turning my head upward.

"No," said Arie. "They're just getting started. Come on." We went upstairs. "Everyone get ready!" he shouted. "Here they come."

As Brady had reported, the western side of the building was now a rubble slide. Parts of the other walls were still standing but were blasted through by ragged voids, and the windows gaped, their glass shattered. We took up positions at the windows. In the dim light, clouds of smoke and dust drifted between the buildings. Everything was still. I peered into the shadows.

"Look!" I shouted.

In the moonlight, I saw squads of dark-clad troops creeping up the street in our direction. The Lotus kids opened fire, and I saw a few of the Agency troops fall and falter back. But within a few moments they returned fire, and I realized how outnumbered we were.

Bullets slammed into the building, sending concrete and brick fragments flying. I saw another squad of Agency soldiers coming toward us from another alley. I fired at them, and they dodged out of sight. Arie called out orders, spotting the incoming troops and shouting directions.

"Brady, watch the right side! They're coming up through the alleyway!"

Enemy fire was pouring into the ground floor of the building. The concrete walls and floors were disintegrating almost before my eyes, like a swarm of insane rock-eating locust had descended on us.

"We've got to move," I shouted at Arie. "We've got to fall back!"

"No, it's way too soon!" he shouted back. "Keep firing! I'm going to the radio room to see if we can get some help!"

He sprang up and ran for the staircase, but bullets were snapping and crackling thickly through the air. I raised my hand to pull Arie back down, but he was already halfway to the staircase.

Then he spun around and staggered limply and I knew he'd been hit. He collapsed at the staircase.

Keeping myself practically on the floor, I crawled frantically to where Arie lay writhing in pain. His face was drawn up tight. A volley of gunfire strafed the floor very near me, raising gritty little columns of pulverized concrete.

"Arie!" I cried. "How bad is it? Let me see!"

He only muttered and clutched at his chest and shoulder.

Another burst of automatic gun fire struck the floor nearby. I knew we couldn't stay there on the floor. I dragged Arie further into the building and into the cover of a column of concrete.

"You know, I think you might be right," he grunted.

"What?"

"We should move now."

"I'll tell the others," I said.

"Kill the radios first," he mumbled. His eyelids fluttered.

"Arie!" I said again. "Stay awake!"

"Hurry," Arie repeated. "The radios."

I crawled to the staircase and scampered down into the radio room. There in the fluorescent glare was the red toggle. I heard the static-haunted cries and urgent pleas of the Lotus kids. How many of them were there? How many would there be when the sun came up?

I flipped the toggle. There was a loud crackle of wild electricity, a shower of blinding white sparks, and the radios went silent. I grabbed my backpack and went back upstairs.

I knelt by him. "Arie! Still with me?"

"I'm not sure," he groaned. "I feel awful."

I tried to examine him, to find his wound, but it was too dark. All I knew was that he was covered with blood.

"We have to fall back now," I said.

"You go," he said woozily, fumbling for his pistol. "I'll stay here and cover your ass."

"I don't think so," I said.

I raced between the firing positions of the Lotus kids and told them we were moving out, then returned to Arie.

"Time to go," I said. Then I put my hands under his armpits and hauled him to a standing position. He steadied himself by clutching a fistful of my jacket in his bloody fist.

The others gathered to us. There were only four of them now. Arie wobbled a little, then sat down hard, legs splayed out and his back to the column. The kids kept their weapons at the ready.

"Arie's hit," I said. "But we've got to fall back."

"Which way is 'back'?" asked a girl who wore her brunette hair in pigtails and held her assault rifle braced on her hip.

"Anywhere they're not shooting," said Arie. "That way." He gestured vaguely to the south.

Brady stepped forward and asked, "Where are you hit, man?"

"I don't even know," said Arie, coughing. "My whole body hurts."

"Let me bind him up," Brady said to me. "If we don't stop the bleeding, he'll be passed out in five minutes and dead in fifteen."

We laid Arie down in the rubble and someone switched on a small flashlight. Arie was pallid and shivering. Brady tore open Arie's blood-soaked jacket, then his shirt. I took out my water bottle and rinsed his chest and shoulder, and we saw the wound.

"Ooh, that's gonna hurt in the morning," said Brady. "But we're in luck. It's in and out. Look: entry, exit. Broken clavicle, soft-tissue trauma. You'll be playing tennis in eight weeks."

"What are you, some kind of army medic?" I asked.

Brady pressed his lips into a hard line and sighed. "I'm no medic," he said, gesturing with his head to the gunfire outside. "But I used to be one of them."

Arie feebly poked Brady in the chest with his index finger and said, "I knew you'd come in handy."

"I got no med kit," said Brady. "We need something for a bandage."

"How 'bout a t-shirt?" I said.

"Perfect," said Brady.

I clawed around in my bag and found the shirts I'd packed.

Brady unsheathed a hunting knife and cut the t-shirts into long strips. With these he applied a pressure dressing to Arie's wound.

"Pretty basic," said Brady.

"This is taking too long," Arie said. "I'll be okay now. You guys go. Give me a rifle. I'll cover you."

"Just another second," said Brady.

He adjusted the dressing while I gave Arie a few gulps of my water. Brady shucked his coat and carefully helped Arie put it on. He was still pale, but his breathing was not so ragged now and he was already looking better.

"Let's get you up," said Brady.

We helped Arie to his feet.

"That's better," he said. "Yeah. I think I can keep up."

Just then, something arced into the room.

It was small and dark and metallic, and it landed on the floor nearby with a muted clank, rolled noisily in our direction, and came to rest almost at our feet. The kid with the flashlight pointed his beam, and there on the concrete was a black metal canister stenciled with white letters. More of the canisters flew into the room.

Someone screamed, "Grenade!"

There came a blast of light and noise, and again I found myself enveloped in whiteness. My ears rang with the high, keening note of an angel choir, and I seemed to float away on a dull, muffled sea of insensibility. I was dead, apparently.

No.

The beams of six or eight military-grade, rifle-mounted flashlights swept with dazzling menace through the dusty air, and behind each one a dark figure came rushing into the building. Over the ringing in my ears, I heard their hoarse, savage voices.

I struggled to my feet, dizzy, head pulsing in pain as though I might have bounced the back of my head off the hard floor when I fell. My ears rang unceasingly. Dark-clothed soldiers streamed in. Arie lay on the floor beside me, not moving. I saw the other Lotus kids stupefied and reeling, rising up like boxers under a referee's ten-count.

I looked down at myself to see if I correctly remembered that I was carrying a pistol. I was. It was in a holster. I groggily removed the pistol and pointed it. They would not take Arie. They would not take me.

A man with a rifle approached me, calmly swung his weapon end-for-end, and with the hard metal butt of the stock he struck me in the face with a quick, effortless precision. Everything went black.

CHAPTER 33

They'd bound our hands, the six of us, and placed us side-by-side and face-down on the floor like luggage.

Arie lay next to me, Brady was on the other side of him, and the other Lotus kids were on the far side of Brady. Arie's face was turned away from me.

"Arie," I said, "you all right?"

He flinched and turned his head to face me. He looked tired and gray.

"I think I'm good," he said. "But we're screwed."

"Just stay with me," I said.

"Shut up over there," said a gruff voice. "No talking."

"Can we at least sit up?" I said.

"No. Now shut the hell up."

And that's how they left us until Rachel arrived.

An armored vehicle pulled up close to the building, and a soldier jumped out and came around to open the hatch. From there he helped Rachel down to the rubble-strewn street. She'd chosen her ballcap-and-fatigues ensemble again, looking again like a ladies' fashion magazine conception of a military field commander. She'd added at least one accessory since I'd last seen her in this ensemble, however. It was a sleek black holster and pistol strapped to her thigh.

"I want something lethal, but tasteful," I imagined her telling an underling.

She picked her way toward us through the rubble without compromising her commanding posture. Two riflemen preceded her and followed her, escorting her to a place where the exterior wall was torn open. She ducked through the gash and came inside. From the pocket of her jacket she fished out a flashlight and shined it on us.

"Is this all of them?" Rachel asked.

"Yes, ma'am," said her lieutenant. "Prisoners and area secured."

Rachel came my way and stood above me. I squinted at her flashlight. Lying face-down as I was, I could see her only from the ankles down. She nudged my shoulder with her boot.

"So, uh, were you going to bring Arie to me?"

"Well, I did find him."

She chuckled, then crouched beside me and I could see her face. She brushed some grit from my cheek. "Hard core to the bitter end, aren'tcha?"

I scoffed, and my breath raised a little dust from the floor. I turned my face from her.

"You knew it," she said archly. "You knew these kids didn't stand a chance. Didn't you? Did you come here to see if you could change their minds? Hm? But ended up fighting with them? Is that what happened? God, what I couldn't do with ten or twelve Alisons."

"Just get it over with," I grumbled. "Wipe me, kill me, whatever."

Rachel exhaled harshly and said, "Tell me what is so wrong with my way?"

"What way?"

"My way. Why couldn't you fight this way for me and my plans? What's so wrong about my way of doing things?"

"I think you know the answer to that. Get it over with."

"All right." She nodded and stood up again.

Vehicles approached. Their headlight beams swung through the dark space, and they stopped out on the street, diesel engines idling.

"The transport trucks are here," said Rachel, voice raised. "We'll only need one, as it turns out. Get them ready."

Someone straddled me, grabbed me by the shoulders, and lifted me to my knees.

"Stay on your knees," he said. "Keep still."

Arie and the others were likewise hoisted to their knees. In the glare of the flashlights, the Lotus kids glared up into the dark faces of their Agency captors with unveiled contempt. Were any of them still fired-up and foolish enough to try something?

Rachel stood in front of Arie. "What about you, Arie?"

"What about me?"

"What was all this for? Longer lunch breaks? Foosball table in the lounge?"

He rolled his eyes and gave her a little head shake. "You haven't won," he said.

There came a subtle change in the light outside. Like slow-motion lightning, or a sunrise set at high speed. The strobe spread in the sky to the west, yellowish but bright, the color of hot but distant flames.

Everyone noticed it. All eyes turned to the windows and gaping damage in the walls. It was bright enough to make us squint slightly, bright enough to render the flashlights momentarily unnecessary. Rachel crossed the floor to where the building's demolished western wall lay in a heap. There she stood gazing at the sky as though it were engaged in some act of flagrant disobedience.

The light faded in only a few seconds, but as it did, there came a deep and ponderous boom. I felt it as much as heard it, and then the ground bounced ever so slightly like the floor of a ballroom. A bit of dust drifted down from the ceiling.

"What is that?" Rachel demanded.

Her lieutenant was already muttering urgently into a small handset and pressing on the headphone in his ear. Another flash of the yellowish light brightened the night sky, this time from slightly more southwest. The sky flared and after a few seconds' delay came the boom and the light springiness in the ground.

"Who is firing?" Rachel said, returning to her lieutenant. "We're supposed to be at a cease-fire."

The lieutenant shook his head and pressed his ear piece to hear better. "No ma'am," he said. "That's not ordinance. Those aren't mortars. Stand by." He listened at the ear piece.

Arie bowed his head and snickered quietly, but Brady joined him, and together they laughed louder. The other Lotus kids laughed.

"What is that?" Rachel repeated to no one, to everyone. She left the lieutenant and came to where the Lotus kids knelt. "What is that?" she snapped at Arie, pointing at the western sky.

"It's just what I told you," he said. "You haven't won. You've lost."

There came another flash and a deep, concussive booming.

"Ma'am," said the lieutenant, splitting his attention between what he had to say and the ear piece, "we got reports of—major demolition charges—out in the western quads. Production structures. The water plant."

From far in the distance a series of drum-like thudding explosions could be heard—*boom, boom, boom-boom-boom*. Like the finale of some massive but faraway fireworks show. The strobes of light from the west had become a warm, yellow-tinged twilight that persisted.

There was another sound, too. High above the resonant, booming rumble of gigantic demolition charges and collapsing factories, I heard the faint noise of voices raised in victory.

Rachel drew her pistol and pointed it at Arie's face. "What have you done?"

Arie turned his face slightly, the pistol's muzzle just inches from his forehead.

"Rachel," I cried, "don't kill him."

"Don't worry, Alison," she said, racking the slide. "You're next."

A burst of gunfire erupted from behind me, and Rachel was knocked back. As a storm of opposing gunfire ensued, Rachel inclined her head to look at her own middle. The pistol slipped from her hand and her eyes flew open as she dipped her fingertips in the blooming of wet redness on her blouse. Next she fell down roughly into a seated position, her dismayed incredulity spreading across her face just as the blood on her clothes spread and blossomed into the fabric. She sank to the floor and lay there motionless.

We dropped awkwardly back down onto our stomachs as automatic weapons fired volleys back and forth over our heads, the noise deafening and echoing flatly off the concrete. Arie and I wriggled with ridiculous desperation to find cover.

Brady rolled calmly onto his back, drew his knees nearly to his chin, and then slipped his zip-tied hands beneath his butt and feet so that his hands were in front of him. He fiddled with his belt-buckle and drew out a small knife blade. He cut the zip-ties and a moment later he freed me and then Arie.

I turned to see who had opened fire on Rachel's troops. They looked in every way to be more Agency troops, coming in from the front of the building. Then I spotted a figure limping doggedly forward and firing a pistol.

It was Gary Gosford.

Two soldiers dragged Rachel's limp form away across the floor, keeping themselves low and firing blindly at Gary's men. I grabbed Arie and we dove for cover with the other Lotus kids.

The number of soldiers in the place had dropped to only a handful, and the up-close gun battle ground them down. Soldiers on both sides dropped precipitously, but Gary's troops were outnumbered, and more of Rachel's men were coming in from her armored vehicle and the transport trucks. Gary and his men pressed forward, but I saw Gary take a bullet and fall. His men faltered back but kept firing.

And then something caught my eye. Something outside, moving fast. A pair of headlights were veering in our direction, straight at the battered building. Something about its shape told me it was not a military vehicle, but it was large and boxy, and as it closed in there was something about it that struck me as familiar.

It was Donna's Winnebago.

The front of the big RV crashed through a bank of floor-to-ceiling windows on the east side of the ground floor. Concrete, window mullions, and what little glass remained in the window panes came flying into the ground floor in a clattering, dusty blast. I saw Donna behind the wheel, blinking behind her Coke-bottle glasses.

From the resulting roil of dust emerged Chase, Woolly, Ruby, and others. Ruby wielded a sawed-off shotgun, which she fired one-handed like a pistol. Chase shouldered an assault rifle and immediately made short work of several Agency troopers. Arie and Brady had rounded up a few rifles from the soldiers who'd been injured or killed, and we joined the melee. I saw Woolly open the cab of the Winnebago, where Donna was still sitting, eyes wide behind her spectacles and gripping the wheel in her tiny fists as though she were still driving. Woolly helped her out and together they hunkered down out of the line of fire.

With the surprise entrance and added firepower of Ruby's gang, Rachel's troops retreated and were driven into the darkness. A few of Gary's men gave chase but, quite abruptly, it was quiet again. At first the only sounds were the gritty rasping of the wounded moving in the debris and the low sounds of their pained groans. But in a moment I realized there was another sound. I looked around and realized that, among the rubble and wounded fighters, eight or ten meowing cats from Donna's Winnebago were prowling.

CHAPTER 34

"Care for a lift?" said Chase with a grin. "Your friend Donna here asked me to drive."

"Yes, thank you," said Donna, shaking her head. "I really shouldn't drive at night with my prescriptions."

"Yes," I cried, "We've gotta get outta here now."

"For once we agree," said Chase. "Pile in."

Woolly had gone out and fired up Rachel's armored vehicle. He flung open the ballistic glass window and hollered, "I can take a few with me!"

We hastily loaded up all the injured troops—no matter who they'd been nominally working for—and with Woolly's new ride in the lead, we tore off to the south.

It appeared that Arie had been at least partially right. There were many road intersections and choke-points where there should have been Agency troops to block our escape, but we found very few troops. Perhaps they had been pulled off their stations to defend the production facilities, canneries, and factories, or perhaps their plans had changed when they learned that Rachel had been shot.

In any case, we took a little fire from a few lightly manned roadblocks, but with Woolly bulldozing a path in the armored troop carrier, we were soon clear of the city center. And after scrounging for fuel and circling back a few times to ensure we were not followed, we got clear of Lotus.

It was very late when we finally set out for the mountain camps. The Winnebago was cramped, but Donna's cats made space and everyone took a place as Chase turned the RV to the east along the decrepit two-lane highway. Arie lay wrapped in blankets on the couch, weakened but apparently stable. I later learned that Brady was treating the other wounded in Woolly's armored vehicle. As we headed toward the eastern horizon, I climbed up into the passenger seat of the RV and sat next to Chase.

We drove along slowly using only the running lights for illumination to avoid attracting attention.

Chase looked into his rearview mirror and said, "Hey Al. Take a look behind us."

I turned and looked out the rear windows.

"Look, everyone," I said, pointing.

Here and there along the dark foothills of Lotus, there were what looked like giant bonfires blazing a few miles behind us. But it was a trick of the darkness and distance, and we knew we were seeing the glare of fires much larger and very far away. It was the factories and production plants that had kept Lotus alive, now consumed by flames. I suspect they burned and smoldered for days and maybe weeks.

After we'd driven what I judged to be thirty or forty miles, Woolly turned off the highway and led us up into the foothills along a packed-dirt road. It was a place, Chase said, where the gang had holed up a few times before. The only way to detect that it was a road at all was that there was just the faintest remnant of tire ruts, and slightly less grass and weeds growing in them than on the surrounding terrain. We went along slowly. Woolly stopped a few times to flip on the headlights to ensure we hadn't strayed off.

The almost imperceptible road ended in a cove among the low hills, where there was what looked like an old sheep camp, complete with a tumbled-down wooden pen and a sod-covered shack with sun-bleached timber walls. There was also a freshwater well with a hand-pump. Chase primed the pump and the water that issued out was sweet and icy cold. We all drank our fill, and then, using buckets and basins, we washed away the dust and blood from our faces and arms and hands.

I sat down on the ground and watched the others washing and drinking in the light of flashlights and lanterns. The stars burned brightly overhead. Crickets sang to us from the shadows. Chase came over and stood by me.

"You okay?" he asked.

"I will be," I said.

"Need anything?"

"Nah."

"Mind if I join you?"

"Have a seat," I said.

He sat next to me, knees up and forearms resting on his elbows. "We'll set out first thing in the morning," he said. "We'll make sure we're not being followed. Then we'll go on. We're not far from the camps. Two, three hours."

I nodded.

"Arie's okay?"

"Seems to be, yeah. He's asleep in the RV."

"I looked at his shoulder. I bet it hurts like hell, but it's nothing Doctor Terry up at camp can't handle."

"You guys really came through for us," I said. "Thank you."

Chase waved his hand. "Eh. You'd have done the same thing." He laughed.

I laughed, too, but then I said, "I'm not so sure about that."

"Nah, I'm sure," he said. "You read the notebooks, right?"

"I did."

"Then you know we've gotten through a lot of scrapes together."

"Yeah," I said. "Hey," I added, "maybe there is something you can help me out with."

"Sure," said Chase. "Name it."

I fished around in my backpack and produced the odd, red-covered notebook that Donna had given me. Chase switched on a small flashlight, and when he saw the notebook, he raised his eyebrows. I was about to ask him if he knew anything about it, but before I could, he snatched it away from me.

"The notebook!" he said. He stood up and thumbed the pages under the beam of the flashlight. "This is it!"

I stood up, too. "It's what?" I asked.

"Arie's encoded, boats-beaten-back, skull-clock, secret Great Gatsby notebook! Oh my god, you don't remember."

"Arie? Boats? Great Gatsby?"

Chase tapped the notebook with the backs of his fingertips. "This is the notebook you found in Arie's room after they took him. It's not mentioned in your journals, is it? No, of course not. You came to Ruby with this notebook not too long after they took Arie.

You thought it might lead you to him or unlock some big secret."

I took the notebook from him and looked at the writing. It was similar to his, but the numbers were so ordered and so unlike ordinary writing, I must have missed the fact that it was his handwriting.

"This is Arie's?" I asked, flipping the pages.

"That's what you told us a couple years ago," said Chase. "I guess we can't ask him what it says, can we? We'll have to get a copy of *The Great Gatsby*.

"What are you talking about?" I asked. My thoughts were whirling like fallen leaves in wind.

He poked a finger at the cryptic lines of numbers. "Your leading theory was that the key to the cypher was *The Great Gatsby*." He stopped and shrugged. "I don't suppose we're likely to find a copy where we're going."

"Oh my god," I sighed.

Chase turned to me with a questioning look.

"I had one. I had a copy of that book. At my house. It's one of the few things I held on to when I moved to Lotus. I know right where it is."

"Mmm," said Chase, "I guess you know you can't go back for it, right?"

"I guess so," I said, shaking my head. "Yeah. No."

"Because I've read your journals, and I knew you before. It's just the kind of thing you'd do. You're back with us now—if you run off and get your memory wiped again, I'm not gonna be happy."

"Is that so?" I said. I turned to him, and we found ourselves again facing each other, bathed in starlight.

"Well," said Chase. "The others would be super pissed-off, too."

"If this notebook was the key to finding Arie," I said, "it might not be so important now. Maybe we can work on de-coding it later."

"I like the sound of that," said Chase.

"Hey," I said. "There's something else you can do for me."

"Name it."

"Kiss me."

He chuckled and shot me a curious glance. "What?"

"You heard me."

"You want me to kiss you," he said.

"Yeah," I said, "on the lips. Don't get any fresh ideas, but yes. I want you to kiss me right on the mouth."

"You sure you're feeling okay?" He put his palm on my forehead to check my temperature.

"Positive," I said. "You don't want to?"

"Oh, I want to. *You* want me to?"

"I want you to."

He moved closer.

As I closed my eyes and raised my face to meet his, Chase said, "Why?"

"Why what?"

"Why a kiss?"

"I don't remember ever having been kissed. I want to remember."

He nodded as though that was a satisfactory reason. I closed my eyes and tilted my head.

Our lips met. Yes, I thought. That's it. His mouth was soft, and there came the renewed tingle of his touch, but this time it spread warmly through my body and to my extremities, like the warmth I felt when we drank the mountain wine. He put his hand gently on the nape of my neck and pulled me closer. I felt my face and neck flushing. After what was a long, satisfying moment, Chase pulled away, just a little, and we sat there almost nose to nose for a while longer.

"How was that?" said Chase.

"Unforgettable," I said.

"Any time," he said. He put his hand on my shoulder and rubbed it fondly. "I'm gonna go help everyone bed down for the night."

"I'll help," I said.

"No, why don't you sit here and rest a bit?"

Ruby's crew withdrew a small stash of blankets and sleeping pads from the old shack, and these were distributed. The wounded were given priority space inside the shack and the vehicles. We'd picked up four of Gary's wounded men. Two of them had died during the short drive, and they were given perfunctory burials.

Gary himself was in very serious condition. They wrapped him in a heavy wool blanket and laid him on the floor of the shack. I went in.

Brady was trying unsuccessfully to get Gary to take some water. He looked up at me and said, "I'm not sure there's much we can do outside a first-rate trauma treatment facility. He's been shot three times. Nothing else I can do."

I thought Gary was unconscious, but in a raspy whisper he said, "It's okay. Thank you. Thank you for everything."

"Gary?" I said, "Can you hear me?"

He didn't open his eyes, but he nodded.

Brady seemed to sense some intimate moment might be pending between Gary and I, and so he went out of the shack. There was a small candle lantern hanging from a nail on the wall. I took it down and placed it on the floor beside Gary's head. In the flickering light of the flame, Gary's face was bloodless and clammy.

"Gary?"

He stirred and opened his eyes and looked at me.

"Hey," I said. "Stay with me."

He shook his head slowly, his eyes narrowed to mere slits. "I've had it," he whispered.

"Why'd you do it?" I asked. "Why'd you come after me? Why'd you help?"

He blinked his eyes wearily. "I didn't do it for you," he muttered.

I smiled. Obstinate 'til the end.

"I did it for me," said Gary, his breathing labored. "But you were right. I didn't want to be on the wrong side anymore. So, thanks. Thanks for that."

I nodded at him, and he closed his eyes. I had to cry a little. Brady came back in and sat with us. Gary seemed to have gone into a very deep sleep. Brady felt his pulse. Then he looked at me and gave me a grave nod. A few minutes later, Gary's breathing became very shallow and rapid, and then it stopped. Brady covered Gary's face, and then I followed Brady out of the shack.

On one side of Donna's RV there were ladder rungs that led to the roof. I climbed up with a sleeping bag and a foam mattress and made myself a bed. Then I sat there with my feet hanging over the side of the RV.

Chase said it was best not to have any fires, but a few lanterns were lit, and an almost peaceful atmosphere descended. Down between the vehicles I could hear Ruby and the others quietly good-nighting each other. One by one, the lamps and lights winked out.

The last light was Chase's. I saw him making himself a pallet just outside the door of the shack on what remained there of a wooden porch. He lay down, a rifle practically under the blanket with him, and then switched off his light.

"Night, Chase," I called to him.

"Night, Al," he said. "See ya in the morning."

I lay down on the roof of the RV. I pulled a knit cap down over my ears, zipped up the jacket Chase had returned to me, and drew the heavy sleeping bag up to my chin. The stars looked down on me. My limbs were heavy, and I could only just keep my eyes open. And yet I felt alive. My entire soul felt as though it were electrified with new life and purpose. I let my eyes close and felt myself falling softly into the bosom of a deep and restful sleep.

Get Book Three

The story continues in
Maybe We'll Remember. Available Now.

https://www.amazon.com/dp/B083HB1PW5

To be notified of new releases,
sign up for Amanda's newsletter
on her website:

www.amandaluzzader.com

CREEP FACTOR

by Amanda Luzzader & Chadd VanZanten

https://www.amazon.com/dp/B07J3X1CM5

It's the feeling that something isn't quite right. The glance of a stranger that lingers too long. A coworker who appears out of nowhere. Creep Factor is thirteen deeply creepy short horror stories that explore the awkward, unnerving, and the terrifying. From backstabbing roommates to vicious pets, from murderous spirits to soul-wracking nightmares, Creep Factor covers the savagely weird to the merely ghastly.

Acknowledgments

Many, many thanks to Chadd VanZanten who is my husband and developmental editor and makes the story so much better with his help. He fills in the pieces that I leave blank. Thank you also to my mom, Barbra Yardley, who edits and proofreads on fast deadlines and catches all the errors I miss. Thank you to my sister Melissa, who helped me when I got "stuck" on the storyline. Thank you to my other sister, Jennifer, and to my dad, Bob, for their support and encouragement. Thank you to my children, Hudson and Dawson, who support me in pursuing my dreams. And thank you to Ingrid, Dez, and Gretchen, for coming to my writing events. I appreciate you showing up for me.

About the Author

Amanda Luzzader writes upmarket science fiction, horror, and middle grade books. She is a self-described 'fraidy cat. Things she will run away from include (but are not limited to): mice, snakes, spiders, bits of string and litter that resemble spiders, most members of the insect kingdom, and (most especially) bats. Bats are the worst. But Amanda is first and primarily a mother to two energetic and intelligent sons, and this role inspires and informs her writing, which frequently involves mothers and women as main characters. As Amanda likes to say, "Moms are people, too."

Amanda has worked as a technical writer and a professional editor and is currently employed as a grant writer for a Utah nonprofit organization. She was named Writer of the Year for 2019 by the League of Utah Writers.